Zélie Isabelle Richaud de Préville Colvile

Round the Black Man's Garden

Zélie Isabelle Richaud de Préville Colvile

Round the Black Man's Garden

ISBN/EAN: 9783337080648

Printed in Europe, USA, Canada, Australia, Japan

Cover: Foto ©Andreas Hilbeck / pixelio.de

More available books at **www.hansebooks.com**

ROUND THE BLACK MAN'S GARDEN

BY

ZÉLIE COLVILE, F.R.G.S.

*WITH ILLUSTRATIONS FROM DRAWINGS BY THE AUTHOR
AND FROM PHOTOGRAPHS*

" Qui suit son chemin
Arrive à la fin "

WILLIAM BLACKWOOD AND SONS
EDINBURGH AND LONDON
MDCCCXCIII

À MON FRÈRE,

ANDRÉ RICHAUD DE PRÉVILLE.

JE te dédie ces souvenirs, à toi qui aime tant les récits de voyage, et dont la pensée nous a suivis pas à pas durant notre promenade de huit mois.

ZÉLIE COLVILE.

PREFACE.

I AM sitting in a bamboo thatched house some twelve feet square, perched on four upright poles, somewhat after the manner of a pigeon-loft, and listening to verbose explanations in three languages on the positions of the Lois, Pums, or Taungs, as mountains are called by Katchins, Burmans, or Shans respectively. My stylographic pen has just rolled through the chinks of the split bamboo floor, into the stew which Miguel, my Goa " boy," is brewing below, and Miguel's grumblings would have been very long-winded but for the timely appearance of a Katchin runner, who, mounting the notched pole by which my front door is approached, offers me a paper parcel with both hands as if it were a draught of water, while Miguel, a little behind the times, exclaims, through the floor, "Postman coming, sar!"

The packet contains, among others, a letter from my wife asking me to write a Preface to her book 'Round the Black Man's Garden.'

It is a far cry from a hill-top overlooking China to Afric's golden strand, and the intricacies of Katchin topography have pretty well banished from my mind all memories of our African coasting trip. But I do remember that it was I who, in an unguarded moment, and taking no thought for the morrow, suggested the title while the late Government was in power; and I feel that the least I can do is to openly avow my fault, and bow my devoted head to the vials of wrath which will doubtless be poured on it. In justice to myself, I must say that, on the result of the late general election being made public, I at once suggested the substitution of "Gentleman of Colour" for "Black Man"; but a friend of my wife's who understands English composition and those sort of things, said the title was clumsy; an artistic acquaintance of mine said black was not a colour at all; and my wife objected that she could not describe as a gentleman a person who was in the habit of hanging his relations, by hooks through their heels, over a pit full of spikes,

as some one she met at Bonny did. Knowing
nothing of the rights and wrongs of the technical
objections, I wisely held my peace with regard to
them, but was obliged to admit that the conduct of
the person at Bonny was not in the best of taste,
and would certainly have been taken notice of by
the committee had he been a member of my club.
So there was nothing to do but let the obnoxious
title stand; and here from my highland fastness I
send forth to the expectant millions an avowal of
my guilt, my only hope being that the charm of
the book may avert a portion of their philonegric
wrath from the unhappy cause of its title.

Having thus confessed my fault, I may come to
the more pleasant task of showing that I am also
the primary cause of the book itself. But for me
these pages would never have been written, for it
was only by my contracting (at great personal inconvenience) pneumonia, pleurisy, and a few odds
and ends of complications, that I obtained the long
period of sick-leave which enabled me to perform the
grateful duties of guardian and companion to the
authoress, on her travels; and it would be false
modesty on my part to doubt, when after a hard
day's travel she penned her diary by the midnight
dip, that her weary vigil was cheered by the har-

mony of my snores, without whose help perhaps the following pages would have lacked that sparkle which I am sure they must possess.

When the book is presented to me, neatly bound and comfortably printed, I hope to put this matter to the test; but in the meanwhile I can assure my fellow-readers that if the authoress is only half as good at writing as she is at roughing it, we have a treat before us.

H. E. COLVILE.

PANKAW, KATCHIN HILLS,
   UPPER BURMAH,
     March 21, 1893.

CONTENTS.

ILLUSTRATIONS.

FULL-PAGE ILLUSTRATIONS.

ILLUSTRATIONS IN THE TEXT.

MAPS.

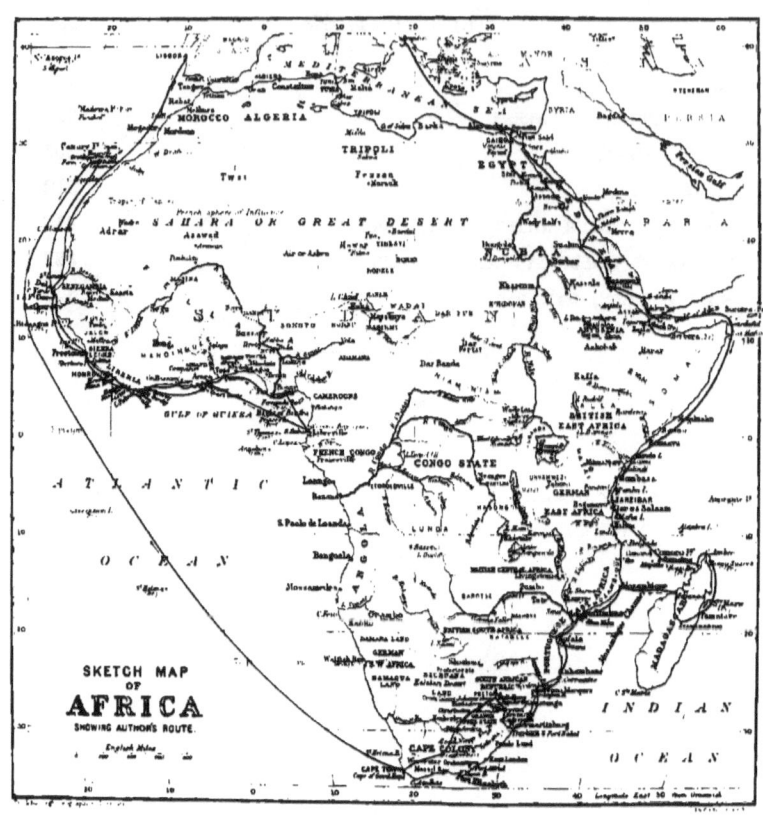

SKETCH MAP
OF
AFRICA
SHOWING AUTHOR'S ROUTE.

ROUND THE BLACK MAN'S GARDEN.

BOOK I.

THE SEA OF ISLAM.

I.

THE doctors having decided that we must winter in a warm climate, I brought the big family atlas to Harry, who dreamily turned over the leaves until he came to Africa. After sitting for some time watching the smoke from his cigarette, he looked up,—" What do you say to the Cape ?" "Charming!" I replied, quite forgetting what a bad sailor I was; "but how shall we get there from Bohemia?" We had promised some friends to spend the month of August with them in that country. "Let us go round by the back way," he suggested, and so it was settled; and the 12th of September 1888 found us at Venice, where we embarked for Alexandria.

A

On the 21st we arrived at Suez, very tired and be-grimed, after twelve hours in that dirtiest, slowest, and shakiest of all known means of conveyance, an Egyptian night-train.

After a good wash and a substantial breakfast in that curious little oasis of Anglo-Indianism, the Suez Hotel, we began to feel more at peace with the world,—a feeling which soon disappeared on dis-covering that our light clothing, guns, &c., which had been sent by sea to meet us here, had not arrived. So the morning, which I had hoped to spend in peace, had to be devoted to rushing about the dirty little town, followed by a swarm of would-be guides, and trying to collect a few necessaries and comforts for the voyage.

As I was anxious to see the Red Sea ports, we had settled to go by the Khedivial Line of steamers, which touched at all of them, but which, we had been warned, had no other advantages. On going to book our passage by this line, we were agree-ably surprised to find that the agent, Mr Campbell, had received a telegram from a friend of ours at Alexandria requesting him to do all he could to make us comfortable, to secure the ladies' cabin for us, and to have an extra supply of ice put on board.

At about three o'clock, after a quarter of an hour's journey in the train, which runs over a causeway through the lagoon, we found ourselves on board, and were received by Mr Campbell, who showed us

our cabin, which seemed large and airy enough,
being intended to hold eight passengers, and having fair-sized windows on two sides, opening on to
the quarter-deck. I must say my heart sank a little when I saw how small our steamer, the "Messir,"
was: it seemed as if the slightest sea would make
itself felt, and subsequent experience proved that
my conjecture was not far wrong.

When we first got on board it was quite impossible to move—the little hurricane-deck, the only
part reserved for saloon passengers, being taken up
by a curious-looking crowd that had come to see the
Governor of Suez off on one of his official rounds;
so we both sat in a corner and watched the proceedings, which, from the variety of the costumes and
the manners and customs of their wearers, greatly
interested me.

One man standing near us had on a *tarbush*, a
check shooting-suit, a white waistcoat, a shirt that
had not been washed for some time, evening patent-
leather pumps, blue-and-white-striped cotton socks,
and a thick gold chain : while talking to his friends,
he was telling his beads behind his back. Another
in the regulation Stambuli black - broadcloth suit
might, but for his *tarbush*, have been taken for a
neat young English curate. A third with a sly
sallow face, a pen behind his ear, and a yellow-
striped dressing-gown, was his Excellency's Coptic
clerk. All looked thoroughly out of keeping with

two magnificent old grey-beards, who, in ordinary
native dress, were capital samples of the "fine old"
Arab "gentleman all of the olden time." Among
the smaller fry the Circassians were the only people
who looked clean and attractive, with their beautiful
eyes and pleasant faces. One of them seemed much
amused at the interest I took in the leave-taking
between the Governor and his friends, the form of
which varied according to the social position of the
latter, and to their different degrees of friendship.
The Governor kissed those with whom he was most
intimate on one cheek and one shoulder—or rather,
after kissing his friend's cheek, bobbed his head over
his shoulder. The next in degree was kissed on
both shoulders. Those in the highest social scale
took the Governor's hand; just as they were going
to kiss it, he snatched it away, as a sign that he
accepted the civility, but would not permit them to
lower themselves to such a degree. The highest of
all bowed very low, the Governor returning the
bow. Lastly came the lowest grade, who were
permitted to kiss his hand, some on the back only,
others on the palm as well, afterwards raising it to
their foreheads. His portly Excellency meanwhile
looked very important and self-satisfied.

At last the bell rang, and the crowd went ashore.
I was quite sorry, for I should have liked to have
seen more of them and their peculiar ways. We
had, however, plenty of fellow-passengers on board

for me to study : these soon went below to don their travelling attire, which appeared mainly to consist of the garment in which Christian people go to bed. The ladies of their harems were not treated to the luxury of a cabin, but were encamped on the hurricane-deck, taking up half of the already scanty space at our disposal. They were kept in an enclosure of canvas walls, which, being open at the top, must have afforded a fine view of all the family arrangements to the officer on duty on the bridge.

There were two of these harems on board, one belonging to the Governor of Suez, and the other to a splendid-looking old man, who with his family was starting on the pilgrimage to Mecca. What a way to do a long and fatiguing journey, cooped up in a little enclosure, and never allowed to show one's nose outside! Harry told me that even on desert journeys the women are shut up in a sort of gipsy-tent pitched on the top of the baggage on a pack-camel. I am told that formerly their lords and masters used to sleep on deck near the harem enclosures, but they have now so far advanced with the times as to treat themselves to a cabin. They, however, did not have their meals below, but squatting in a circle on their shoeless heels, ate out of one big dish with their fingers. When not so engaged, or saying their prayers, they smoked a never-ending succession of cigarettes, and played at cards, chess, or backgammon, in which they were joined

by the officers and crew, who, with the exception
of the engineer, were all natives. He, I was glad
to find, was an Englishman, for the natives are
curiously casual in their duties; and even the
man at the wheel thought nothing of leaving his
post to say his prayers.

Our party at meals consisted of three Englishmen,
—Captain Lewis of the Egyptian army, hurrying
back to Suakin, having heard that fighting had
begun again; and two brothers, Mr Wood and Mr
A. Wood, the elder of whom was going as Consul to
Jeddah,—an Egyptian officer, and a young Circassian,
who looked quite mad, and, as it turned out, was a
good deal off his head.

As soon as we were under way, I lay down, very
thankful to get possession of the dirtiest of divans;
for the motion was far from pleasant, and I had
already learnt that if one takes these sort of journeys
one must begin by striking all antipathy to dirt out
of one's composition. Our Captain, a good-natured
fat Egyptian, came and chatted with me in English. I
asked him if his boat always rolled as much as she was
doing at that moment; he assured me, "That was
nothing to what she could do." He said this with
such evident pride that I could not help smiling.

After dinner we sat on deck trying to get cool,
and enjoying the fast-fading view of the African
coast, whose jagged rocky peaks stood out in sharp
relief of darkening purple against the sunset sky.

TOR.

During the night we were to cross over to the Arabian coast, and touch at Tor, a little Egyptian port and quarantine station at the northern end of the Sinai peninsula. The night was not a very pleasant one, the heat being intense. Two of our cabin-windows opened on to the forward part of the ship, in which was encamped a portion of a Sudanese regiment going from Cairo to Suakin, accompanied by their wives and babies; whilst between them and us were heaped up in crates the wretched fowls, destined to be killed one by one, though many of them were already dying from the intense heat. With a slight head-breeze we got the full benefit of their combined odours.

Next morning we were up early, and found we were only going six knots an hour, the pilot having all the time to keep a sharp look-out for coral-reefs. At nine we anchored off Tor, but had to lie some way out, the reefs making it dangerous to go very near.

Captain Lewis assured us there was nothing worth seeing on shore, a statement which the view from the ship certainly did not discredit; so we remained on board, and I sketched the settlement, consisting of three palm-trees and what looked like a few mud-walls dropped on the seaward edge of a burning plain of yellow sand, bounded at a distance of some ten or fifteen miles by the range of Sinai, a mass of sharp-cut peaks and rocky gorges, now in the fore-

noon mostly in a deep purple shade, relieved by a
still darker shadow in the clefts, with here and there
a glow on some pinnacle that had caught the sun.
Except for those lonely palms, on shore there was
no sign of life—all looked so dead and burnt that one
could hardly even imagine there could be sound;
though, judging by the inhabitants who soon boarded
us, I have no doubt I should have been disillusioned
had I gone ashore.   Hardly had the anchor dropped
than a dozen big-sailed native boats were racing
towards us, dashing full speed, until it seemed as
if their bows were on the point of being crushed in
against our hull, when by a dexterous turn they
were swung round alongside; the big sails flapped,
and the crews were scrambling over the bulwarks,
each urging us to come ashore in their own boat—
the best of the flotilla—almost before one's heart
had ceased to jump in anticipation of their disaster.
They were wild, picturesque-looking fellows, with
the scantiest of clothing, their only ornaments consisting of fish-bones stuck through their hair.   From
their appearance I should have thought them a
match for anybody; but one of them, who came on
board with a basket of dates for sale, got so terribly
worsted in a passage of words with an old Sudanese
hag, who was in some way attached to the troops,
that he had completely to surrender and let her
take his goods at her own price.   I must say the
way she pinned him into a corner and heaped in-

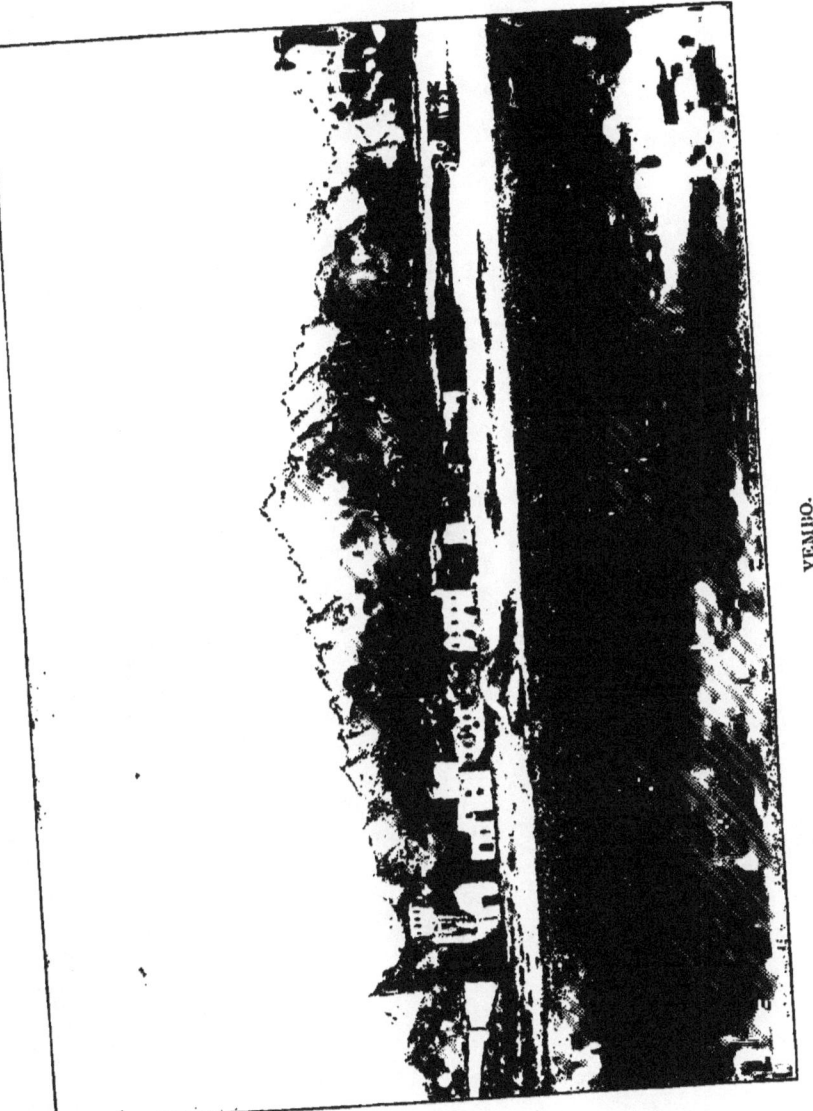

YEMBO.

vectives on him, whirling her withered arms about his face, was enough to frighten the bravest man.

Here the Governor and his harem left us, thus placing a little more of the deck at our disposal.

At noon we started again with the wind dead ahead, passing Shadwan Island at five o'clock in the evening, and the Dædalus reef and lighthouse at six on the following morning. The Captain told me that the two lighthouse - keepers spent nine months out of every twelve on that bit of rock, hardly as large as a good-sized room. What an existence !

In the afternoon I made an expedition forward among the Sudanese, and greatly delighted one proud young mother of about fifteen by taking her baby in my arms; it was certainly a nice little thing, with bright eyes, white teeth, and head like a black egg. They all seemed very happy and cheery together, and, in spite of their ugliness, there was something very taking about them. The men are splendid, and looked remarkably smart in their snow-white uniforms.

At 10.30 A.M. on September the 24th, we sighted Yembo. After passing through an opening about 300 yards wide between the reefs, we entered a wide lagoon forming a fair-sized and safe harbour. Nine other vessels of various tonnage were at anchor. Looking at them through my glasses, they appeared like ant-hills, overrun as 'they were with black fig-

ures. The Captain informed us they were all pilgrims
who had done the double journey to Mecca and Medina ; those who only go to Mecca re-embarking at
Jeddah.

As we got nearer, the din of voices was indescribable. Most of the men looked perfectly wild, rushing about trying to secure some corner on their
respective homeward-bound vessels. I never saw
such a scramble in my life ; they looked more like
a troop of monkeys than anything else, as they
bounded over any cargo that happened to be in their
way, swinging themselves from rope to rope about
the rigging.

We anchored not far from the wharf, which was
black with a moving excited crowd. The tall well-
made Arabs in their *burnouses*, with their well-
defined features and graceful movements, were a
great contrast to their more ragged fellow-pilgrims.
On a French vessel alongside of us, bound for the
north of Africa, were some very wild-looking men,
worn and emaciated, with their clothing in rags.
The Captain told us the pilgrims have to pay so
highly for what they want on the journey that they
soon get to the end of their resources. How strong
and beautiful must be their faith to cause them to
leave their home without having the slightest idea
when they may return ! Some of them come from
the west coast of Africa, walking across the desert
through totally unknown lands, guiding themselves

by the rising sun,—men and women, old and young,
enduring such sufferings and privations that many
die by the way. Death on the return journey is
considered perfect happiness, as then they feel sure
of attaining the Paradise for which they have for-
saken everything. Among them we saw many so
crippled that they had to be carried; others were
almost skeletons.

Soon after we anchored the two brothers Wood
went on shore, but soon came back, saying it was
dangerous for me to go into that crowd. They
had been pelted with stones in the town. As we
were anxious to see the place, however, their experience did not stop us. So I put on a thick veil
notwithstanding the heat, out of respect to native
prejudice, and soon realised how much veiled women
must suffer! Many of them are entirely covered
with a cotton stuff thrown over their heads, reaching to their feet, and tied round the neck, only
leaving two small holes for the eyes. When they
eat in public they loosen the string round the
neck, and pass the food up underneath this long
garment.

Having secured a very rickety canoe manned by
two fierce-looking natives, we landed after several
perilous encounters with boats crammed to over-
flowing with shouting pilgrims, who certainly looked
more like wild beasts than human beings, but, all
the same, very picturesque from the brilliant colour-

ing of their cotton garments. On landing we had great difficulty in getting through the crowd ; and the odours that filled the atmosphere were over-powering. By dint of wriggling under bare arms and over sprawling forms, we managed to get into the heart of the town, which we found entirely deserted by all except a band of very unpleasant-looking dogs in search of food. The inhabitants were either safe in their flat-roofed mud-houses, or seeing those unwelcome birds of passage—the pilgrims—off the premises. I never saw streets so empty or houses in such a tumble-down condition. But for some awnings here and there on the flat roofs, made of rough sticks with some rags thrown over them, evidently for the convenience of the women when sitting on their house-tops, one would have imagined one's self in a city of the dead.

A few minutes' walk brought us to the eastern wall of the town, at one of the gates of which we came across a drowsy sentry sitting on his heels and hugging his rifle, as he pensively contemplated three rusty guns, which from their appearance might have come out of the Ark. Then following a narrow street to our left, we found ourselves in the bazaar, where the crowd was so dense that it was almost impossible to pass. However, by winding through various dirty streets, we at last reached the wharf, or rather the edge of the crowd that was on it.

Before making our way home I was anxious to

photograph some groups; so with great difficulty we edged our way to a shady corner of the square, stepping over camels' necks, piles of goods, and shapeless heaps of rags, which, from the groans that issued from them as we passed, I suppose hid human beings. Opposite us was a well-built house with lovely *mushrabieh* windows, through which we could see three veiled women in white, evidently watching the departure of the pilgrims. As I had taken the precaution of putting on a dust-cloak to conceal my camera, my proceedings attracted no special attention; and I managed to get some very good shots. The people were certainly not such as I should have cared to run the risk of alarming by levelling a strange-looking instrument at them.

I had seen enough of native crowds for one day, and as we returned on board I looked forward to the comparative peace and purer air of the "Messir," and was therefore anything but agreeably surprised to find our ship overrun with pilgrims. Our steward, Ibrahim, tried to explain that the Captain had at first refused to take them; but finding there were *only* three hundred, he had given in. Three hundred to occupy a space which would only hold a few dozen ordinary mortals! It took so long getting them on board that we had to put off our departure till the following morning. Sleep was quite out of the question for that night—the din of voices never ceasing, not to mention the heat, mosquitoes, and the homely flea, of which last a cargo had been shipped with no extra charge.

At 10.30 A.M. we steamed out, passing close to the "Malacca," an old P. and O. liner, which the Sultan of Zanzibar had bought for the use of the pilgrims belonging to his dominions. She was so crowded that several of the Haajis had taken refuge in the rigging, where they were perched like Japanese acrobats on a pole, sheltering themselves from the burning sun under small cotton European parasols of various colours. Towards luncheon-time we were rolling so tremendously that our Captain, who was not a first-rate sailor, being anxious to have an hour's quiet for his mid-day meal, turned the vessel's head round, causing her to pitch so that certainly one passenger—if not more—went without lunch; besides which, we lost an hour. But what is an hour to the son of the East?

Later in the day I went forward to make acquaintance with our new fellow-passengers—a miserable sight. They were a ragged hungry-looking crowd of all ages—many of the men seeming as if they had parted with all their worldly goods except the daggers, splendidly mounted in silver, which they still wore.

Life on board ship is monotonous at the best of times; but when it is too hot to sleep, and one is too ill to read, it becomes doubly so. On the following day, however, our Circassian fellow-passenger provided us with excitement enough and to spare. He had been gradually getting wilder in his manner ever since he came on board, spending the whole of his time writing letters, which he tore up as soon as they were written. He confided to Mr Wood that he had been crossed in love; whether that had turned his head, or whether it was merely a delusion, I do not know, but at any rate he in some way connected Harry with his misfortune. He was "sure the Englishman knew his thoughts even before he put them on paper," and the result was that he glared most unpleasantly at Harry whenever he met him. I tried to make friends with him at meals, as he sat next to me; but as he only burst out laughing whenever I spoke to him, I gave him up as hopeless.

On the morning after leaving Yembo I was on deck talking to Mr Wood, when up rushed our madman. He stood for a moment in front of us, muttering something in French, meanwhile taking off his coat. Then with a bound he jumped overboard. Mr Wood just got hold of his foot for one moment, thereby checking his fall. Instinct seemed to make the wretched man catch at a rope, to which he clung out of reach, his feet dangling, dragging along in the water. We tried to persuade him to come up again, but he only shouted back that we were all his enemies, and were trying to put his people at home against him. After a time he

thought better of it, and scrambled into a safer
position, watching the waves, and leaving us in
doubt whether he would not again throw himself in.
At last, after much talking and persuasion on our
part, he was induced to climb up and get on deck,
apparently thoroughly shaken, and having for the
time being frightened himself back to his right
senses.   Our usually quiet, indolent Captain was
a sight to see, rushing about asking what he should
do with such a madman on board.   We were all
of one mind, that the Circassian should be landed at·
the first place we touched at; and the steward was
in the meanwhile told to keep a close watch over
him, for which I was thankful, as, knowing his hatred
of Harry, I felt a little nervous.   At lunch, to my
astonishment, the poor man came quietly up to me
and begged my pardon for having given me such a
fright.   He very rightly remarked that if Mr Wood
had let him have a dip it would have done him
worlds of good.

In the afternoon the venerable owner of the harem
and his men-followers appeared on deck with their
loins enveloped in what looked like bath-towels, but
wearing nothing on their heads, arms, or legs, having
divested themselves of their usual travelling attire.
Ibrahim explained to me that we had that afternoon
passed a place called Sherm Ràbigh, at which point
all pilgrims going to Mecca had to clothe themselves
in that species of sackcloth until they had accom-

plished their pilgrimage. What tortures town-bred natives accustomed to European clothes must endure with so little to protect their bodies from the burning sun!

We were due at Jeddah that afternoon, and as all the pilgrims and future pilgrims were to land there, the collecting and sorting of their different goods caused an indescribable bustle on board. Out of the harem appeared the old man's two wives, dressed entirely in black, having over their faces a piece of muslin so thin that their features were distinctly visible. Both were evidently Circassians. The elder, who still showed traces of good looks, seemed to act the part of handmaid to the younger wife, who, conscious of her youth and beauty, quite took it as her due. With them was a lovely little girl—the daughter of the old man—with magnificent eyes, clear complexion, and well-cut features. She was allowed to run about amongst us. It was sad to think of such a lovely delicate child having to undergo all the hardships of that long journey.

Towards two o'clock we anchored some miles from the town, only small boats being able to sail in and out among the coral-reefs. This was Mr Wood's destination; and on leaving, he invited us to come and see his future home, should we go ashore. As we were to remain at anchor till the next morning we accepted, but waited patiently

B

till the crowd had gone ashore, which they only
accomplished after many disputes with the boatmen
about the high charges. It was a pretty sight to see
about thirty little sailing-boats, clumsily made, but
going a good pace, racing each other among the
reefs. Dotted about were small canoes, each dug
out of one tree, their owners fishing for coral.
We secured a nice sailing-boat with a jolly, bright-
faced black boy, as quick and active in his movements as a monkey. Certainly he needed to be so,
for in shaping his course through the zigzagging
reefs, he had constant changes of wind and current
to contend with; and it was only by continually
raising and lowering the sail, sometimes rowing
with all his might, or by suddenly touching the
rudder with his foot, that he finally brought us to
Jeddah in safety.

As we approached I took several photographs
of the town, which looked most imposing with its
high square houses, most of them whitewashed,
and thus bringing out to advantage the large
unpainted *mushrabieh* windows. To the wharf
were fastened a great number of crooked-masted
dhows. There being no pier, our boatman carried
us ashore on his back. Before we left him he
gave us a ring made of a bit of silver wire twisted
like a rope, so that when we returned we should
hold it up as a signal of recognition. This was
all settled by signs and many smiles on his part.

After passing through a very busy crowd loading
and unloading cargo, we soon found ourselves in
the bazaar, the largest I had ever seen. It is
in a wide street; but the rays of the sun are
excluded, and a cool and mysterious appearance
is given by an ingenious arrangement of roofing.
On poles placed across the street from house to
house, at a height of about twelve feet from the
ground, is laid a network of bamboos, with varied
pieces of canvas and other stuffs scattered on the
top, the whole being supported by occasional upright poles. On each side are the shops, which
are raised about three feet from the ground, and
resemble nothing so much as a row of pigeon-
holes, averaging seven feet by five, but varying
somewhat in size according to the wares contained
in them; at night they are made secure by shutters,
which during the day are kept beneath the floor.
The merchandise was very varied: fruit of many
sorts; beads which were unmistakably from Bir-
mingham; cotton stuffs as clearly from Man-
chester; carpets, of course; black coral cigarette-
holders made by the natives; scents of many different kinds. A *narghilé* was generally to be seen
in a corner, and a pair of red slippers close at
hand. Most of the owners were sleeping or smoking, the only busy ones being the metal-workers
and the tailors; the latter not only making the
clothes, but generally embroidering the material

as well. We were soon followed by a crowd offering us their wares; but we did not stop, being anxious to reach Mr Wood's house, and afterwards to visit Eve's Tomb, the great sight of the place.

After leaving the bazaar we walked through many streets, all of them very short, with sharp turns to the right and left, until we accidentally hit upon a house on which waved the British flag. There, sure enough, we found the new Consul. He showed us over his future abode, which certainly might be made very picturesque, with its airy rooms and pretty look-out on the sea; but a few tables and chairs, left by the last tenant, were then the only pieces of furniture.

Mr Wood offered to send his *cavass* to escort us to the tomb; and soon there appeared a very imposing-looking old man, with bare feet, a short red coat embroidered in gold, and white breeches, having at his side a long sword in a beautiful silver sheath, and carrying a stick with an elaborate silver knob, which he flourished in the way so familiar to us in the drum-major at home. We sallied forth, and soon found these weapons were most useful—the stick for the horrid famished dogs, and the sword to threaten the crowd of little black urchins who would follow and throw stones at us. Our guide hurried along the narrow streets to a gate in the town wall, whence we walked on for a quarter of a mile ankle-deep in sand, passing by

the barracks, in front of which several Turkish
officers on horseback were drilling their men, all
dressed in white cotton uniforms. At last we
reached Eve's supposed resting-place, a strip of
land a hundred feet long by twenty broad, enclosed
between low walls, with a small gate at each end.
After going about three-quarters of the length
between these walls, we came to a small mosque,
which our guide told us was built over our first
mother's heart, and in which two men kneeling on
mats were praying very earnestly and in loud tones.
When we expressed our surprise at the length of
the tomb, our guide was ready with his answer,
"Having been the mother of us all, she was naturally very tall." As it was getting late we hurried
back to the shore, and after some time found our
nice boy, who had several native passengers in his
boat ready to be taken on board.

While waiting for dinner I stood on deck watching a boat being laden with cargo, in the bow
of which were two men repeating their evening
prayers. Unfortunately for them they were just
on a level with our waste-steam pipe, which the
inconsiderate engineer suddenly opened, causing the
boiling steam to fly straight in their faces. A
roar of laughter was all the sympathy they got,
and they soon ended by joining in the merriment,
quite forgetting to finish their devotions.

The next morning Ibrahim asked me if I would

go marketing with him. I gladly accepted, being
always ready for sight-seeing; so five o'clock
found me again going on shore, chaperoned by our
Egyptian steward. Although so early, it was very
hot, and the bazaar was more crowded than the
day before by natives in all kinds of coloured
costumes. We first went for our provisions to a
bazaar I had not yet visited. If the heat had not
for many days past deprived me of all wish to
touch meat, the sight I saw there certainly would
have done so, the butchers' shops being simply
black with flies. I speedily deserted Ibrahim, and
turned my attention to the more tempting vegetable
and fruit stalls, where he afterwards joined me.
There were pyramids of pomegranates, some split
open, showing their lovely crimson seeds; next to
them were water-melons of curious shapes; while
among the vegetables I seized upon an old favourite,
the purple fruit of the egg-plant. Ibrahim com-
plained that in consequence of my being there they
asked him double the usual price for everything.
This made him very angry.

Having got hold of a boy to convey his purchases
to the boat, he took me into a narrow street where
the metal-workers lived in dirty little shops. I
bought several silver charms, but on the whole
there was little worth purchasing. On our way
back we stopped at a scent-shop to buy some attar
of roses, which was very cheap; the man covered

my hands with all kinds of scents, each more delicious than the other. Seeing a fruit-stall opposite covered with beautiful grapes, bananas, and limes, we got another small boy, and loaded him with these tempting spoils. I was beginning to feel very hot and hungry, so Ibrahim took me to a *café*. I could not help laughing to find myself sitting *en tête-à-tête* with Ibrahim drinking delicious black coffee at a small marble table in a cool and spacious room full of strange men. It was twelve o'clock before we got back to the vessel.

II.

During our absence there had been several new arrivals. Among them was Father Luigi Bonomi, the Roman Catholic priest—a tall handsome man with a kind intelligent face—who escaped from El Obeid in June 1885. Harry and he recognised each other directly, for after his escape he made his way to the camp where Harry was at Dongola.

That afternoon we left for Suakin, and got into a nasty cross-sea, which made the "Messir" roll even more than ever; and as we were already nearly mad with prickly heat, the night was one of misery. The next morning early a welcome little yellow bird flew past our port-hole, a sign that land was near. It remained some time on the ship; and Captain Lewis, thinking it was thirsty, told his

black servant, Mustapha, to give it some water in
a plate. The intelligent youth brought up some
thick cabbage-soup!

Soon afterwards we sighted the African coast, and
steamed along about fifteen hundred yards distant
from it for some miles. As we passed abreast of
Sheikh Barud's Tomb, which was visible in the far
distance, the sailors threw a bucketful of fresh water
overboard, providing, as they believed, some water
for the holy man to drink, there being no fresh
water on any part of that coast. It is a barren-
looking country, with its hard line of rocky hills
overlooking the narrow sandy plain dotted with
stunted mimosa-bushes, which the dervishes found
so useful as cover during the fighting, crawling like
snakes from one to the other.

Suakin was now in sight, and the excitement was
great on board, as we did not know what reception
we should meet with. For all we knew, the enemy
might be in possession. Some one thought he saw
smoke in the distance. Was it Suakin burning?
Should we be able to get into harbour? Many
were the conjectures. Captain Lewis, who had
been very unwell all the voyage, was now quite a
different man, looking forward with joy to more
fighting. Suddenly we heard a cannon-shot; and
by looking through his glasses, Harry made out
that a shell had been fired from Fort Handoub.
Evidently Suakin had not yet surrendered. While

HADENDOWA ARABS.

we were anxiously listening another gun was fired, this time from a man-of-war in the harbour.

At about three o'clock we steamed into the sheltered little harbour, passing on the left the native cemetery, and on the right Quarantine Island, which contains the European graveyard. Before the anchor was lowered a crowd of natives, with long curious wooden spikes sticking in their curly heads, scrambled on deck; and as soon as we were brought to, Captain Lewis went ashore, soon returning with Mr Bewley, the owner of a large house in Suakin, who kindly offered to put us up during our two days' stay. This offer we gladly accepted; and after putting a few things together, we were rowed ashore. No one who has not experienced the discomforts of a small dirty Egyptian steamer can realise the delightful feeling of finding one's self in a clean and airy house.

I was shown up to a big room opening on to a wide balcony overlooking the harbour. Two little black boys were deputed to wait upon us. With great trouble I got rid of them and began to unpack, but every few minutes the door was opened and a little black grinning face peered in. While we were at lunch we heard continual firing on all sides. Mr Bewley told us that H.M.S. "Gannet," at anchor not far off, had been firing the whole of the day before, but that now she was running short of ammunition, and was anxiously awaiting the arrival of another man-of-war. Most of the firing had to be done from the forts, situated at various distances from the town. About fifteen hundred dervishes were hidden in trenches, ready for an attack on the town, which was expected at any moment; and it was believed that they had strong reinforcements on the hills to support them. Their supposed object was to make for Quarantine Island, on which were the condensers. The fresh water once in their possession, they knew full well the town would soon have to surrender. The hospital is built on that same island. Some nights before, the enemy had come quite close; and two prisoners, who were not so ill as they made out, escaped and joined them. Osman Digna used to mark any deserters from the Egyptian ranks by cutting off a finger, so as always to know them. I do not know whether Osman Naib, who was then in command of the dervish force outside Suakin, carried out the same agreeable custom. This general had superseded Osman Digna by order of the Khalifa, by whom Osman Digna had at that time been recalled to Khartum. Two of the enemy had deserted the week before and come into the town. The trenches, they said, were full of the dead and dying, and with the heat were becoming pestilential. The dervishes worked all night making these trenches, but stupidly dug most of them in a line with the forts, so that the guns could sweep right down them, causing great havoc.

This night-work was stopped by the electric light being turned on. It seems the first time the dervishes saw themselves all lit up by it there was a panic among them.

After lunch Captain Lewis came to take Harry round the outer forts, one of which was not more than four hundred yards from the enemy's trenches. I was most anxious to go with them, but it was thought to be too risky, as casualties were constantly happening; so during their absence Mr Bewley rowed me across to one of the nearer forts on the south side of the harbour, where, after making our way through the hedge of wire entanglements that surrounded it, I followed him up a high and very lightly made ladder into the guard-room, and thence on to the parapet. There I got a good view of the enemy's intrenchments, in which the dervishes, looking like black specks, were moving to and fro. At the foot of the fort, just inside the town wall, was a tennis-court, in which a game was going on; and as I could see it and the enemy's lines at the same time, the picture was a curious mixture of homely everyday life and the excitement of war. On the one side of the wall, the two men wholly absorbed in their game; on the other, the fanatics only waiting for a favourable opportunity to rush and cut all our throats; in the middle, the Egyp-

tian soldiers in the fort, rather bored with their
day on guard, and, purely as a matter of business,
potting the Arabs as occasion offered.

We were invited to dine at mess by Captain
Lewis, and on our arrival at the roomy verandah
overlooking the harbour were received by ten
English officers. There were two other guests—
the *Commandant* and the Lieutenant of a French
man-of-war at anchor in the harbour. I was at
once introduced to them, and they were very much
surprised to meet one of their countrywomen in this
out-of-the-way place. The *Commandant* told me
they had broken down in the Red Sea, and put
in at the nearest port, not knowing there were any
disturbances. They steamed in straight for the
farthest end of the harbour—as it happened, just
placing themselves between H.M.S. "Gannet's" guns
and the enemy. He laughingly said to me, " Every
one thought that we were mad. I soon backed
out, having been informed what was going on."
We had a long talk about " La Belle France," and
became great friends.

Mr Gordon, General Gordon's nephew, was the
moving spirit of the party. Always hard at work,
at that time he was very busy putting up electric
light on the big town gate, which he had built.
He had also put up several telephones—one connecting the mess-room with the " John Pender," the
telegraph ship then at anchor in the inner harbour,

which he set going to ask them to turn the electric
light on the enemy for our amusement. Unfortunately something had happened, and it could not
be done.

A bevy of small Hadendowa boys waited at table,
each more cheeky than the other. The smallest, a
bright-eyed little monkey, who kept watching us,
was a great pet of one of the officers. When
he was asked which he thought was the nicest
of us, he pointed at me, saying, " Zu takes the
cake ! " Some time before, a boy had deserted
to the enemy, and shortly afterwards his master,
who had just returned from leave with some new
uniform, finding himself at rather close quarters
with the dervishes in a skirmish, heard a voice from
the bush saying, " You've got them all on ! " and
looking up, recognised his former servant.

After dinner Mr Gordon made the boys dance and
sing music-hall songs. At ten o'clock we rowed
home, glad to get a night's rest in comfortable beds.

I was awakened very early by the continual
firing, and as my bed faced the window, I could
watch the forts enveloped in smoke. The two little
black boys brought us all we required, and requested
I would let them wash some clothes ; so I gave them
a few pocket-handkerchiefs, hoping that would keep
them quiet and out of the way during my dressing.
No such luck ! They were very soon back, and
creeping in noiselessly, came and stood by my dress-

ing-table, where they amused themselves by examining all the contents of my dressing-bag, poking each other in the ribs with delight; but what seemed to fascinate them most was to watch me curl my fringe. I am sure they must have inspected the lamp with care after I had gone to breakfast. At nine Mr Bewley took me to see the town, which was kept most scrupulously clean by the convicts, whose morning duty was to sweep the streets. We met men carrying skins full of water, which they sell in small quantities. We passed over the drawbridge and causeway that connect the island of El Kaf, on which the Government buildings are situated, with the town proper. The shallow water beneath was black with little urchins grovelling in the mud. A little way farther on we reached the big square, where the day before two women had been killed by the enemy's shells. On the other side of this square stands one of the town gates. I was only allowed to walk two paces outside it, as one immediately becomes a mark for the dervishes, who are all day on the look-out for pot-shots.

The remnant of the rolling stock of the Suakin and Berber Railway was at that moment returning from its round of carrying food and ammunition to the forts. It consisted of an engine and two carriages; the driver was concealed and protected by sheets of iron, a very necessary precaution, as the enemy constantly fired at the train on its daily rounds, without however seeming to cause much damage. I shall always regret not having gone to the forts in it; it would not have been a bit more dangerous than many other things I did during this journey.

Walking home, Mr Bewley gave me a description of a Greek funeral he had attended the week before. The coffin was taken in a boat from the town across to the cemetery, where, after landing, the friends removed the lid, exposing the corpse to view; it was that of a young bridegroom dressed in his wedding-suit, with his wife's bridal wreath of orange-blossoms tied round his forehead, her bouquet over his hands. All the friends stooped to kiss him three times, and then in turn poured claret, incense, and ashes over him. The body was then lowered into the grave; and a friend being helped down, knelt on the corpse and tore the clothes from off it before screwing down the lid. To finish up this ghastly ceremony, they all drank liqueurs standing round the grave.

Just before lunch the Governor-General, Colonel Holled-Smith, came to call on us, and invited us to dine with him that night. In the afternoon Captain Lewis took us in a boat to visit the "John Pender," on which we were shown the cables and dynamos. There were two delightful monkeys on board belonging to a nice old sailor, who made them show off all their tricks. On leaving the "John Pender" we rowed back round Quarantine Island to the extreme end of the harbour, where H.M.S. "Gannet" was anchored. The Captain being on shore, Lieutenant James did the honours of his ship, and showed us the big gun which they had been using to fire at the enemy. With the help of a strong telescope the trenches were distinctly visible, and while standing on deck we saw a wounded soldier carried on a stretcher from one of the forts to the hospital. Similar casualties were constantly happening, although the firing had greatly diminished that day. During the night the enemy's fire always ceased.

At eight o'clock we walked over to Government House for dinner. The only other guest was Captain Bradford of H.M.S. "Gannet," a nice cheery sailor, delighted to have a chance of dining with his fellow-creatures. We were given an excellent dinner out in the cool verandah, a fresh breeze keeping the flies and insects away. It is rather distressing, until one gets used to it, to find one's soup and wine black with them in a second. Before leaving, which we did soon after dinner on account of our early start next morning, our host showed us the improvements he had made in the house.

September the 30th, 6.30 A.M., found us on board again, and steaming out saluted by the enemy's firing, which was incessant. In about half an hour we passed abreast of the place between Suakin and Tamai where Baker's zereba was made in 1884, and McNeill's in 1885. Suddenly there was a great excitement, the crew rushing to the side of the ship and eagerly pointing at something in the water. The Captain called us, and we hurried after him in time to see part of the body of some enormous sea-monster arching itself out of the water in a semi-circle, and only to be compared in appearance to the coils of a gigantic eel. The crew called it a *batàn;* but if it was not our friend the sea-serpent, it must have been some near relation. The Captain told us he had seen it before alongside the ship, some hundred feet long. The large portion we saw certainly led us to believe there must be a great deal more under water.

Though there was a strong breeze, the heat was intense, and the old divan was my one consolation; I lay there for hours watching the Captain and the steward sitting on their heels playing backgammon. As we were passing abreast of Trinkitat, the latter kindly interrupted his game to point out to me several *sambuks,* mostly engaged in smuggling and the slave-trade, which was said to be very flourishing at that time.

The heat in the night was intolerable; everything damp, and our clothes were more fit to be wrung out than worn. Pitching was again added to all the other discomforts, and the wind was so strong against us that our poor little boat could only make four and a half knots an hour, so that all hope of reaching Massowah by daylight had to be given up.

It was seven o'clock in the evening and pitch-dark
when we at length steamed into the harbour. The
rows of lights on shore gave one the impression of a
big town with many *boulevards* running in different
directions. Several boats were soon distinctly visible
making towards us, entirely lit up by the most vivid
phosphorescence I had ever seen. It was a fairy-like
scene, the oars starting ripples of light every time
they were dipped in the water. Ibrahim told me he
thought if we could that night interview General
Bordighera, commanding the Italian troops, he might
allow us to go and visit the fort at Saati, some miles
inland. Being anxious to see as much of the country
and its colonists as possible, we agreed to go ashore
at once, and try what could be done. There was also
another great inducement—an iced drink, which Ibrahim said could be got at any of the little *cafés* on
the wharf. The ice on board having been finished
days before, we had suffered a good deal from the
want of it. We left him no peace until he had got
us a boat and escorted us to a regular Italian *café*
with little marble-topped tables outside.

The iced drink quite refreshed us, and having
found out that the General's headquarters were on
the other side of the harbour, we again got into
our boat, and were rowed across to a well-built
landing-place, escaping on the way several imminent
collisions, thanks to the brilliancy of the phosphor-
escent light, none of the boats having lanterns on

board. Making for a large, square, whitewashed house with battlemented walls, we ascended a double flight of steps leading on to a terrace where sentries were walking up and down. Passing through large double doors, we were met by an officer, who received us most cordially, and after hearing our request, wrote an order which would enable us to see all we wanted, and gave us leave to go by the train which starts at an early hour every morning for military purposes. He told us at the same time, that as the General was out, he would take it upon himself to telegraph to the Colonel commanding the fort to be in readiness to receive us.

We returned to our uncomfortable little ship, proud of our success. That night was the most terrible one we had as yet experienced. Sleep was out of the question; the sheets seemed to burn one's skin, and there was not a breath of air to relieve the feeling of suffocation. As Harry expressed it, " We were like pats of butter in July." Next morning Ibrahim, having taken French leave, accompanied us. Starting at 5.30, and passing on our way the picturesque old galleried hospital-ship " Garibaldi," we soon reached the landing-stage.

The town presented quite a different appearance by daylight, being by no means so imposing as when lit up. All the European houses are small, and built on the quay, taking up most of one side of the harbour. On reaching the little wooden pier leading to

the station, we had to wait in our boat some time,
the whole place being taken up by a large cargo of
ice, the daily consumption of the Saati garrison.
The station was a large hut, copied from those used
at Suakin; close to it were great store-houses. All
the daily stores having been placed on the trucks,
we started, our fellow-passengers being several non-
commissioned officers and men, most of them looking
pale and worn. We had to travel twenty-five kilo-
metres to reach our destination. The first part of
the journey was through an alluvial plain, which
might well have been cultivated as far as Monkullo,
but there were only native camps dotted about without a vestige of vegetation near. Ibrahim told us
that soon after the Italians came to Massowah
a large fire broke out in the native quarters, which
were entirely composed of huts. Since then all
natives had been ordered to live in properly built
houses, to which most of them objected, prefer-
ring to camp out in the plain. The Italians have
dug a good many wells for the benefit of their
various forts; and all the water in the town is
brought by means of pipes from these wells, which
are worked by horses. We stopped at several
stations, or rather store-houses, to deposit provisions
for the outlying posts. Leaving the plain behind
us, we reached a rocky and hilly country, where
we were shown Dogeli, the scene of the Italians'
first battle against the Abyssinians. The line of

railway has been most skilfully made, notwithstanding all the difficulties which must have been
encountered. On reaching Saati station—well built
and kept beautifully clean—we were received by
a young officer, who in very good French told us
that a telegram announcing our arrival had been
received, and that his Colonel was at that moment
coming down the hill to meet us.

The Colonel soon appeared, a short, cheerful-look-
ing man with white hair and charming manners,
who at once made us welcome. His French was
somewhat difficult to understand, but we soon became great friends. The young officer we had first
met asked if I should mind riding a mule without
a side-saddle, as the road was all up and down hill,
and I should find it very hot walking. I was delighted at the offer; so several mules were brought
for the party, mine being led by a young soldier
who had been chosen on account of his having
been brought up in England: he told me that his
father still lived in London, but that he had been
obliged to return to Italy to serve his time in the
army. Off we started, the Colonel leading the way
up a steep hill, on the top of which was a battery
containing six big guns, two Gardner guns, and
a detachment˙ of about one hundred men; close
by were the telegraph office, a pigeon-house full of
pigeons—in case of siege—and the infirmary, containing twenty-four beds, of which nineteen were

then occupied. There is always less sickness here than at Massowah, owing to the fresh breeze which is constantly blowing on this elevated spot.

We then rode down a very steep place to a small iron bridge over a ravine, in which runs a Decauville line connecting an outlying pepper-box fort with the railway station. After crossing the narrow bridge, we climbed to the top of a second hill, where barracks are built for a company of infantry, with another battery containing ten guns pointing to the west, the direction in which the enemy last appeared. The soldiers were just receiving their rations of tinned meat, ice, and wine, with which they all looked very contented. From this hill we rode to a small plateau overlooking the railway station. Here was the soldiers' mess-hut; opposite to it another hut for the kitchen; and behind this a small theatre where the non-commissioned officers act every Sunday. The Colonel told me there was always great competition for the women's parts. Close to the theatre, on the brow of the hill, we were shown a life-sized statue of a soldier who was killed while fighting the Abyssinians, made in red clay by some of his comrades; it was quite a work of art. On a separate little mound stands the officers' club, a pretty, well-furnished little hut, with open verandahs all round; in the centre was a large table covered with newspapers, and at one end a bar at which every kind of iced drink could be bought. After partaking of the latter, we left our mules and walked across to the mess-room, a large airy hut, made, like all the others, of bamboo. The Colonel persuaded us to remain for breakfast; and as the morning train was returning to Massowah in a few minutes, the officers all advised us to stop till the evening, and travel back in the cool, a proposition to which we gladly agreed.

Breakfast being ready, and the punkahs in full swing, we sat down, twenty-two in all. The officer who sat next Harry was full of energy, and after we had finished an excellent meal, wanted to take us to see his company of Bashi-Bazouks; but the Colonel said it was too hot, and that we must put it off till the afternoon. So after some cigarettes had been smoked, it being the usual hour for a siesta, our kind host took us to his hut, composed of two rooms, which he put at our disposal. He ordered the young soldier who spoke English to sit outside in case we required anything; and he himself, before leaving, saw that everything had been properly prepared for us—a big wooden tub, a little camp-bed in each room, scent-bottles and *articles de toilette* beautifully arranged on the table. The hut had double walls of matting, and was kept perfectly cool by a strong breeze blowing through the passage between them.

We slept from eleven to three o'clock, and were only awakened then by our sentry informing us that the young officer had come with mules to take us to see his company; so dressing hurriedly, we soon mounted under a broiling sun. I was beginning to wish the Bashi-Bazouks had never existed, when, on turning a corner, we came upon an Abyssinian caravan which had just arrived. It was a curious sight : there were about five hundred dark, wild-looking men and women, their hair curiously entangled, and wearing little or no clothes; the children, though very dirty, were bright-eyed and intelligent-looking. This was said to be the largest caravan that had passed since the Italian occupation. There were a great number of camels and mules, which are used chiefly to carry the skins and *dhurra* these people bring to the coast to exchange for European wares. Our friend then took us to see his black soldiers, mostly very fine strong-looking men. Their women were in a separate camp at some distance from the men's huts.

As the train started at 4.15, we went straight to the station, where the Colonel and other officers came to see us off. I was given a basket with oranges and lumps of ice : the latter turned out most useful, as in our carriage was a non-commissioned officer who that morning had had a sunstroke, and appeared very ill. At the last station but one a young officer got into our carriage, and,

saluting Harry, said in very good English he was
the General's A.D.C., and had been sent by him to
invite us to dinner. On reaching the pier he insisted on our getting into his boat, and being rowed
to our ship to dress. Seven o'clock found us landing again near the General's quarters.

The General, Antonio Bordighera, was waiting to
receive us on the quay—a tall, dark, handsome man,
with a firm look and soldier-like bearing. He
graciously offered me his arm, and conducted us
to the house we had called at on the previous
evening, and which had been built as a palace by
a brother of Arabi Pacha. At the top of the
steps were a number of officers, to whom we were
introduced *en masse*. The General then led us
into the dining-room, a large whitewashed room,
placing me on his right hand and Harry on his
left. The band, which usually played only on
Sundays, was ordered out in our honour, and
played beautifully during the whole evening. I
told the General how I envied him having such
good ice, and he asked if we had any on board; and
hearing that such a luxury had long been exhausted, he promised to send a hundred kilos the
next morning, and kept his promise. He then explained to me how, their ice-machine having broken
down two summers ago at the very hottest time,
they had persuaded their Government to make a
contract with an English company, which sent them

ice regularly from Norway, so that they might never
be without a good supply, as, when the ice failed
them, the men who were down with fever died from
the want of it. None of the officers seemed the
least disheartened by the bad climate and the
many deaths that had occurred among them. The
General said that the great thing was to keep all
ranks well occupied, and that he had set the men
to tree-planting and gardening. A good concert-
room and theatre had been built for their amusement in the evenings. The only guest besides ourselves was the Italian consul at Hodeidah, who was
introduced to us as our future fellow-passenger. It
was getting late when we took leave of our host,
who insisted on escorting us to our boat.

The next morning about forty Indian merchants
came on board, and at 7.30 we started. The sea
was perfectly smooth, and a strong south-east wind
was most refreshing by day, but had its disadvantages when we slept on deck at night. To prevent
my sheet from being blown away altogether, I had
spread my dressing-gown over it, tucking it well
in : I was somewhat aghast the next morning to see
that the dressing-gown had been blown up into the
rigging, and that one of the native passengers had
spread his carpet within a yard of our mattresses.
At 10.30 next morning we steamed into Hodeidah
harbour. The Italian consul very courteously asked
us to breakfast with him, adding that he was a

coffee merchant, and could give us the best Mocha
coffee that we had ever tasted. So it was settled,
and his boat having come to meet him, he took us
to the shore, which was a mile and a half off.
The little pier was crowded with natives, a few
Europeans, and a good sprinkling of Indian merchants. Our friend told us that they so rarely
see European women that I must not be astonished at their following us.

The little town has a very prosperous appearance; bales of goods are to be seen in all parts,
but the streets are far more dirty than at Jeddah,
and altogether the natives look less civilised. The
houses seem well built, with fine carved doors and
latticed windows. While waiting in the consul's
dining-room for breakfast, I amused myself by
watching a house being built just opposite. The
masons were hard at work on the walls, which were
already about 20 feet high. The mortar—a mixture
of mud and sand—was prepared down below by
young boys, and put into small round baskets,
which they very cleverly threw up in the air with
a circular motion; these were caught by the masons,
who, having emptied them at once, threw them
down again; and so on, with great rapidity, and
apparently no fatigue or effort. In the same way
each brick was sent flying up in the air, immediately caught, and put in its right place. Several
women passed while I was looking out; I noticed

that they were more thickly veiled than at Jeddah.

Besides ourselves at breakfast—which was very plain but good—were an Italian clerk, and a wicked-faced Italian who spoke French very correctly. He had been a surgeon in the Turkish army : a pretty sure sign that he had made things too hot for himself at home. He told me he could procure me any number of cat's-eyes or moonstones, so I gave him an order for several dozen, but I never received them. When travelling in out-of-the-way parts, if you want a thing, lay hands on it at once or you will never get it : in this case he told me the stones would have to be brought from Sana, where he often went, and we were much tempted to go overland to Aden and visit that place, which the consul said was well worth seeing ; but after talking it over, we thought it would be too tiring an undertaking for Harry, who was still an invalid.

We were advised to have a native policeman to escort us about the town, and were also offered an Indian clerk who spoke English. Much against Harry's wish I accepted them both, he having a great dislike to the showman class. I, on the contrary, rather like some one who can tell me about things. When the clerk arrived, he proved to be a shabby, mean-looking youth, with features exactly like a hawk, the same flat head, and nose hooked like a beak. We sallied forth, the policeman behind, and a few steps in front "the Hawk," deluging us with uninteresting information in a low unmusical voice. Everything was so mean and sneaky about the man that I could see it was all Harry could do not to dismiss him on the spot. He, however, contented himself with some sarcastic remarks, which the other either did not or would not understand. His one aim was to hurry us through the streets until we came to a miserable little European warehouse, to him the chief object of interest in the town. He informed us that over a hundred years ago an old woman lived in this place quite alone, keeping a coffee-house, no one ever going near her. "Then to whom did she sell her coffee?" asked Harry in a very sarcastic tone, which was noticed by our guide, who nevertheless continued, saying her name was "Hodeidah," and "all this place came out of her," which he evidently considered a triumphant ending.

Harry being most anxious to see a wretched man who had been chained to the ground for the last twenty years for some criminal offence, we passed through an open bazaar with nothing interesting in it, and came to a burial-place just outside the town, at the end of which was the prisoner. He was lying on the bare earth with no clothes or shelter, and a thick iron chain fastened to one foot. The kind-hearted inhabitants had often built him a shed, but no sooner was it done than he pulled it down.

There can be little doubt that he is mad. He is now looked upon as a martyr and a saint. It has become a superstition that if the inhabitants want to ensure success in any enterprise, they must supply him with food for a certain time. Harry having photographed him, we returned to our host, whom we found in his office, and who soon afterwards took us on board with a Parsee friend of his who was going to Aden, and for whom we at once conceived a violent dislike. I shall never forget the journey back in the dusk in the rickety open boat. The two boys set sail, and the boat heeled over so much that it was only by constantly shifting our positions that we saved her from capsizing. The tacking we had to do in order to reach the ship took us so far out to sea that we were buffeted unmercifully by enormous waves, which dashing over the boat drenched us to the skin.

On the morning of the 5th of October we left Hodeidah, the last port we were to touch at in the Red Sea, and passed Perim Island on the afternoon of the following day. The place is English territory, and is separated by a narrow channel from Sheikh Seyd on the Arabian coast, where the Turks have built a fort which completely commands the island. The temperature had cooled considerably, being now only 88°. A strong current against us reduced our pace to four and a half knots an hour. The Captain expected we should reach

Aden in the middle of the night; but it was not till six o'clock next morning that we woke up and found ourselves at anchor off this fiery-looking spot. I, lying on my mattress feeling utterly tired out and unwilling to go below, never noticed that the sun was striking on my uncovered head, when suddenly feeling sick and giddy, I realised that I had got a touch of the sun; so I hurried down, dressed, and packed all our things in readiness to leave the wretched little "Messir" for good.

Our Parsee acquaintance, who till then had been obliged to keep to his cabin, suddenly made his appearance, wearing his curious head-dress made of shiny American cloth shaped like an exaggerated mouthpiece of a whistle. He tormented Harry with all sorts of questions, and was most gushing in his offers to take us ashore; so Harry came down and proposed that we should remain in hiding until, tired of waiting, the man had gone without us. Having the day before us, there was no necessity to hurry. We settled our bill with Ibrahim, who, I need hardly say, was a rogue of the first water. He made us pay £20 for our food alone, and having written out his bill in Arabic, he felt safe, especially as we had made no contract beforehand.

BOOK II.

THE LAND OF ROCKS.

On the 7th of October we landed at Aden, a place so well known that I shall not describe it in detail. My first thought on seeing it was, "What shall we do with ourselves if we have to wait here several days for the next boat?" As it turned out, we were quite sorry to leave it in the end.

We secured at the Hôtel de l'Univers a large and airy room, opening on to a long wide balcony, at the farther end of which were two beds entirely enveloped in mosquito-nets. We sat looking out until attracted by a little scratching noise on the wall close to my head. I discovered that it was caused by a scorpion, whom I at once tried to dispose of by pushing him over the balcony. The noise I made in my excitement must have been too much for the unnoticed occupant of one of the beds, who unceremoniously emerged from under the folds of his net and walked leisurely past us to his room.

ADEN.

The effects of the sunstroke were making me feel so ill that the nice, one-eyed old Arab servant who was seeing to our luggage proposed I should let him give me a foot-bath of mustard and hot water, which I agreed might do me good. He came back with all the necessaries, and was soon busy trying to induce me to put my feet in the scorching water, when the door was opened very quietly, and in glided our objectionable Parsee, who sat down un-invited opposite Harry. After a short silence he began asking innumerable questions about our plans. I could see it was all Harry could do to keep his temper; luckily the breakfast-bell rang, so the man had to go. But his visits were not to end here; for later on I was lying down while Harry was writing home letters, when in he came again, with-out knocking, and took possession of the most com-fortable chair, silently making an inventory of all our worldly goods. In vain Harry said that he was busy and I was ill, but our friend only answered, " Oh yes," and never stirred; at last Harry, unable to stand it any longer, took up his hat, murmured something about posting letters, and showed him the door.

Soon after, Harry went to write his name in the Governor's—General Hogg's—book, and as soon as he was gone, our old Arab came in and asked me in very good French " why that *Pharisee* was always walking into our room? " I told him I did not

know, and that I wished he could stop him doing
so. The old man shook his head threateningly, and
promised to keep his eye on him; and certainly
that one eye did its work well, for we never saw the
detestable man again.

Some time after, Harry returned, not having
found the Governor; but a little later a message
came from Government House saying General Hogg
would like to see him. Finding we were likely to
remain a few days, the Governor at once invited us
to go and stay with him, which we did, spending
ten happy days under his hospitable roof, taking
life easily, so as to recruit our strength for the
discomforts that were surely awaiting us. As we
drove to Government House we passed him on his
way to the town, where he had suddenly been
called, the news having just arrived that the Somalis
had attacked Berbera, which required the immediate
despatch of a man-of-war, so that if necessary the
British subjects might have the means of getting
away.

Usually in the early morning the General gave
me a sketching lesson, I being only a beginner, and
very anxious to make as many sketches as possible
during our journey. Aden is a wonderful place for
beautiful lights and shades. In the afternoons we
drove—the first day to see the tanks overlooking the
town proper. It is always supposed to rain only
once every three years at Aden; and this was the

THE TANKS, ADEN.

end of the third year during which not a drop had
fallen, so that the tanks were entirely dry, and we
were able to see their great depth and the ingenious
arrangements for catching every drop of water as it
trickles down from the overhanging rocks. Oddly
enough, two nights after, I was awakened by feeling
a most refreshing drip falling on my face. The
long-waited-for rain had come, making its way
through the parched roof. I woke Harry, seeing
most of our things were getting wet, but the only
remark he made was, "Never mind. You can't
stop it, so go to sleep again." It was so true, that
the only thing left for me to do was to push my
bed into a drier corner and keep quiet. The rain
must have got into some of the bamboos and disturbed the white ants, which began increasing their
already loud scratching. They are ingenious insects, and build lovely little mud tunnels, looking
like veins, along the walls, wherever they cannot
find ready-made dark passages.

I had noticed that the Somalis often wore skin rugs
thrown round them, and I was anxious to buy one;
so one day we did a little shopping, and, in spite of
their decided smell, I was pleased to secure a couple
made of antelope-skins, beautifully tanned, with the
edges cut and plaited into long fringes.

One evening we were taken to see some acting in
barracks, and on another beautiful moonlight night
we steamed about the harbour in the General's

launch. That was the first time I had ever seen the Southern Cross, and I own I was disappointed, as I had quite expected something far more brilliant and definite in form.

The morning of October the 17th found me again packing and getting ready for a start, with the help of "Qui hai," as, from hearing the General call him, I always named his Indian servant. I only found out afterwards that it was not the man's name at all, but simply the Hindustani for "Who is there?" a call equivalent to "Come here." This of course remained a standing joke against me, like something of the same sort that happened to me up the Nile, where I was riding a donkey which was followed by its foal. The donkey-boy would continually beat the poor beast, making it go too fast for the baby-legs to follow; so airing my best Arabic, I said to him, "*Beshwaish*" (gently), to which he replied, "*Hádir*" (meaning, "I am here to obey your commands"); but this was a little beyond my Arabic, and thinking he was answering me in English, I said, "No, not harder, but softer."

After lunch the General took us in his steam-launch on board the "Java," bound for Zanzibar. Some of my friends who know Aden will smile when I tell them we were very sorry to leave the shelter of its barren rocks; but then perhaps they did not stay with that most charming and kind of hosts, General Hogg; nor had they probably had the experience of sixteen days in the Red Sea in one of the hottest months, on such a miserable little cockle-shell as the "Messir."

Our new Captain, a cheery old salt, took me down to see our cabin, which looked terribly small. The first thing that caught my eye was a large basin under my berth full of a moving mixture of treacle and live cockroaches! I had been flattering myself that, now we were on board an English ship, I should no more be haunted by these brown monsters that come creeping all over one the moment the lights are put out, eating even one's boots and gloves: almost the only thing safe from their ravages being real Russia leather. I told the Captain that nothing would induce me to sleep in my cabin, but he tried to console me by telling me they caught hundreds every night.

I then took a look round at our fellow-passengers, and soon made out with the Captain's help who they all were. Two young men sitting together were Mr Gedge and Mr Jackson—the latter a naturalist —who were joining the East African Company. Then came two young missionary girls, chaperoned by a converted black boy of eight in European clothes. Besides these were two other missionary passengers—one a layman sent out to teach the natives to build houses, and the other a young clergyman full of energy at the thought of all the converts he was going to make. There was also a

German naval officer on his way to Zanzibar to take charge of a man-of-war; and lastly, a Turk, the ex-governor of Hodeidah, sent by his Government on a mission to the Sultan of Zanzibar.

Every nook and corner in the forepart of the ship was taken up by Indian merchants and cargo, so that we could not get away from the stern; and there being generally a head-wind, the odours that reached us were sometimes overpowering.

I was thankful to find that besides our being allowed to sleep on deck, our meals were all served on the top of the big skylight, ingeniously converted into a table; for, although the weather was very fine and warm, there was a continual chopping motion which very much upset some of us.

That night the steward made up our beds by putting two long benches side by side, which reminded me of a wooden cot. Harry and I had ours put under the lee of the Captain's cabin, while the missionary girls were settled alongside the skylight, on which the men's mattresses were strewed about. It always amused me to watch the layman taking possession of the place next the girls, and tucking in the one nearest to him, for the nights were very cold. After retiring to our cabins we all reappeared in our night-attire. The poor young women, being very shy and modest, always covered themselves with a lot of useless garments to make the journey from their cabin to their im-

CAPE GUARDAFUI.

provised beds—wraps which, as soon as they had
jumped in and got under the bed-clothes, had to be
dragged out piece by piece. The worst of sleeping
on deck was having to turn out so early on account
of the swabbing which began at daybreak. This
did not matter to the men, who walked about
in *pyjamas* with bare feet till nearly breakfast-
time; but we poor women had to go down to
the fusty cabins and dress at once, feeling more
dead than alive.

We soon made friends with Mr Gedge and Mr
Jackson. The latter had already been twice on this
coast; and after his first trip he was shipwrecked
on his homeward journey, losing all his possessions,
amongst them a valuable collection of birds and
butterflies. He said that Rider Haggard's account
of the shipwreck in 'She' was founded on his
adventure, and that "The thing that bites" in
'Maiwa's Revenge' also really existed. It had
been brought to the east coast of Africa by some
Englishmen for the purpose of trapping lions; and
when they left the country they gave it to a chief,
who made use of it to punish his concubines by
putting one of their hands in and maiming them
for life. The description he gave us of Kilima
Njaro, and more especially of Tavata, the settlement
at its foot, made us seriously think of joining their
party, and going so far with them; but when he
said it would take quite three weeks to get the

necessary things and porters together, we found
our time was too limited. I am glad now we did
not go, as, had we done so, we should—as it turned
out—have missed our trip across Madagascar.

On October the 19th we passed Cape Guardafui,
and got our only glimpse of the Somali coast—an
uninteresting mass of bare stratified rock, the appearance of which fully justified the want of interest
the land-grabbers of Europe have hitherto taken
in this—nearly the only unannexed—part of the
African littoral. So small is this interest, that
Cape Guardafui—a point made by all ships bound
southwards and eastwards from the Red Sea—does
not even boast a lighthouse. It, however, affords
shelter to a nice little anchorage on its south side,
which might be of use in the northern monsoon,
but for the fact that the natives have an unpleasant
habit of boarding all unarmed ships that bring up
there, and murdering their crews. In justice to the
Somalis, however, it is only fair to say that this
custom originated in the behaviour of a certain
crew, whose ship having got into difficulties put
in for repairs, in which they were helped by the
inhabitants; but on the latter demanding pay-
ment, they were politely pushed overboard, and
threatened with a closer acquaintance with the
ship's muskets if they ventured to return.

BOOK III.

THE LAND OF BONDAGE.

AT 2.30 P.M. on the 23d of October we crossed the equator, and on October the 25th, at 8 A.M., we anchored at the entrance of Lamu harbour, the water being too shallow to admit of our going in. On our right was Manda Island, covered with low bushes and baobab - trees; and on our left Shella Point, the extreme end of which is a sandy hillock which used to be covered with skulls, the result of some native battle, but now only a few are to be seen, as most of them have been taken away by the doctors of the English coasting vessels. The town of Lamu could not be seen from our anchorage, being hidden by the land jutting out into the harbour on which Shella village is built — a picturesque spot, its low square huts roofed with dried palm-leaves of rich grey and brown tints. Just behind the village is a grove of cocoa-palms, beneath which grows very luxuriant vegetation.

The Captain telling us that we could not get

away before night, Harry and I decided to land on
Shella Point, so as to leave the whole afternoon for
visiting Lamu. There were several leaky, rickety,
" dug-out" canoes round the ship, whose native
crews were most anxious to take us ashore. We
chose the safest-looking one, an outrigger less than
two feet wide. It is difficult enough under any cir-
cumstances to get into a canoe, still more so when
it is a " dug-out" kept in continual motion by the
sea. Having at last seized the right moment and
safely jumped in, we found ourselves ankle-deep
in water, with nothing to sit on but our wet heels.
The owner set the sail, if it could be called a sail,
being only about three feet square, and made out
of dirty rags put together anyhow; nevertheless, it
tilted our canoe to a most unpleasant angle. As
soon as her old cracked bottom touched the beach
we were encircled by a troop of natives, all most
anxious to carry us ashore, which they finally
did.

We had never met a more cheery lot of natives,
amusing themselves like children with a baby por-
cupine, which they abandoned to escort us through
the village. I noticed it was the women who
carried the water from the wells and did all the
heavy work. We photographed a group round a
well, a proceeding they did not at all appreciate,
for most of them ran away; while some of the
younger ones left their great round earthenware

SHELLA POINT.

water-pots to follow us, dancing and singing round
us.   Most of them had the hem of their ears
pierced, and a quantity of small silver rings in-
serted.   They also make a hole where earrings are
usually worn; and their object being to get it as
large as the lobe of the ear will stretch, they insert

Natives of Lamu.

rolls of rags, and increase the size of the roll until
the hole is as large as a two-shilling piece. Some of
the richer ones had flat pieces of roughly worked
silver fixed to these rolls.   All the married women
wore a small silver button passed through the nos-

tril, taking it out only if they become widows.
They all plait their short woolly hair in ridges
going from the forehead to the nape of the neck,
and the hair not being more than an inch long,
the plaits lie flat to the head. I saw a few men
sitting on their heels in one of the huts sewing, but
most of them seem to spend their time smoking in
their doorways. As we passed, they got up and
came forward to shake hands with Harry in the
most solemn and ceremonious way.

After a rather perilous return journey we reached
the vessel in time for lunch ; after which the Captain sent us to Lamu in his boat. It took us
three - quarters of an hour's sailing to get there.
Opposite the town, and about half a mile from it, is
a mangrove-swamp of a most beautiful green, which
was very soothing to our eyes after the glare of the
sea, but I fancy rather a dangerous neighbour to live
near.

We were carried ashore by the crew through
deep mud and over heaps of decomposing matter,
and found ourselves at the English Vice-Consulate.
One wondered how any civilised being could live in
this dirty unhealthy place, and yet I was told that
Captain Haggard, who was consul here for some
time, was quite sorry to leave it. One part of the
town is composed of well-built Arab houses, whose
overhanging upper storeys give a twilight gloom to
the streets even on the brightest day. Most of the

MOMBASA HARBOUR.

commerce is carried on by the Indian community, who, whenever we passed any of them, ran into a doorway or crouched near the walls, dragging their children after them, I was told for fear of our casting the evil eye on them. We then walked through the native village and bazaar, causing great excitement —the women peeping at us from their huts, calling out, "*Bibi, sambo*" ("Good day, lady"); but if we ventured too near, they ran away laughing and screaming. Most of the elder ones wore bright-coloured cotton stuffs thrown loosely round them, making them look very picturesque with their grey hair. The bazaar was a very poor affair; the sellers squatted on the ground before the big, flat, round baskets, filled with seeds and roots of various kinds. Little red capsicums, looking like minute shrimps, seemed a favourite vegetable, if one could judge by the quantity on view.

We met several Somalis, fine strong-looking men, who all wore daggers, beautifully mounted in silver, slung round their waists. Theirs, I was told, was the only tribe whose members were allowed to enter the town armed. Here, again, the men stopped us to shake hands.

Having seen all the curiosities of Lamu, we went back to our boat, thankful to get afloat again. It took us over an hour to reach the ship, the men alternately rowing and landing to tow us. On our return we found on board a black man, dressed as an English clergyman, talking to our young missionary, who looked extremely depressed, having just received orders to go up country with this companion, and take the place of an English missionary at an inland station who with his wife had been murdered by the natives they were trying to convert. Our poor fellow-traveller had already been taken on shore, and shown the bed on which the victims had been murdered. It seemed to me a delicate attention on the part of the black missionary, receiving the enthusiastic young one with all these details! I have often wondered whether, before leaving home, these out-of-the-way places are described to would-be missionaries in glowing colours; for I know they are not entirely at liberty to choose where they are to go, as one of the missionary girls told me she had asked to go to the Mauritius, where she had friends, whereas she had been sent instead to the unhealthy east coast of Africa.

Soon after we anchored, Mr Jackson and Mr Gedge started on a little shooting expedition to Manda Island—to unstiffen their legs, they said. They returned very tired, with one or two partridges, and the hoofs of the smallest gazelle that is to be found in Africa, which they gave me. The bag was hardly worth the long rough walk in such stifling heat.

The next day, at 8 A.M., we got under way—a

most glorious morning, with a cool breeze; but no
sooner had we left the shelter of Shella Point than
a heavy swell came on, making some of us feel we
liked solitude; and, selecting retired corners, we
sat silently expecting the worst, which, alas! often
came.

On October the 27th, at 8 A.M., we approached
Mombasa, and steered straight for a pillar erected
by Vasco da Gama; then turning sharp to the
right through a very narrow passage, we entered
the lovely little harbour in which Mombasa Island
is situated. In it was a ship at anchor belonging to the Sultan of Zanzibar, and lent by him
to the East African Company to enable them to
communicate with his island in case of emergency.

The view of the island from the ship was lovely.
The part of the town that overlooks the harbour
is built on the crest of a high rocky bank rising
abruptly from the water, in every crevice of which
hung festoons of creepers laden with flowers of brilliant colouring. The old fort, with its bastioned
walls towering over all, looked most imposing, though
probably useless against modern weapons. The
houses, seen from the ship, appeared well built and
clean with their whitewashed walls; while a little
to the right the native village spread itself under
the shade of cocoa-palms and mango-trees. On the
mainland, which is connected with the north of the
island by a short causeway, is the mission station

with its little houses built like Swiss *chálets* in beautiful park-like grounds.

On the south side of the island is a very broad channel, which we were told will be the entrance when the new harbour is made, which, besides being more easy of access, will be far more sheltered and roomy than the northern one now in use. The coral-reefs fringing this coast make the entrances to all these ports very difficult. In the lagoons formed by them the water is most beautifully calm, but not always deep enough for vessels of any size; so that only the native dhows can take advantage of them to carry on their coasting trade in all weathers.

As soon as we anchored, the mission boat was seen putting off and coming towards us. In her was the founder of the mission and one of the ladies, who came on board to carry off to the fold the two young girls, their little black chaperon, and the layman. When they had left, the Captain took us ashore to see Mr Mackenzie, who was managing the British East African Company's base, and so was the connecting-link between the explorers and England. We landed on a steep stony incline, leading up to an open space overlooking the harbour, which Mr Mackenzie afterwards told us he intended to plant and make into a shady square; then walking down a clean wide street, we soon reached the head-quarters of the Company, a good-sized, white-washed, airy Arab abode.

MOMBASA.

While we were sitting with Mr Mackenzie, three men came whom there was no mistaking for any persons but explorers. The first we were introduced to was Count Teleki, a tall handsome man, with a charming, weather-beaten, sunburnt face, hair cropped quite short, wearing an Arab skull-cap, his flannel shirt unbuttoned in front, and sleeves rolled up over the elbows. I was told afterwards that when he and his companions arrived at Mombasa after two years of hard travelling up country, they had worn all their clothes to rags, and that the Count had made his entry into the town in a pair of curiously made red cotton breeches, and nothing else. He owned that, finding himself so near civilisation with only rags to his back, he allowed two of his men to put together this useful and picturesque-looking garment.

His companion, Herr von Höhnel—a young naval officer who had been sent by the Crown Prince of Austria to survey the country—was a tall, intelligent-looking young man, who looked quite civilised in a good European suit of clothes which he had taken the precaution of leaving at Mombasa on his way up country. They undertook this journey to try and discover the actual position of the Lake Samburu in the Massaï country, and found there was no such thing as a *Lake* Samburu, but that Samburu was the name of a district in which were two lakes. I unfortunately have forgotten the native

E

names, but they meant the "Black" and the
"White" Lakes. Count Teleki rechristened them
Lake Rudolph and Lake Stéphanie, by which names
they now appear on the map. The explorers had
several times to fight their way, having encountered
various unfriendly tribes who would not let them
proceed.

The third man to whom Mr Mackenzie introduced
us did not belong to their party, and it was only
afterwards we heard all about him. He had arrived the day before from Kilima Njaro, where he
had been sent by the German East African Company
the year before; and when the quarrels began with
the natives, he, like all the others, came down to the
coast, thankful to escape with his life. He looked
quite the wild man of the woods, with his long hair
and beard, and a little monkey nestling in his arms,
a faithful little companion that he had taken up
country with him, and that never left him.

He was said to be a Pole, whose father had been
sent to Siberia for some political offence, and whom
the son had succeeded in rescuing, when they were
overtaken by Cossacks, who shot the father. The
boy roamed about Siberia, keeping himself alive for
seven years by the help of his gun; but at last he
managed to escape to Austria, where later on he
accepted the offer of the Germans to join their Company in Africa.

I have rather drifted from my description of

Mombasa. Mr Mackenzie sent us to see the place with a black boy, who asked Harry at once if he was ever in the Sudan. It turned out that he was a Sudanese, who had been up the Nile during the fighting, and thought he recognised Harry. He took us through a street where all the shops were; but finding nothing interesting, we walked on till we reached the outskirts of the town. There the thick and luxuriant vegetation, with its tangle of creepers from tree to tree, effectually blocked the way, and obliged us to retrace our steps.

Coming back, we met our Captain in the town, who told us we must start early that afternoon. I was very much disgusted at this news, as Mr Mackenzie had promised to take us to the other side of the island and show us the new slave settlement he was forming. A great number of slaves had been captured and sent there the day before, and he offered me one of the little black boys to take back to England with me, an offer I thought it advisable not to accept.

Again we were nearly tempted to go up country, Mr Mackenzie asking us to accompany him on his trip to the first settlement belonging to the Company; but the limited time at our disposal again forced us to refuse. All the Arab houses in Mombasa had massive carved doors, and we were anxious to buy one to send home; but, thanks to our restless Captain, we had no time to do anything.

We got back in time to say good-bye to Mr Gedge
and Mr Jackson, who were disembarking there,
and soon afterwards I was most interested in watching the Count and his escort coming on board; it
consisted of about one hundred and fifty blacks,
the survivors of the two hundred he had taken
from Zanzibar. The Count told us they had
suffered terribly from famine, and that that was
the cause of the death of most of the men he
had lost. His head man was the intelligent Somali who accompanied Stanley on his first expedition—such a clever handsome face, looking very
picturesque with his many-coloured scarf thrown
loosely round his head. I photographed him, as
well as three of their cannibals—strong, muscular,
square-shouldered men, with as little clothing on
as possible, grinning from ear to ear, showing such
splendid rows of white teeth.

It will be a great feather in the Englishman's cap
if he can establish this new East African Company
without any serious fighting, considering that all
those who have been there before have had to fight
their way through the country. Mr Jackson told
us one day, when we were discussing the character of the natives of this coast, that they were
really very easy to get on with, if one only took
the trouble to understand them and treat them
kindly.

The news had come some days before that a

German missionary had been made prisoner farther down the coast, and that a ransom had been demanded. Not long ago three German sailors deserted and went up country in emulation of Rudyard Kipling's heroes, with the intention of forming a little kingdom of their own, but fared even worse than their antitypes; for the natives not only killed them, but roasted and ate a piece of each, the belief being that if they eat a bit of a white man, it imbues them with his knowledge and power.

The Germans seem to be too unbending to get on well with the natives, and although they may succeed in establishing themselves by force, will, I fancy, always have to exercise it to keep their position. The officials of the British East African Company, on the contrary, are doing their best to make their presence desired : for instance, one of Mr Mackenzie's first acts on arriving at Mombasa was to build a new mosque as a substantial proof of British tolerance. A good deal of care and tact was required in the then state of affairs. Nevertheless this picturesque little place will some day be very important, and before long the English will have made a line of railway which will enable one to skim over the unhealthy band of the coast, and find one's self on healthy ground with plenty of big game, which will soon become a necessity to the Englishman, whose one pet home sport seems to be marred by barbed wire.

Dinner that day was enlivened by our new fellow-passengers, who appeared most amused at coming back to civilised ways. The Count, while smoking his pipe that evening, gave us a most interesting account of his journey, describing that they had got as far as a place which Emin Pacha's outposts had reached.

On waking on October the 28th, I was delighted to find that we were in smooth water, having entered the channel, thirty miles wide, which is between Zanzibar and the mainland. The latter looked flat and uninteresting in the far distance, while the island of Zanzibar, close on our left, was hilly and covered with well-grown trees and thick bush. On one of the hills a big house was pointed out to me which had been built by the late Sultan for his many wives, on his return from Bombay, where he had been exiled by one of his thirteen brothers, and had there acquired civilised ideas. These to some extent he tried to work out in his little kingdom when, after his brother's death, he resumed his reign. At his own death he left each of these wives a small private fortune and the big house to live in all together.

At 11 A.M. we dropped anchor a short distance from the town of Zanzibar. Several English and German men-of-war were already in the harbour, collected there on account of the disturbances that were continually springing up on the mainland, and

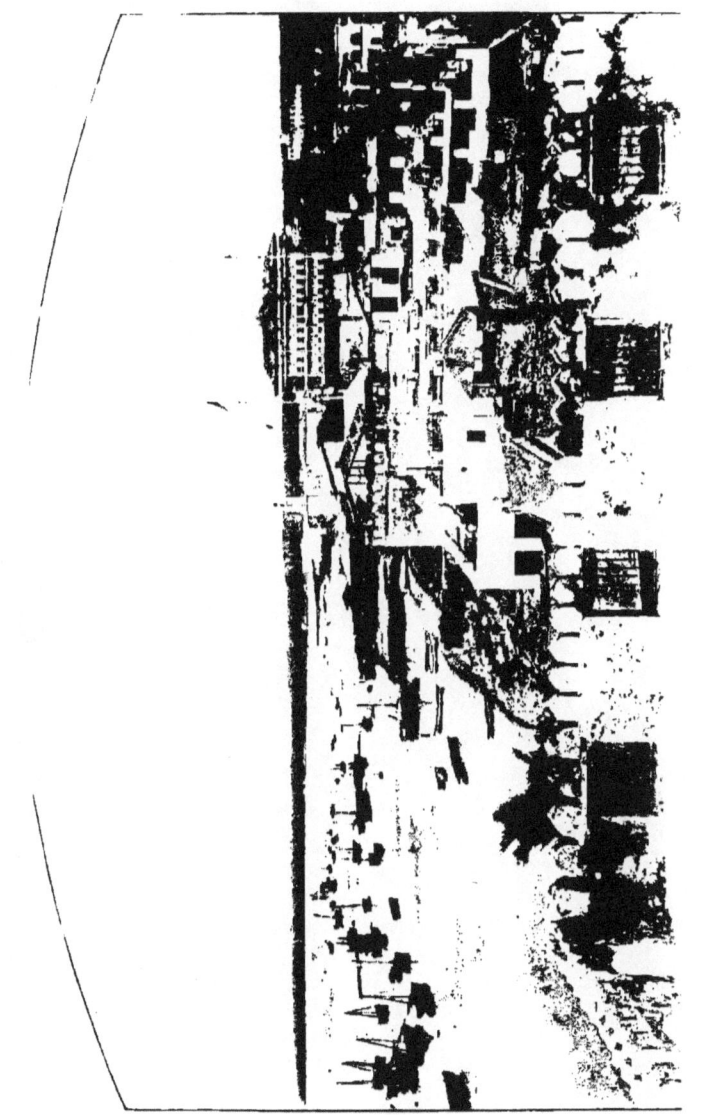

ZANZIBAR FROM ROOF OF BRITISH AGENCY.

our fellow-passenger, the German officer, received
an order from his Admiral that he was to take command at once, and go and inspect some place down
the coast.

Having sent the letter of introduction General
Hogg had given us for the Consul-General, Colonel
Euan Smith, we decided to wait for the answer
before going ashore; so I set to work and sketched
the town, which looked very picturesque, although
rather spoilt as a picture by the Sultan's hideous
palace,—a high, square, whitewashed building, with
a narrow wooden gallery running round the first
floor, looking entirely out of proportion to the rest
of the building. It was a decided contrast to the
English Consulate. This was built on the extreme
point of land, so that the waves were ever dashing
themselves on to the walls of the terraced walk
surrounding the house; and, unlike the palace, it
had a wide, covered, and cool-looking verandah.
The Captain told me the latter had been added by
Colonel Euan Smith, and that it had certainly improved the look of the house, as well as making it
cooler inside. Not far from the palace was a most
hideous erection of brick and mortar in the shape
of a dhow, which the late Sultan had had constructed as a tank, resting on the ground, looking
more than anything like a gigantic sarcophagus.
This Sultan was, from all I heard about him, fond
of spending his money and starting new ideas.

He had sent to Europe for an ice-machine, and had electric light put on the top of a tower, both of which soon got out of order, when, having no one among his people who could repair them, he let them go to pieces. He had also a curious mania for clocks, and ended by hanging numbers of them round his reception-room. I only hope, for the sake of his visitors, they were not all kept going at the same time. Imagine cuckoo-clocks, chimers, and others let loose in the same room, trying to keep pace with each other!

I noticed not far from the "Dhow" tank the English flag-staff planted in the ground, while those of other nations were on the roofs of their representatives' houses. It was explained to me that this permission to plant the English flag in the ground was a special mark of the Sultan's favour.

My sketch finished, I amused myself watching Count Teleki and his escort go ashore. It was a wonderful sight to see all his ivory piled up, nearly covering the whole quarter-deck; some of the tusks were over eight feet long; and there was besides a great collection of heads and skins, which were very pretty. His men were all the time singing and laughing, delighted to get back after their two years of hardships up country.

Early in the afternoon an invitation came from the Consul-General, asking us to go on shore and dine with him and his wife, and expressing a regret that their one spare room was occupied till the following day, when he hoped we should go and stay with them until the arrival of the Messageries boat, which was to take us to Madagascar. The heat and glare on the ship were so trying, that we gladly accepted our Captain's offer to take us ashore at once.

Landing at the little pier of the British Agency, we soon found ourselves in a cool and wide inner passage on the first floor, encircling and overlooking a covered central court. There we were received by Mrs Euan Smith, her husband being busy with the mails which we had brought. I cannot describe my delight in sitting comfortably at the tea-table, with everything pretty round me ; for there were some lovely things in the house which our hosts had brought from India. We were introduced to the private secretary, Mr Berkeley, and to the Vice-Consul, Mr Churchill ; and, soon after, Admiral Fremantle and Colonel Euan Smith joined our cheery party. As most of them were going to church, and I was advised not to go myself on account of the stuffy heat, I was very glad when Colonel Euan Smith proposed he should take us for a drive in one of the Sultan's carriages. That potentate kept about a hundred horses, only reserving for his personal use six white thoroughbreds, and willingly lending any of the others to whoever asked for the loan of them. So we started in a comfortable landau, on what seemed

to me a most perilous journey for any inhabitants
that happened to be walking in the narrow streets.
Our native driver simply charged down upon them,
turning the sharp corners as one would in a sleigh,
shouting at the top of his voice to the people. At
one moment I thought we must run into a group
of women sitting round a little bonfire, over which
they were cooking and selling fish; but by some
miracle they escaped, as we all did, and soon after,
we had left the town behind us.

After passing the barracks, built on an open
grassy space, we drove along a lovely road, over-
hung on both sides with large mangoes, palms,
bamboos, and many other sorts of trees and shrubs.
Everything seemed to me to grow to a huge size;
even the snails with their pointed spiral shells were
quite three inches long, and four in diameter. The
mangoes looked at their best, covered as they were
with their large plum-shaped fruit. No other trees
to my mind came up to them in shape or colouring,
having, as they always do, the autumnal and spring
tints growing at the same time; and curiously
enough, these patches of tender green did not seem
out of place against the background of dark-green
and autumnal shades. One tall tree attracted my
notice, as I had never seen it before: it is called the
papaw-tree, and has a tall bare stem like that of a
palm, with marks all up it left by the old leaves
dropping off, and right up at the top was a bunch

of large green leaves cut out and shaped like a fig-leaf, nestling under which were clusters of fruit exactly like green figs. This fruit when green is cut in half, and the milky-white juice it gives out is rubbed on meat to make it tender.

A summer residence belonging to Colonel Euan Smith was the object of our drive: it was a little house surrounded by well-laid-out grounds, which had all been planned and planted by his predecessor, Sir John Kirk. Everything had grown so rapidly that it had become too deeply shaded, and felt damp. After going to see some wonderful coffee-plants with berries three times the usual size, and a plantation of pine-apples, we walked to the edge of a slope overlooking the sea, whence could be seen a lovely view of the bay, with the projecting tongue of land on which the town is built, charmingly lit up by the setting sun. Never having tasted the juice of a fresh cocoa-nut, a native was sent to climb a palm-tree for one, making him look more than ever like a monkey. On his returning with the nut, it was cracked, and a hole was made in it, through which I sucked the transparent tepid juice. I cannot say I appreciated it. I had fondly imagined it was thick and white, like milk, and tasted strongly of almonds; but no such thing, and one sip was sufficient to satisfy me that I did not like it. Had it been kept on ice for some hours, and had I been very thirsty, I might have thought more highly of it.

We went a different way home, so as to have a
look at a summer residence built by the late Sultan,
an imposing-looking building, which it made one sad
to see on closer inspection, as here again all was
going to rack and ruin. Not being able to get into
the house, we walked about the grounds, where a
start had once been made to mark and plant out
a nice garden, which was then left to become a
wilderness. Strewed all over the place were drain-
pipes which had been intended to carry the water to
two enormous uncovered tanks, built side by side
as swimming-baths, against the east end of the
house, and having flights of steps to go from one
to the other. Why there should have been two
of these swimming - baths, one next the other,
I cannot imagine, if it was not that the author
of these brilliant ideas preferred to do everything
regardless of expense. Near the front door—like
preparations for a fair — were swinging-boats and
a huge merry-go-round, all in good preservation.
The guardian of the place set the organ going,
which immediately struck up "The March of the
Men of Harlech."

We got back a little after dark, the hedges lit
up with thousands of fireflies illuminating our road,
and producing a beautiful fairy-like scene without
the little fairies, who I felt would have been quite
in keeping had they appeared.

That night, after the luxury of one of the best

dinners I ever could wish to taste, and some very good music—our hostess being a real artist on the piano —I found it hard to have to return to our moving home, alive as it was with cockroaches. It did not take me long to undress that night, and rushing up on deck, treading on a goodly few of these monsters, I took refuge in my improvised bed, where even in the open air the heat was so suffocating that sleep was out of the question.

The next morning I joyfully finished our final packing, and bade adieu to the "Java"; being, all the same, sorry to leave our kind Captain, who had done all in his power to make us comfortable. As we were being rowed ashore a welcome and homelike sound reached us, "God save the Queen" being played on the Admiral's ship.

In the afternoon Mrs Euan Smith took me out in her pony-cart. Passing the mission, I saw a number of little black boys dressed in European clothes playing football. The missionaries educate and keep the boys and girls till they are thought old enough to marry. Then having chosen among themselves mates suited to their own tastes, they are given a bit of ground to cultivate, on which they erect a little hut, and are there left to increase the community of little black Christians to their hearts' content.

That evening we dined on board the flag-ship, and had a most cheery time. The Admiral settled to come and fetch me next day, and take me to see a clove-plantation; so having secured another carriage-and-pair of the Sultan's, we set off, passing through the northern end of the town with the same reckless sort of driving. Some of the streets were much broader, and lined on both sides with little shops, mostly containing European goods. Here I noticed that many of the women wore broad silver anklets, which, from the way they dragged their feet after them, appeared to be very heavy. These slow movements greatly accentuated their usual look of indolence. The inhabitants of this island are such a mixed race that it would take pages to describe them, but I fancy the Arab blood predominates. Having got to the plantation, thickly planted with clove-bushes, the fruit of which was beginning to ripen, making the air heavy with its strong aromatic perfume, we got out and walked about along the shaded paths, collecting many curious little plants.

That evening, when dining with Mr Churchill, I was told of a sad tragedy that had happened not long before in Madagascar to a German naturalist and his wife. After landing at Tamatave and collecting their porters, they started for the capital. Taking advantage of a wild uninhabited part, their men stopped and asked for more money, which we are told is a way they have, and that it is always best to give in to them in moderation, as one is entirely at their mercy; but instead of doing so, the rash naturalist threatened them with his gun, which simply made them take to their heels. After waiting a long time and finding the porters had deserted them, he told his wife to wait for him while he walked on in search of a village where he could get other natives. The day passed, and he never returned. Still she waited for fear of missing him, when on the second day her baby died. After burying it in the sand, she determined to retrace her steps in search of their last halting-place—many weary miles back—which she reached at last, and remained there till she was found by other travellers, who took her up to Antànan-arivo, where after some time her husband turned up, having on leaving her completely lost his way.

As we had found it rather unpleasant walking in thin shoes in the pitch-dark street, Mrs Euan Smith and I went home in a sort of *chaise à porteurs* carried on men's shoulders, making one feel rather top-heavy.

Every morning on getting up I looked out of my window to see if the Messageries was signalled, always hoping the evil day was not yet come when we should have to leave our comfortable quarters; but it came at last.

BOOK IV.

THE ISLAND OF MYSTERY.

I.

On the 1st of November a message arrived that we were to sail at 1 P.M. After taking leave of our kind hosts, we went on board the "Amazone," escorted by Mr Berkeley. At the head of the gangway the Captain—Commandant Masset—received us most graciously, and the French Consul, Monsieur Lacaux, whom we had met on land, came forward and introduced us to Monsieur Le Myre de Vilers, the French Resident - General in Madagascar, a tall, handsome-looking middle-aged man, who welcomed us like old friends. When Monsieur Lacaux told him we were anxious to see as much of the Malagasy island as was possible, he kindly volunteered to take us under his protection, which offer he certainly carried out, and we can never be sufficiently grateful to him for all the trouble he took about us.

The size of the "Amazone" delighted me, as did

MONSIEUR LE MYRE DE VILERS.

THE "AMAZONE" AND HER PASSENGERS.   81

our scrupulously clean and airy cabin, opening into
the spacious and comfortably furnished saloon.   In
this ship I felt we should at last have plenty of
room to walk about, although—as is always the case
in French ships—the second-class passengers are
allowed on all parts of the deck, thus crowding up
the first-class accommodation.   Those on the "Amazone" chiefly consisted of Mauritius trades-people
returning from visiting their French relations.
Their children were most trying; and the worst of
them all was a weedy spoilt boy who was continually sneaking round one's chair, treading on or
knocking against one's favourite corn, while his
peevish mother was for ever screaming after him
in a voice that set one's teeth on edge.   He would
then attack the poor old seafaring piano, always
left on deck, and with one finger bang out the old
familiar tune, "*J'ai du bon tabac dans ma tabatière*,"
to the delight of his adoring parent.   I fear I was
less admiring, and would willingly have wrung his
scraggy little neck.

It was soothing, on the contrary, to watch the
Sœurs de Charité, with their gentle movements and
contented peaceful expressions, spending most of
their time telling their beads.   One of them was a
very pretty young girl—as some of the officers
seemed also to think, for they were often having a
chat with "*Ma Sœur*," who looked so bashful and
bewitching under her spotless, large, white linen

F

cap with its turned-up points. Her destination,
poor thing! was to spend the rest of her life on the
deadly coast of Madagascar. There is something
very beautiful in the thought of these young nuns
leaving their native land and going out to such
unhealthy climates, there to remain as long as they
live—and some do live to a good old age up country,
but rarely on the coast.

The first day on board, while walking up and
down the deck, our attention was attracted by over-
hearing English spoken by a man and woman. The
latter Harry recognised at once by her dress as a
Malay from the Cape. We were very much puzzled,
wondering what they could be doing on this French
ship bound for Mauritius. I determined, if a chance
offered itself, to enter into conversation with her,
which occurred the next day. As I was taking a
look round the second-class cabins I passed her, and
gathered that she was trying to make the steward
understand that she wanted some soup for an invalid. As she evidently could not speak a word of
French, and he was equally ignorant of English, I
stopped and offered to interpret for her. After I
had explained to the man what she wanted, she told
me the soup was for her sister-in-law, pointing to a
very delicate-looking woman, who, unlike my dark
friend, had a pure white skin, but was attired in the
same Dutch-Malay fashion—a coloured cotton print
dress, inflated by an exaggerated crinoline, the bodice

and skirt all in one, shoulders covered by a bright
silk handkerchief folded in a point, and another to
match encircling the head and forehead, passing
behind the ears, entirely hiding the hair, and crossed
loosely under the chin. The dark one turned out
to be most communicative, and after asking me to
sit down with them, she explained that they were
on their way home from Mecca. Her husband, who
was also on board, was a well-to-do livery-stable
keeper and cab-proprietor at Kimberley. They
had for some time contemplated making the great
Mohammedan pilgrimage; and being also anxious
to see the capital of England, decided to go
to Mecca *via* London, taking with them their
little daughter of nine, and their young sister-in-
law, whose husband undertook to carry on the
business at home in their absence. They had accomplished both the pleasure-trip and the pilgrimage; but harrowing were the descriptions they gave
me of the miseries and hardships they had to contend with. The dark one told me in a curiously
happy tone that her little girl had died on the way
back, but that she could not mourn for her, as she
had luckily died after the pilgrimage was over.
She then told me that her companion, a few days
before reaching Yembo — they having done the
double pilgrimage of Mecca and Medina—gave birth
to her first-born, and that it was with great difficulty that she had been revived sufficiently to reach

the coast. I could well imagine the sufferings of
the poor woman laid up in the desert, with no resources, and obliged to keep moving towards the
coast, riding on a camel—a beast that at the best
of times shakes you till you feel like a bagful of
loose bones. At Yembo they apparently took a
ship at haphazard, which landed them at Aden,
where they had been ·advised to take the French
boat to the Mauritius, whence they were told they
would get the English steamer bound for the Cape.
Rather a round-about way, it seemed!

I had often heard travellers complain that they
never got enough food on French boats. It was certainly not the case on the "Amazone"; for in the
morning an excellent cup of coffee was brought to
us before getting up, *déjeûner à la fourchette* was
served at eleven, and at half-past one there was cold
luncheon for any one who wished for it; at four
o'clock, tea; at seven, a first-rate dinner; and a
good cup of coffee to finish up with, which the
Captain often asked us to drink in his cabin, where
he always kept a good supply of most excellent
liqueurs, to which he treated his favourite passengers. At nine we finished up with tea and
biscuits, or *un grogue* for those who preferred it.

Having been introduced to Monsieur le Vicomte
d'Anthouard—Monsieur de Vilers's secretary—and
to Monsieur George, the French Chancelier at Tamatave, we five made a select little circle, and often

discussed the *pros* and *cons* of our Madagascar trip;
Monsieur de Vilers being most keen about our
undertaking to cross the island from east to west,
going as far as the capital with him.   The difficulty was to get from the west coast of the island
back to Africa, there being no communication from
that side except by native dhows.   We, however,
made up our minds to go, and take our chance of
finding some boat to carry us across the Mozambique Channel.

Early on the second morning after leaving
Zanzibar we sighted the green slopes of Mayotta
Island, one of the largest of the Comoro group, and
by eight the low black cliffs in which they termin-
ated had risen well above the water.   Closely skirting the land until we reached the eastern end of the
island, we turned to the right, and wound our way
through the reefs which nearly bar the narrow
channel between it and Zaoudzi Island, to the
north-east of which we dropped anchor.   While
entering the harbour our most erratic of Captains
nearly ran down a native boat.   The poor owners
were in a terrible fright, but the Captain, taking
it for granted that the natives must always make
way, never even slackened his pace, and carried
away their sail and broke their rudder.

From our anchorage the three islands of this group
were well in view : Mayotta, green and hilly, dotted
with sugar-plantations and red-roofed white houses

nestling under tall trees: Zaoudzi, a mere rocky islet, which has attained an undue importance by being selected as the headquarters of the French settlement, and contains the Government buildings, coal-sheds, workshops, &c. : and Pamanzi, a miniature repetition of Mayotta, connected with Zaoudzi by a stone causeway running across the shallow channel, and broken by two rocky islets.

There were two French men-of-war at anchor in the harbour : " Le Destin," commanded by Commandant Michel, then acting as Admiral of the station ; and " Le Beautemps-Beaupré," commanded by Commandant Le Dos. We met the latter at lunch, he being a great friend of our Captain ; and as he had asked us to visit his ship, we promised to go and see him after we had been ashore : so he settled to send his boat to meet us on our return.

A few strokes of the oar brought us to the little stone pier. Passing several Government wharfs, we came to the *Place*, out of which runs a short wide street, where there was one shop, a *café*, grandly called " Hôtel de France," the hospital, and the barracks. At the end of the street, turning to the right, we found ourselves in " L'Allée des Crabes," as the before-mentioned causeway is called. Having plenty of time, and seeing that the two little rocky islets were inhabited, we strolled on. The first contained an Arab village, whose inhabitants looked clean and healthy. We were so accustomed to hearing the natives salute us in English wherever we had been, that it seemed funny to hear them say, "*Bonjour, monsieur.*" Continuing our walk along the next bit of causeway as far as the second islet, we entered a Malagasy village, which was not nearly so clean. The people were copper-coloured, and the women had long, straight, jet-black hair, which they plait very tightly; their one garment of cotton stuff they wore loosely draped round them.

On our way back we met Monsieur Le Myre de Vilers walking about with the Governor, Monsieur Papillon, who took us to his pretty little house, surrounded by a verandah, and having a thatched roof, which kept it beautifully cool. In his garden were some splendid pomegranate-trees, the fruit of which was just ripe. I was allowed to feast on them, finding the acid juice most refreshing.

Monsieur Papillon told us that the drinking-water for his own use was sent out to him from France, he not liking to trust to the water which is brought over by the natives from Mayotta, there being none on this island.

Commandant Le Dos having sent his boat, Harry and I went on board the "Beautemps-Beaupré." She was a small ship, but everything was made very comfortable on board. The *Commandant* was most hospitable, and brought out his best champagne to drink to the success of our journey.

At four we steamed out of this fine harbour

by the southern channel. Several green and well-wooded small islands were passed before we found ourselves well out to sea. We then directed our course towards the north-west coast of Madagascar.

After a gloriously smooth night, we anchored off Nosy-Bé at 7 A.M. on November the 4th, in a well-sheltered roadstead, with green islands dotted around us. (*Nosy* signifies "island" in Malagasy.) The scene was enlivened by many native dug-out canoes with outriggers attached, sailing about at a tremendous pace, looking like butterflies with their many-coloured sails.

Nosy-Bé is a few miles west of Madagascar, and is very varied in appearance, some of the mountains being rocky and barren, while others are covered with dense vegetation. It is considered a more healthy spot than Mayotta, and there is also a greater rainfall. We were taken ashore to the little town of Hellville by a French official who had come on board to fetch his letters. He replaces the Governor, as the latter now lives at Diego Suarez, on the east coast of Madagascar. After landing on a fine stone pier, we walked up a slight incline shaded by lovely mango-trees to Government House, where our companion introduced us to his family. They all seemed perfectly well and happy in their well-built and beautifully kept home; in fact he told us he had requested his Government to leave him as long as possible on that station. As we

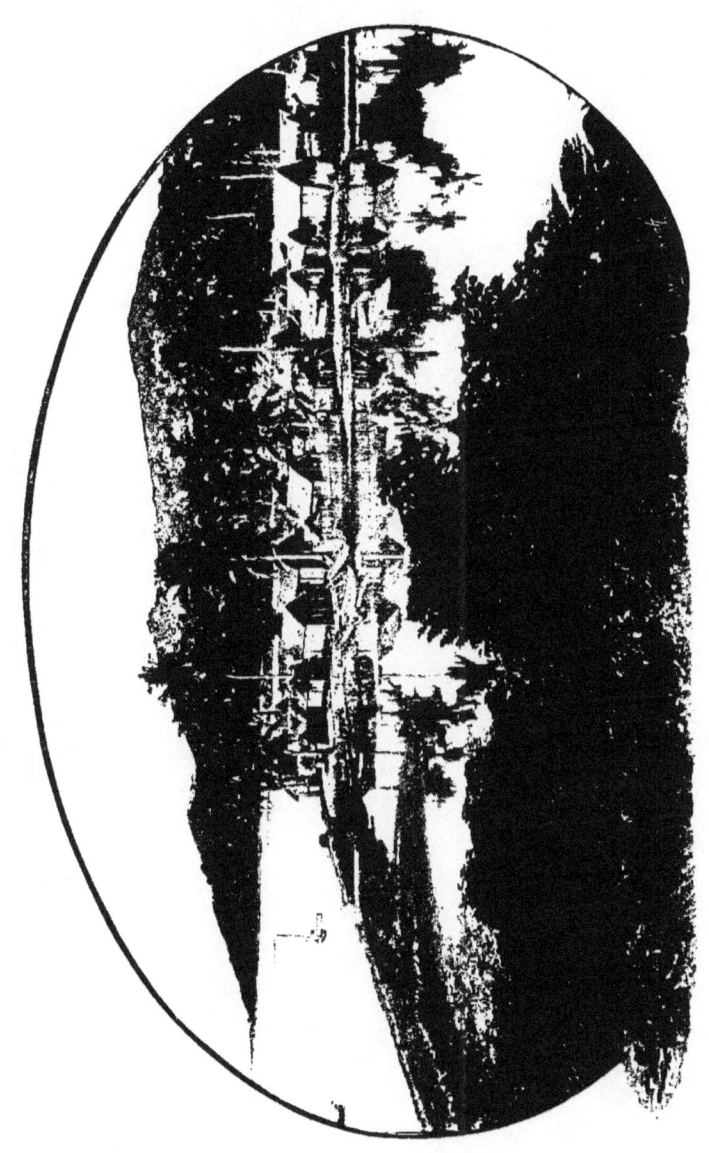

NOSY-BÉ.

wished to explore the neighbourhood, he insisted on our being accompanied by one of his native servants, which bored us extremely, so we got rid of him as soon as we could politely do so.

At the back of Government House is a wide, long *boulevard*, with double rows of trees. Looking on to it are the French Government buildings and mission-schools, each with its own little garden full of bread-fruit trees, and that acacia with bright scarlet flowers that the French call *flamboyant*.

We walked on for about a mile, until we reached a Malagasy village, the best-built native village I had yet seen, all the huts being constructed of bamboo, raised on piles about three feet high, and roofed with palm - leaves. It was inhabited by bright and healthy-looking people, who were particularly civil to the strangers. The married women wore the same silver button in the nose that I had noticed on the east coast of Africa. A little farther on we came to an Arab village. These two races, though living so close to each other, never mix nor intermarry, but nevertheless are always on good terms. Beyond this we came to a pretty fountain, always running, and providing plenty of good drinking - water, which is brought by means of pipes, from lakes on the hills, to the town.

After walking for some way through profuse vegetation, we sat on the edge of a bank overlooking the sea, and affording a view of the

northern wooded slopes of the island. At our
feet, on the tide-washed mud at the mouth of a
little river, was a Sakalava settlement. Like the
other Malagasy village, it was built on piles, and
with far more apparent reason, for at high tide it
must have stood in two or three feet of water,
reminding one of the prehistoric lake - dwellings.
These piles, however, were its only point of resemblance to its neighbour, for it was as dirty, untidy,
and miserable-looking as the other was clean and
prosperous. It was curious to find three distinct
communities, whose habits and modes of life were
so wholly different, planted within a stone's-throw
of each other on this little island.

Near us was a children's school where they were
hard at work, as one could tell from the hum—a
familiar sound that is ever the same, no matter in
what country you hear it. Some of these copper-
coloured little brats came and had a peep at us;
but otherwise the natives were so accustomed to
seeing white people that they did not follow us
about as in most other places.

We then sauntered quietly towards the pier by
narrow paths cut through a thick growth of many
kinds of ferns, by which time the heat had become
so intense that it was a relief to get back to the
ship and rest.

We steamed out of the harbour at 5 P.M., through
a narrow passage between two islands, one of them

a high cone covered with a magnificent virgin forest. Never before had I seen such a densely packed mass of different varieties of trees; and as we passed, I got peeps through the foliage of soft green mossy banks, and of little streams trickling down towards the sea. They told me that this forest is a boon to Nosy-Bé, as it attracts so many clouds, and more or less regulates the rainfall.

On November the 5th, at 6.30 A.M., we passed Cape Amber: nothing very striking about it, for a line of low hills is all that seems to mark the northernmost point of Madagascar. We then steered to the south-east, losing sight of land until 9 A.M., when we changed our course, and seemed to be making straight for the coast lying due west of us. The captain pointed out to us a hill called "Windsor Castle," from its resemblance to a distant view of that edifice. This hill is used as a landmark for entering the Diego Suarez harbour by getting it in line with some point on the eastern shore. As it happened, our Captain, who had never been there before, missed his mark, and before there was time to realise what was happening, a great bump was felt, women shrieked, and every one rushed about to try and find out what had caused the crash. Looking overboard, we soon saw there was no danger of our sinking altogether, for we could clearly see the bottom, the sea being so shallow. It was soon found that the vessel had struck a rock right amidship, leaving her bow and stern free, and that there was no possibility of her getting off until the tide rose. The Captain, however, made the second and third class passengers crowd to the stern to see if that would help to float her; but nothing came of it, and anchors had to be thrown out on all sides so as to keep her from drifting ashore when the tide rose. The Captain knew it was a very windy corner, and that the tide runs with force through the narrow entrance into the harbour; so that even with the help of the anchors, we risked being dashed against the sharp bank of rocks on Point Orange to our left.

Soon after we had struck, a small native canoe put off to us from the island which blocks the centre of the entrance to the harbour. In it were five Frenchmen, so sunburnt that they might easily have been taken for natives. One of them climbed up the side of the vessel, and said that, seeing we were in trouble, he had come to know if he should communicate with Diego Suarez by means of his heliograph, so that they might send their steam-launches to our assistance. He explained that he was Lieutenant Sauvage, and that he was encamped on Point Orange with forty *disciplinaires*, four of whom he had in the canoe—strong, healthy-looking men, although they had been in that climate four years. Some of them had very forbidding expressions, and the Lieutenant said it was often very difficult to

manage them, for they were always ready to rebel
at the hard work they were made to do. Our Captain having accepted his offer, he scrambled down
into his canoe, hoisted his sail, made of an old sack
attached to two rough poles, and soon reached the
Point. All had been done so smartly that one could
not help admiring his energy in such a relaxing
climate.

While we were waiting for the launches, we had
plenty of time to take in a view of our surroundings. We had struck at the mouth of a narrow
channel, barely two hundred yards wide, which
forms the entrance to Diego Suarez Bay. On our
right was the barren rocky "Isle de la Lune," against
which the surf was breaking in a continuous line of
foam. On our left were the almost precipitous cliffs
of "Point Orange," surmounted by a heavy crown of
tropical bush. In front was the broad expanse of
Diego Suarez Bay, with "Windsor Castle," and the
lower peaks of the range on which it stands, breaking the sky-line in the western distance; while behind us was the surf-marked circle of coral-reefs
surrounding a network of shallow lakes, which
sparkled in the sun in every shade of blue and
green, from the milky hues of the turquoise, and the
cool bright green of the spring grass, to the more
brilliant sheen of the emerald.

As there was nothing else to be done, Harry and
I went down to lunch: everybody else, except

Monsieur de Vilers, seemed too anxious about what
might happen to feel any hunger. The bumping
got more frequent and more violent, and as the
tide began to rise, there was a greater strain on
the anchor-cables. At one time it was thought
advisable to send the women on shore; but by
the time the steam-launches were sent out, the
sea had got so rough that they could not safely
approach us. One of them got such a bump against
our ship that she was disabled, and had to take
shelter within the harbour. Suddenly there was
a terrific crash: a cable had snapped against the
strength of the rushing tide dashing on the rocks
not many yards from us. The engines worked to
their full power trying to keep the ship off the
shore. It certainly was a very critical moment,
but luckily the wind was not so strong as is usually
the case at this point; if it had been, she would certainly have been knocked to pieces against the rocks,
for her engines could never have withstood the force
of both wind and tide combined. Terror was im-
printed on many faces, mothers clasping their children, but the nuns were calm and composed, de-
voutly telling their beads. Monsieur de Vilers was
getting decidedly anxious about the women—having
been in several shipwrecks, he knew how fatal a panic
was—when, after a tremendous thump and rise, which
nearly threw us off our feet, the "Amazone" seemed to
shake herself together, and was afloat again. It was

DIEGO SUAREZ.

a great relief not to hear that continual crash at short
intervals, which ended by getting on one's nerves.

We struck the rock at 9.55 A.M., and it was 2.30
P.M. before we steamed to our anchorage at the
mouth of the "Baie des Cailloux Blancs," narrowed
at its entrance by the promontory of Diego on our
right, and the slightly projecting coast-line on which
the settlement of Antiserane is built. On the former
—a high table-topped mass of rock indented at its
foot by little sandy bays—stands the hospital, for
which its breezy heights and the good water-supply
to be found there make it very suitable. The
latter—at a much lower level—presents a flat and
uninteresting sky-line, broken here and there by
the red-tiled-roofed barracks and other Government
buildings : these are continued down the steep slope,
in which the plateau ends, to the sea-shore, which is
connected with the table-land by good zigzag roads.
Opposite us on the shore were wharfs, coal-sheds,
workshops, and piles of stores ; while farther down,
built on either side of a narrow ravine, was the
civil town, inhabited by a mixed population of
Malagasies, Indians, and Mauritius creoles. Like
the military settlement, it was almost entirely
built below the crest of the plateau.

Though man had given a certain air of life to
the place, the whole scene was singularly dreary
and monotonous. Not a tree was visible to break
the straight horizon, and almost the only bit of

colour was that given by the red tiles imported from France.

Soon after we had anchored, Monsieur d'Anthouard took us ashore to see the Colonel of artillery commanding the station ; but as we landed, we met that officer just stepping into his boat to call on Monsieur Le Myre de Vilers. He, however, kindly wrote a note to one of his subordinates directing him to show us round. So, trudging up the face of the bank by one of the zigzag paths, we arrived —with the help of a private we met on the road— at the officer's hut, and sent in the note. The occupant of the hut presently appeared, evidently just awakened from his siesta, and not too pleased at having to act as cicerone to two strangers in a blazing afternoon sun. He, however, did his duty manfully, and showed us all the lions of the place, which consisted of the barracks, mule-sheds, and terminus of the Decauville railway. The barracks, which had been built entirely by military labour, are constructed of perforated bricks, and stand on brick piers, raising the ground-floor some six feet above the soil. The mule-sheds contained a good many animals, employed for all transport purposes, and for working the Decauville railway, which, as we had some experience of it on the following morning, I shall describe in its proper place.

We had just completed our round of these sights when we were overtaken by the Colonel, accom-

panied by four men bearing a kind of chair made
of an iron frame, covered with canvas, attached
to two poles. This was my first acquaintance with
the *filanzana*, in which I was afterwards to travel
many miles before I left Madagascar. The front
ends of the poles were lowered to the ground, the
other ends being held up by two of the men at
a convenient height for me to sit down. On doing
so, I found myself hurled up into the air on the
shoulders of the men, who went off at a gallop,
making me feel at every moment that I must be
pitched out, the only support for my feet being a
piece of board swinging on two ropes. Having
no shelter over my head, I was obliged to hold
up a parasol, clutching on to the chair with my
other hand. I thought to myself, never shall I
be able to go a long journey in this uncomfortable vehicle; for I had not been in it ten minutes
before I had such a stitch in my side that I should
have preferred walking miles in the blazing sun.
I, however, managed to make the round of the
town in it, and then proceeded to the Colonel's
quarters, a pretty little house in a shady garden
on the edge of the steep bank facing Diego Point.
His cool little sitting-room was prettily hung with
native mats, and just outside the window was a
big tree covered with bottle-shaped nests made by
the weaver - birds, which much resemble yellow
sparrows. To protect their eggs from bigger birds

G

they interlace green branches over the entrances
to their little homes.

After a short visit we returned on board, accompanied by our host, who had been invited to dinner
by the Captain of the "Amazone." Commandant
Moussu, whose gunboat was then anchored near
us, was also of the party.

Monsieur de Vilers had set his heart on our
taking a ride on the "Montagne Russe," as he called
the Decauville line we had seen. He declared it
was the very thing we should enjoy; but the
Colonel did not seem equally keen. However, we
all begged so hard that he promised to send us
word if he could manage it. As there was only
one train a-day, starting at 5.30 A.M., to take provisions to Maattinsinzoarivo fort, we retired to rest
early in hopes of having to be called before sunrise
for our trip. After we had gone below, Monsieur
de Vilers heard from the Colonel that our expedition
could be arranged; so he sent us a message, which,
however, never reached us. Had it not been for
his kindness in getting up to call us at five
the following morning, we certainly should not
have awakened in time to catch the train. As it
was, we had only ten minutes to tumble out of
bed and into our clothes, eat a crust, and jump
into the boat, which he had had manned while
we were dressing. In less than twenty minutes
from the time we were called, we were walking

up the pier steps, where the Colonel received us.
The little train had already started up the hill, so
we had to take a short cut and meet it at the
barracks. There were three trucks, two laden with
provisions, the third for passengers with two seats
placed—outside car-fashion—back to back. On
this Harry and the Colonel took their seats; but
I preferred sitting on a provision-box in the foremost truck, between the driver and a private, who
were most entertaining, and told me about their
everyday life.

Two mules, each led by a native, were hooked
tandem-fashion to the side of the leading truck; the
leader being ridden postilion, while the other native
scrambled on to the train behind. We started at
full gallop, holding on like grim death to avoid
being jerked out by the jump which the cars gave
as they passed, in rapid succession, over each joint
of the roughly laid rails. The line runs through
low prickly shrub over an undulating plain, the
steeper slopes of which are avoided by curving
round the spurs and valleys; but no levelling has
been attempted, and the track consequently passes
over a succession of ups and downs. On arriving
at the beginning of one of the latter the mules
are cleverly unhooked without stopping the cars,
which speed down the incline, while the animals
are galloped at full speed by a short cut, to rejoin
them ere they lose their impetus on the next ascent,

when, without slackening their pace, they are hooked on again until the next descent is reached. At one point where the line crosses a ravine by a causeway too narrow to allow of trucks and mules passing together, the engineer has taken a hint from the character of the ground, and built the embankment with a dip in the middle; so that, when the mules are detached, the impetus given by the descent takes the train up the opposite bank, where they can again be hooked on. In spite of the jerks, and the fact that the dust and wind almost prevented me from seeing, the sensation of rushing through the air at such a pace was a most delicious one; and I was quite sorry when, after a journey of twelve *kilomètres*, the line ended abruptly at the foot of a steep hill, whence we were told we had three *kilomètres* to walk. Just before we began climbing this hill, we crossed by a good stone bridge " La Rivière des Caimans "—here a clear boulder-strewn stream, looking far more like the home of trout than of crocodiles, though I am told that a little lower down, where the stream becomes broader and more sluggish, the latter are plentiful enough to justify its name.

I was thankful it was so early in the morning, for at that hour there was a deliciously cool breeze, which gave us strength for our tedious walk. After an hour's toil up the newly made military road, zigzagging up a steep bank covered with sparse low

shrub, we reached the fort, a stockaded enclosure
in which were a two - storeyed stone building, a
number of detached huts, and a kitchen-garden,
in which a good many men were at work, and which
seemed to provide an ample supply of vegetables.
My ideas of a fort being based on what I had seen
in Europe, and the very pretentious works at Massowah, I confess I was rather disappointed at this
very unpretending little stronghold; but I was told
it was quite strong enough for the purpose for which
it was intended—to ward off the attacks of evil-
disposed Sakalavas; though even they, so far, had
never tested its powers of resistance. Whatever
its qualifications may have been from a military
point of view, it certainly afforded a charming view
of the surrounding country. To the north, the broad
plain over which we had just passed, with the
gradually widening "Rivière des Caimans" winding
through it, till it lost itself in La Baie de Diego
Suarez; beyond it the red roofs of the Antiserane
barracks, from which the heliograph flashed us an
occasional message, and in the distance the high
summit of Diego Point. To the east, at our feet,
lay a green valley, through which wound the upper
waters of "La Rivière des Caimans," bounded on its
farther side by a steep wooded bank, between the
top of which and the sky-line was visible a narrow
strip of the Indian Ocean. To the south, the view
was bounded at a short distance by a bush-covered

range of hills; while to the west spread a succession of barren hills and valleys, terminating in the rugged range of which "Windsor Castle" is the highest point.

The Captain in command having been informed by heliograph of our intended visit, came to meet us. The poor man looked very ill, having just got over a bad attack of fever. The Lieutenant, on the contrary, although he had been there eighteen months, was perfectly well, and told us he had never once had an attack. This elevated spot, swept by sea-breezes, certainly seemed as if it ought to be more healthy than the low-lying town of Antiserane; but I was told it was these very breezes which, fever-laden from the mangrove-swamps in the plains, caused it to be unhealthy. The men, a hundred and forty in number, were *disciplinaires,* and I should think rather a handful, as a big dark room used as a prison, which was shown us when we went round the huts, was said to be often quite full with men who had to be confined for insubordination.

After resting a short time in the officers' mess, we had to hurry back, as our ship was to start early. I think the poor Colonel did not at all appreciate our expedition, for it became intolerably hot before we got back, and, like us, he had probably started without his breakfast.

At eleven we steamed out of harbour with a

pleasant cool wind ahead, which, however, became
unpleasantly strong when we got outside, and I
soon had to disappear, and spent a wretched night,
as the vessel pitched terribly. At one o'clock next
day we got into calm water, as we entered the
channel, about ten miles wide, which separates the
island of Sainte Marie from Madagascar. The
former island consists of a high ridge running
north and south, some thirty miles in length and
two in breadth, on the western coast of which the
harbour is situated.

We cast anchor at 2 P.M. off " Île Madame," the
inner of two islets in the harbour, which contains
the Government House, hospital, and workshops, and
is connected with the main island by a ferry-boat
running on a wire cable. Île Fourban, the outer
island, is uninhabited, and is only used as a coal-
depot. Owing to the unhealthiness and excessive
mortality in this station, the European garrison and
civil *employés* have been reduced to a minimum ; the
only representative of the former being, I believe,
an artillery sergeant, who acts as caretaker to the
fort on Sainte Marie ; while the latter do not, I
think, number more than half-a-dozen.

We went on shore with the post-bags, and after
landing them on "Île Madame," were rowed to Sainte
Marie pier ; then walking along a beautiful shady
road with glorious vegetation on all sides, we
reached the Roman Catholic mission station, easily

recognisable by the hymns which we heard the little native children singing inside. Then after looking at the church, which stands in a pretty garden, we climbed up a steep slope to the fort, perched on the ridge of the island at its narrowest, and overlooking the harbour to the west, and a broad stretch of swamp to the east. We knocked at an open door, and getting no answer, walked in and found the whole place deserted; there had evidently been no troops there for some time. We were afterwards told that this elevated spot was the most unhealthy part of the whole island, owing to its being exposed to the winds that sweep across the marshes. Continuing our walk some distance along a good road shaded by large overhanging trees, we arrived at a collection of native huts, near which was a little *café* kept by a Frenchman who looked wretchedly ill. He sold us some cocoa-nut milk, and talked to us in a desponding manner of the vanished prosperity of Sainte Marie. Between the huts and the sea fringing the shore is a lovely avenue of cocoa-palms, under which sat a group of natives, from whom we bought some leechees, a delicious slightly acid fruit contained in a hard shell, which on being removed reveals a substance that from its translucent appearance might be taken for a hard-boiled plover's egg. In a little garden close by I noticed a splendid cacao-shrub, its reddish pointed pods full of my favourite nibs.

TAMATAVE.

As there did not seem much to make it worth while walking any longer in the hot sun, we retraced our steps and returned on board. This island is pretty, but without any particular interest, and is said to be a hotbed of fever; even at the time of our visit—the end of the dry season—it was extraordinarily green, and one could hardly imagine to what further degree of rankness the vegetation would reach by the end of the rains.

The next night was spent at anchor, a great relief after the last restless one at sea! Early on the following morning, however, we started again, and twenty-four hours' steaming brought us to Tamatave, November the 8th, 6.30 A.M. Just before entering the harbour we passed " L'Île des Prunes," whose green foliage offered a striking contrast to the withered tree-trunks, evidences of the force of the hurricane which had swept over it in 1885, blowing off the roofs of houses, uprooting and killing the trees, and driving on shore the ships at anchor in the harbour. I was told that the British consul, Captain Haggard, was at the Mauritius during this storm, and on his return found that the roof of his house had been lifted off like the lid of a box and deposited half a mile away.

The ships have to anchor a longish way from the shore, making it very inconvenient for loading and unloading cargo. The poor bullocks, of which a considerable number are continually exported to the

Mauritius and other islands, go through a terrible ordeal. Several of them are tied by the horns to a rope, which is fastened to spars placed athwart the canoes; they are then driven into the sea with many shrieks and blows from the natives, and have to swim for dear life, towed by the canoes, to the ship which is to convey them. When they arrive at the ship's side, a rope is passed under them, and they are hoisted on deck. It seemed terribly cruel, for I am told they do not even use a rope thick enough to prevent its cutting into them. I saw one clever animal get himself free of the ropes and swim to the reefs, where he seemed perfectly happy, stumbling about out of reach of his persecutors.

A great many people came on board from the town; among them was Monsieur Baissade, the doctor belonging to the French Residency, to whom we were introduced, and under whose care we were placed for the journey up country. Soon after anchoring, our Captain came up to us accompanied by an English officer, who had come from H.M.S. "Penguin" for their mails, and who kindly invited us to lunch on board. On arriving there, however, we were introduced to the Captain—King Hall—who asked us to lunch with him. On sitting down I was surprised to find that my neighbour, the first Lieutenant, was Mr Stanhope, whom I had not seen since we were both little children at Pau; while Harry's last meeting with him was at Dongola.

The "Penguin" is a smart little gunboat; but I honestly confess I was not happy while on her, as she was continually rolling.

After lunch we went ashore with Captain King Hall, taking the "Amazone" on our way to say good-bye to Commandant Masset. From the beach, on to which I was carried by a couple of blue-jackets,

Doctor Baissade in his filanzana.

we walked to the hotel by the long, straight, sandy street, which is practically the whole town. In spite of its length and straightness, and that most unæsthetic of objects, a tram line — which runs down its centre — it was not without a certain picturesqueness. The houses, in all varieties of shapes and sizes, were mostly built of wood, while their projecting eaves, supported on tall wooden uprights, gave a plentiful variety of light and shade, but, unlike those of Arab towns, afforded none of the latter to the street itself. In spite of the dust, and the glare of the mid-day sun, there was a fair amount of life in the street, both native and European : white-robed, straw-hatted Hovas of the middle class sitting near their verandahs, or sauntering barefooted through the dust; the coast negroes, bareheaded, in loose sacks of coloured home-spun, also on foot ; Hova officers and Europeans perched high on men's shoulders in their *filanzanas*—the former in the most correct and uncomfortable-looking black frock-coats and tall black hats, and the latter for the most part with the loosest of white cotton suits. We, imitating the humbler of the natives, proceeded on foot; and although the walk was not very long, we were glad to escape the vertical rays of the sun, and to take shelter in our inn, grandly called "Hôtel de France," where our travelling companions had already settled down. It was a small single-storeyed house surrounded by a verandah, and separated from the sea on one side and the street on the other, by two strips of untidy garden.

We found Monsieur de Vilers holding a *levée*—all the Europeans in the place, and the heads of the native population, having come to pay their respects

to the Resident-General, dressed in their best European clothes, top-hats, and gloves. His rooms were
on the right of the verandah, and ours on the left;
so I amused myself by watching the mixed procession going in and out.

As it was hoped that the porters for our journey
would be procured by the following morning, Doctor Baissade proposed that we should go with him
and buy camp - beds, stools, &c., which we should
want on the journey, having come without any of
these necessaries. I was offered a *filanzana*, but remembering my previous experience of that conveyance, preferred to walk ankle-deep in the sand. However, I soon got tired of this, and began to regret
I had refused the offer of a lift; for in spite of there
being several very good shops kept by Europeans,
it took us some time to find what we wanted—two
folding camp-beds, two iron folding-chairs, a very
large basin with canvas cover, which we filled with
all tubbing necessaries, and two *poncho* waterproofs,
—*i.e.*, square sheets of waterproof cloth with holes
cut in the centre for one's head to pass through. I
was also persuaded to buy a helmet, a head-gear I
detest. So far I had managed with one of Heath's
small sailor-hats. But later on the helmet turned
out most useful in the almost perpetual rain we had
going up country, as it acted as a " sou'-wester," and
shot the water well off the back of my neck.

Our shopping finished, we went to the bank to

exchange our gold into dollars (called *ariàry*), the coin most generally used by the natives, the Malagasy having no coinage of their own. We afterwards had to send some of these dollars to a man who cut each coin into seven pieces of different sizes. It is a most inconvenient way of buying anything, for one is obliged to carry a set of scales and weights with which to weigh out the value of the purchase.

We returned in time for dinner, and retired early, thinking we might have to start in good time the next morning. Our departure depended entirely on the porters, who are all natives of the interior, and who come down to the coast when they hear of a job. Although they had several times before taken up the Resident, his party and goods, and knew perfectly well that he never gave more than a certain fixed sum, still each time they think it necessary to bargain for more pay, and to waste several days before they give in.

Next morning we got up early and packed. Outside I heard a hum of voices, and going out on to the verandah, I saw a great crowd of natives all talking and shouting at once, while Monsieur d'Anthouard answered them with great calmness in their own language, looking as if he had years before him to settle about the trip to the capital; for if he had let them think for a moment that he was in a hurry, they would have held on to their high prices.

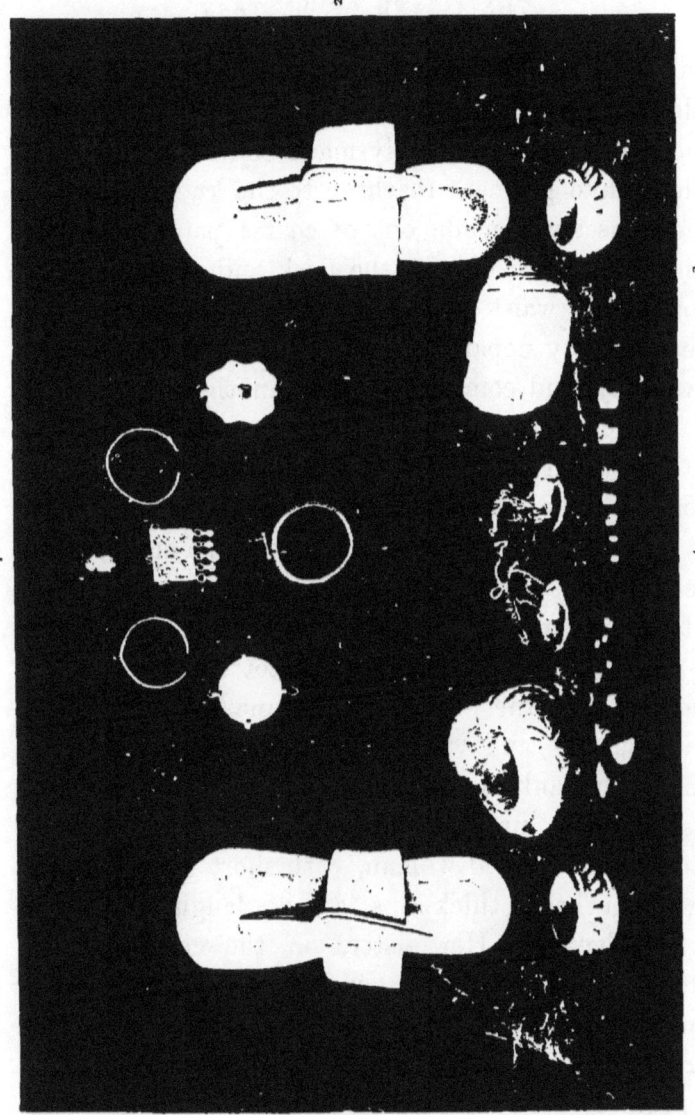

1. Silver charms, Jeddah.   2. Sandals, Lamu.   3. Silver anklets, Zanzibar.   4. Cut silver money, scales, and weights, Madagascar.

Silver Charms, &c.

In spite of their obstinacy, they were rather a pleasant - looking set of men, with dark - skinned faces, and lithe gracefully-made bodies covered by a blouse-like garment reaching to the knees, which in most cases was made out of coarse palm-fibre sacking, with holes cut for the neck and arms, and tied round the waist with a string. After a long discussion they departed, having temporarily got their own way, and condemned us to another day's delay.

While we were sitting under the verandah waiting to know our fate, two *filanzanas* arrived, and deposited their passengers near us. They turned out to be a certain Princess Juliette and her sister, members of the former reigning family, but by a Mauritius mother. In dress they were somewhat similar —wearing loose *camisoles* and cotton skirts which had not seen the wash-tub for some time, low shoes with buckles, and white cotton stockings very loose about the ankles—but otherwise I never saw two sisters more unlike. Juliette, the elder, was an enormously fat old woman, with short grey wool all over her head, thick lips, a loud laugh, and great flabby hands. Her sister, on the contrary, was almost a living skeleton, with a prim, rather serious manner, black wavy hair, and the complexion of a dried-up apple. She appeared to act as a sort of servant to her sister, sitting behind her chair saying nothing, and now and then getting up to attend to " Fatty's " wants.

As it turned out, it was fortunate that we had not started that day, for a frightful storm came on while we were at dinner—a perfect deluge—in the middle of which arrived the American consul, who had come to consult the doctor ; so we left them together, and adjourned to Monsieur de Vilers's sitting - room. As it was getting late, I took an umbrella to cross the verandah and reach my room, in doing which I got quite drenched. To my horror I found everything in our room afloat : trunk, chairs, table, all were dancing and knocking each other about. I called loudly for help. The hotel-keeper swore that such a thing had never occurred before ; but the doctor told him he knew better, for it had happened to him some months ago, and that the same remark had then been made. To sleep in the room was impossible, so all our things were carried across, and our camp - beds made up in Monsieur de Vilers's sitting-room. We had a good laugh over it all, every one carrying some garment or piece of furniture for us. The way we took it delighted our kind friend, for he said now he knew we should not mind any *contretemps;* and he stamped us as good travellers from that moment.

The next morning—November the 10th—we were again uncertain if we should be able to start. The men, as on the previous day, were again assembled outside, making a great noise, without coming to any definite conclusion, although they

H

had begun to come down in their prices.   Nevertheless I packed, having been told that as soon as the natives gave in we must start.   It was fortunate I did so, for they at last agreed to go for 25 francs a-head.   That being settled, there ensued the most amusing scramble.   The luggage-porters made a rush for the rooms, on the principle that first come first served, which in this case meant securing the lightest load.   Monsieur d'Anthouard and the doctor had their work cut out trying to keep them outside, so as to distribute the loads as they thought best, —without, however, much success.   The porters are wonderfully careful — never losing anything, and knowing the exact composition of each bundle. They notice at once if anything is changed in them, as I found out to my cost later on ; for having removed a rug from the roll of cloaks and put it in another package, they made such a terrific fuss that I was obliged to unstrap everything and replace it.

II.

Our departure, which took place at 12.25 P.M., was quite as amusing to witness as that of the luggage. We had ninety-eight men to carry our party of eight, which consisted of Monsieur de Vilers, his private secretary Monsieur d'Anthouard, Doctor Baissade, a native officer, our two selves, and Monsieur de Vilers's French cook and valet.

The porters were all anxious to seize upon the lightest weight, which was myself; so as soon as I appeared there was a rush towards me. It was at last settled who were to be my twelve bearers, and I had scarcely settled myself in my *filanzana*, when off they galloped down the street, leaving my umbrella and mackintosh on the ground. Luckily Harry saw them, and picked them up.

The first start in a *filanzana* was certainly trying to my nerves,—the twelve bearers shouting and running as hard as their bare legs could carry them, jumping over any obstacle that came in their way, and throwing me on to one another's shoulders in a fashion that made me wonder how often during the day I should be landed on my nose. But I soon got used to it, and after the first day or two forgot to clutch hold of the poles. Four men at a time carry the passenger, always keeping step. The men on the left side support the pole on the right shoulders, holding it with their right hands; those on the right side have their heads between the poles, the right-hand pole resting on their right shoulders, while with their left hands they catch hold of their companions' right wrists, and so steady each other. Every half-minute, without slackening their pace, they throw the *filanzana* on to the shoulders of four others, who in anticipation have been running on ahead, so that there should be no pause. They were a bright and cheery set of people, never ceasing to laugh and chatter the whole day, and were like a lot of big children out for a game of ball — the unfortunate passenger being the ball. The sailor's description of his camel-ride over the Bayuda desert —that the beast played cup-and-ball with him the whole way, and only missed him twice—would have been equally suitable to this mode of travelling. The bearers are of a higher class and generally younger than the baggage-porters, and are specially trained to keep up a fast rate of travelling day by day. The latter have, as a rule, enormous bumps on their shoulders, which I have read are hereditary ; but my own impression is that their growth on each individual is the result of the constant friction of the long bamboos on which they swing their loads.

The first part of our route lay through a wide sandy plain, dotted with alternate patches of short grass, low scrub, or fairly thick bush. In the distance to the right was a range of high hills, while to the left the constant roar showed that the sea could not be far off. An hour and a half's march brought us to Anjòlokàfa, a small village built on a tongue of land between the sea and the mouth of the river Ivòndrona, which here empties itself into the lake Nòsy-Vé.

This lake, or rather lagoon, is separated from the sea by a long and narrow strip of land. The latter becomes an island at high tide and admits the rollers, making the lagoon impassable for canoes.

To our disgust we found this to be the case on our arrival; while a strong south-easterly wind was adding to the roughness of the water. We waited a few hours, when, seeing there was no improvement, we made up our minds to spend the night in the village, and at once set to work to choose our huts. These were built of bamboo, and each consisted of a single room, with a mat-covered floor, and a hearthstone in a corner from which—there being no chimney—the smoke from the fire made its way out as best it could through the crevices of the roof. In another corner were several thick bamboos about seven feet long, which, having had their joints bored out, are used as water-jars—an ingenious contrivance, and very excellent for those who are expert in its use, but one which requires considerable practice, any undue elevation of the butt having the effect of sending the whole contents out with a rush, as I found to my cost the first time Harry tried to fill my drinking-cup for me. Our camp-beds were pitched under a beam, from which we hung the mosquito-curtains, so that they reached the ground. We thought sleeping under them rather close and stuffy at first, but on the one or two occasions during the journey up country on which we could find nothing to hang them to, we learned their value, for after a sleepless night we woke up in the morning with hands and faces a mass of mosquito-bites. The beds were a great success: made of the light framework of angle-

iron, they stood any amount of wear and tear, were
set up or folded for the journey in a minute, and
were wonderfully comfortable.

While the French cook was preparing an excellent
little dinner, and after we had set the porters to
collect our goods and put up our beds, we made a
short tour of the village and its surroundings. The
former consists of about twenty bamboo huts, with
palm-thatched gabled roofs, scattered irregularly
about a singularly barren piece of ground; and I
should imagine its only reason for existence was its
proximity to the ferry, in working which most of its
inhabitants found a livelihood, and at which—as in
our case—travellers were very likely to be delayed.
We were not the only sufferers on this occasion, for
soon after our arrival we were overtaken by three of
the *Sœurs de Charité* who had been our fellow-
passengers on board the "Amazone," and who were
also on their way to the capital. The only bit of
vegetation which we could see anywhere near was a
wild-looking thicket, and to this we turned our steps,
and were rewarded by finding a most lovely collection of aloes, cactus, flowering-shrubs, and a great
variety of large ferns, with one or two varieties of
orchids, unfortunately not in flower.

On returning to the village we found Monsieur
d'Anthouard surrounded by the *filanzana* porters
clamouring for money. They are given a few bits
of the 5-franc pieces every night and morning to

pay for their supper and breakfast; but they are
never satisfied with what is given them, and for the
first day or two they try to find how much they
can get out of their employers. Monsieur d'Anthouard was so well up to their tricks that he did
not pay any attention to their demands, but simply
gave them what he thought right, on receiving
which they all went away apparently quite satisfied.

Besides the porters attached to our party were
two *simandous*, or members of the regiment of the
Royal Bodyguard, composed of slaves freed on the
day of the Queen's coronation. They have unlimited
powers wherever they go, as, speaking in the Queen's
name, they can oblige the natives to submit to the
corvée, turn out of their huts for travellers, and
leave any work they may be engaged on should
their services be required as porters. One of their
duties is to carry poison from the sovereign to any
subject whom it may be desirable to get rid of; and
should the poison be refused, they have orders to
use other means to effect the same end. As a rule,
the poor victims gracefully accept the bitter cup
without a word. The poison used, which is very
deadly, is made from the leaves of the *tangèna*-tree,
which I was shown the following day—a tall shrub,
with narrow, pointed, shiny leaves. The *simandous*
wore breeches, a white drapery called a *lamba*,
loosely thrown round them, and on their heads the
hats of the country, very much resembling those

of Leghorn straw. In their hands they carried light
spears, with the butt ends made like an ordinary
spud, which they used as walking-sticks.

We also had accompanying us a young Hova, one
of the Queen's officers just returned from France,
where he had been sent to complete his education,
which, unless he was a very remarkably unpleasant
young man before he started, had certainly not
improved him; for his conceit was overpowering,
and the way in which he treated the other natives
filled me with the perpetual desire to ask some one
to kick him.

The natives on this coast belong to the Bètsimi-
sàraka tribe, and have dark skins, flattened noses,
and curly hair; while most of our porters, who were
of Hova extraction, and who come from the centre
of the island, were copper-coloured, with prominent
cheek-bones, straight black hair, and less flattened
noses. Being so accustomed to travellers, the
former did not show much curiosity on our arrival;
but having learned how generous Monsieur de Vilers
was, the women always came to offer him presents
—eggs and very lean chickens—knowing full well
they would get in return good solid silver. After
presenting their gifts, these women often sang curious doleful songs, never very loud, and going on for
hours, which had on me a restful effect, sending me
off to sleep.

We dined at three little folding-tables placed end

to end, each seated in his own camp-chair, brought folded under his arm, as men used to carry their opera-hats. After dinner, those of the party who had done this journey before related their various experiences for our benefit. Among these was one very characteristic of the morals of the country. The narrator, having stopped on the road to the capital at an important village, in which the Governor of the district resided, found that that officer was absent. He was, however, duly welcomed by the young wife. The traveller, not speaking Malagasy, and wishing to show his appreciation of her civility, patted her on the cheek, saying in French that she was very pretty. Soon after, he noticed a discussion going on between his hostess and his interpreter, at the end of which the latter informed him with a deep bow that the lady accepted. Thinking that his interpreter — as often happened—had made use of the wrong word, he thought no more of the matter. Soon after his dinner he retired to rest, when, to his surprise and embarrassment, *Madame la Gouverneur* made her appearance, evidently with the intention of making a prolonged visit. Then, and not till then, did he connect the interpreter's remark with the harmless little flatteries which had placed him in such an awkward position.

There was heavy rain during the early part of the night, which, besides keeping up an incessant

patter on the palm-leaf roof, managed to find its
way through it, falling in occasional big drops all
over the floor and beds. Once or twice I managed
to sleep by drawing my waterproof over my head;
but I suppose the stifling heat made me incautiously
throw it off, for in spite of all precautions I was continually being awakened by a cool splash on my
cheeks. The consequence was, it was well into the
small hours before I fairly fell asleep. It was therefore with anything but pleasure that I heard Monsieur de Vilers's voice at the door telling us it
was half-past four, and time to get up. Tumbling
out of bed more asleep than awake, I had begun
leisurely to dress, thinking—if I thought at all—
that there could be no real hurry, when in rushed
the whole troop of porters, who began packing up
everything we possessed; and it was with the greatest
difficulty that I managed to get them out of the hut
comparatively empty-handed. Even then they got
no farther than the door, on which they kept up a
continual tattoo, occasionally opening it to see how
we were getting on. This performance was repeated
on every morning of our journey, but not always
with so much success on our side; for every now
and then a porter would get into the hut when we
were not looking, and triumphantly carry off the one
bag containing everything necessary for dressing.

We must have made a funny picture to our
visitors, if they were capable of appreciating it: I

struggling to dress and to find my things; Harry
trying to shave—a ceremony he never omitted, however early the start,—all by the light of one little
wax candle, which for want of a table had to be
stuck on the floor by means of a drop of hot wax,
and which was constantly being blown out by the
wind and toppling over. I must own I was not
very keen about these early starts, but I soon found
out that it was a hobby of our host's to go the
round and wake everybody up before daylight. We
therefore put up with them with a good grace,
and hastened to thoroughly wake ourselves up with
the excellent cup of black coffee of which we
always partook before the start; but the pleasure
of drinking it was rather marred by the dose of
quinine which the doctor insisted on serving out at
the same time.

These swallowed, we were hurried off to the
water's edge, where we had to wait a good half-hour
while the porters loaded and got ready the canoes,
—unwieldy-looking things some thirty feet long and
three broad, with pointed stems and sterns, hollowed
out of the trunk of a single tree. A curious mixture
of types were collected by the misty lake-side on
that grey Sunday morning, all—except Monsieur de
Vilers, who was always wide awake and full of energy
—equally sleepy, and desirous of being back comfortably in bed, and each trying to pass the tedious time of waiting in a different way: Monsieur

d'Anthouard giving directions to the porters, and generally making himself useful; the doctor carefully stowing away in a canoe some bags of specie of which he was taking charge for the Malagasy Government; the three nuns telling their beads; Harry lying on the bank trying to pick up his lost half-hour in bed; I munching a crust of bread and a piece of chocolate; while the porters shouted and danced, and carefully threw all one's most perishable baggage into the wettest part of the canoes.

At last all was ready for a start. The first to move off was the doctor with his money-bags. I followed next in my *filanzana*, and was deposited in it at the bottom of the canoe, thus avoiding the alternative of sitting in water, or perching on the top of a pile of baggage which already looked as if it must overbalance the narrow keel-less craft. Somebody gave a shove from the shore, and I found myself alone with my twelve porters—temporarily turned into boatmen—who, shouting at the top of their voices all the time, paddled for dear life. After about a quarter of an hour we came to the part of the lagoon directly across the bar, where, in spite of the comparatively low tide, the sea was rolling in with decidedly unpleasant force. As each roller swept under us, the canoe lifted her pointed prow into the air, falling again into the trough of the next wave with a splash, and shipping sea after sea, till, finding

that the water had risen to the footboard of my *filanzana*, I thought it was about time to take some
steps to get rid of it, and accordingly, doffing my
brand-new helmet, set to work to bale her out, a proceeding which seemed much to amuse the men;
but nevertheless the one nearest to me followed my
example, and began trying to ladle out the water
with his old sieve-like straw hat. I am afraid my

Crossing Lake Nòsy - Vè.

efforts and the disfigurement of my helmet were not
of much avail, for the canoe seemed to get heavier
and heavier, and in spite of the men's redoubled
shouts, as with their heads between their knees they
strained at the paddles, the canoe refused to make
any headway against the sea. The situation was
getting decidedly critical, and our difficulties were
increased by our drifting into some weeds, among

which the starboard paddles could not be worked,
so that we got broadside on to the sea. I was
preparing at any moment for a capsize, and
to exchange the company of my Malagasy boatmen for that of the crocodiles that infest the lake,
when, realising it was a case of now or never, the
men gave another shout, and by a supreme effort
shot the canoe into smooth water.

On approaching the shore I looked in vain for
the doctor, whom I had expected to find waiting
for us; but seeing nothing but the usual collection of *lamba* - clothed natives, I began to fear
that some mishap had befallen his canoe. It was
not until our craft had actually touched the shore
that, hearing his voice, I looked up and discovered
him disguised in a bath-towel. It seemed that he
had such a drenching in his passage, that he had
taken off all his clothes to dry them, and had improvised an imitation of a native costume. Soon
afterwards I was thankful to see the other canoes
appearing in sight, for the tide and wind were rapidly rising, and every moment rendered the passage
more risky.

As soon as the last canoe had come in, our temporary boatmen resumed their usual duties, and lifting our *filanzanas* on to their shoulders, started off
at a brisk trot, leaving the baggage-porters to dis-
embark our luggage and follow us,—the only exception being made in favour of the cooking-utensils,

which, with the French cook and valet, pushed on
ahead with all possible speed, that our breakfast
might be ready at the mid-day halting-place—
Ampàniràno—which we reached after a five hours'
journey among thick woods, and across miasmic
swamps exuding fetid vapours at every step, as our
bearers, wading knee-deep in water, stirred up the
black mud beneath.

Our halting-place was a straggling and rather
dirty village of the usual bamboo and palm-leaf
huts, two of which, however, set apart for the use
of travellers, were fairly clean. Here we partook
of an excellent breakfast, provided by that treasure
Alphonse, and which I for one had been wanting for
some hours.

After a short rest we started again, travelling for
two hours over ground similar to that passed in the
morning; after which the character of the country
suddenly changed, and our road lay through a
lovely park-like district, the ground covered with
crisp green turf, broken here and there by clumps
of stately trees, and dotted with smaller patches of
palms, mimosa, tree-ferns, and shrubs that looked
like rhododendrons, intermingled with the growth
of small plants and creepers. Here and there a
pretty peep was gained of Lake Rasòabè and its
farther well-wooded shores, while to the left we
could hear the sea breaking on the beach in the
distance. Animal life was singularly deficient, a

few little birds being, as far as I could see, the
only inhabitants of this lovely region.

After travelling through this park for a couple of
hours, we bore to our left and marched along a
glaring sandy spit which lay between the ocean
and the chain of lagoons. On our right was a
curious and dismal illustration of the partiality of
cyclones. In the region through which we had just
passed not a branch was missing from the trees;
but here was a forest absolutely stripped of all but
its upright stems, which rose gaunt and bare out of
the sand-dunes like the time-worn mainmasts of a
sunken fleet; yet only three years before they had
stood covered with foliage and bound together with
creepers, seemingly an indestructible jungle.

On the beach grew a curious creeper with ivy-
shaped leaves and a violet flower, which I was told
only grew in the sand. I got my men to pick me
some of the black seeds, resembling those of a
convolvulus, and took them home with me to
England, where, however, we never succeeded in
making them flower.

After an hour and a half's march, an opening in
the lagoon, with a steep wooded bank on the farther
side, blocked the direct route along the sea-shore,
and made us again turn inland, crossing the channel,
through which the porters waded waist-deep, seemingly with much enjoyment, as they tucked up
their one garment, and splashed and sported in

the water in a way that made me feel that at any moment I might unexpectedly join them. In course of time, however, they carried me over, safe and dry, and we entered a tract which, though well wooded, was less lovely than that of the earlier afternoon, and which stretched as far as Vavony, our resting-place for the night, where we arrived at six o'clock, having done about forty miles.

The next morning we started at 4.50, travelling through very much the same sort of wooded country, and only passing one village—the little hamlet of Andàvakamenaràna—until about seven, when we reached Andèvorànte, the most important town, after Tamatave, on this coast. As the nearest point to the capital, and that from which the road begins to run direct, it would seem to be the natural port of Antànanarìvo; and there can be little doubt that it will become so if the road is ever opened to the latter place. The mouth of the river Thàroka forms a fine harbour, at present rendered inaccessible by the bar stretching across it. This, however, is probably not more formidable than many similar ones—such as that at Durban—which have been opened as soon as the exigencies of trade demanded it.

Monsieur de Vilers stopped at Andèvorànte to inspect the guard of honour that had been formed up to receive him; and although we pushed straight on, we had time, as we passed, to note its appearance, which was decidedly picturesque, though rather wanting in uniformity. Officers and men were dressed in every variety of what had once been uniforms—coats of blue or red or green, facings of equally various hues, trousers long and short, and in some cases wholly absent, and caps and helmets of every conceivable shape. After leaving Andèvorànte, we journeyed for about half an hour along the sand-spit which separates the river Thà-roka from the sea, till we arrived at the place where the canoes for our passage were supposed to be collected. But only three were there, and consequently the transit of ourselves and baggage was rather a lengthy operation.

The latter was sent off first, and while waiting for the canoes to return, I took a stroll along the bank with Monsieur de Vilers in search of flowers. Nearly all were strange to me, and so beautiful that I should have liked to dig up a whole sackful, but, bearing in mind our limited means of transport, had to content myself with some lovely small red-and-black seeds of a creeper which was very abundant. On our return to the boats my porters brought me a curious yellow fruit, the size of an orange, with a hard shell, which on being opened disclosed a pulpy interior. I was not allowed to eat it for fear it was poisonous; but I afterwards learned it was the delicious juicy *voavontaka*, which is so prized for its refreshing qualities.

When our turn came to cross, we found that even
the few canoes available were of the most aged
and unseaworthy kind. The one in which I was had
so big a hole in her bows that when she was fully
laden the water poured in. My boatman, however,
thought nothing of such a little defect, which he soon
remedied by the simple expedient of sitting down in
the hole! The country on the farther side of the
river was a flat alluvial tract covered alternately with
cultivation and thickish bush, and intersected here
and there by streams, one of the largest of which we
had to cross by a bridge formed of two slender tree-
trunks, so narrow that the bearers had to lean outwards with feet and hips touching, and bodies overhanging the stream on either side—rather nervous
work until I got accustomed to it; but I soon found
that the men never lost their footing with a light
weight on their shoulders, and I ended by feeling
that they would take me safely over every obstacle.

At 9.50 we halted for breakfast at Tànimàn-
dry, a stockaded village with a small Hova garrison, and the first telegraph-station on the line from
the coast to the capital. After a good breakfast, and
a siesta on the flat of our backs—which we all found
was the only position that thoroughly rested us after
sitting upright for so long in the *filanzana*—we
started again in a westerly direction, through a
marshy country, where here and there a little rice is
grown; after which we began to ascend the first steps

of the great table-land occupying the centre of the island—a very irregularly formed plateau of red clay hills covered with scant grass, and almost wholly treeless. The most curious feature of the country is the apparent absence of valleys : the hills struck me as being more like a number of gigantic bubbles or blisters than the ordinary undulations one is accustomed to see ; and the depressions between them, having no outlets, are consequently very swampy and difficult to pass. They, however, made up in vegetation for the barrenness of the hill-tops ; and each was filled with a lovely thicket of fern-trees, palms, and wild pine-apples, mingled with a wealth of such tropical flowers as love these sheltered airless nooks.

Late in the afternoon we came to the river Mahèla, a rapid stream about a hundred yards wide, with steep clay banks fringed with a thick growth of the small-leaved bamboo. On the right bank, near the ferry, were a few very miserable native huts, whose occupants were only able to produce three of the smallest of dug-out canoes for our passage across. The crossing consequently took a long time ; and when finally we all got to the opposite shore, our porters had to put their best feet foremost to get to the next village before dark.

It is extraordinary what these men can do when they set their minds to it. They had been going, on and off, since long before daybreak—the early part of

the day through heavy swampy ground, and afterwards up and down steep wet clay hills, at times so

Down-hill.

slippery that the back pair of each set of porters had

to sit on their heels and act as a drag during the
descent.   In spite of all this, from the time we left
the Mahèla until we reached our halting-place for
the night, I do not think they ever ceased running,
chattering, and laughing for a moment, keeping up
a good jog-trot up the hills, a steady run on the flat,
and literally taking away one's breath by the pace at
which they slid and bounded down the slopes.   The
country on this side of the river was far more regular
in character than that on its eastern bank, and consisted of a series of hills and valleys, mostly running
north and south — that is, at right angles to our
route.   At the bottom of most of the valleys were
streams, some fairly broad and easily fordable,
others narrow with abrupt clay banks, down the first
of which the *filanzana* had to be lowered, feet first,
at such an angle that one expected it would topple
over the "leaders'" heads ; while the next moment
the ascent on the other side found one reclining
gracefully on the back of the chair, one's head resting on the "wheelers'" bare shoulders.

The valleys were luxuriantly clothed with palms
and bamboos.   Among the former I noticed quantities of the useful and ornamental *Rafia*, and, for
the first time, the "Traveller's tree," bare-stemmed
and with banana-like leaves.   These, however, only
grow near the top, and, unlike those of other palms,
which grow all round the stem, are in two vertical
rows on opposite sides of the trunk.   The effect

when facing it is that of an outspread fan. The stems of the leaves being hollowed at their junction with the trunk, form the troughs for the collection of rain - water, from which it earns its name. Of bamboos, the graceful small - leaved variety was most plentiful, some of them rising in single stems to over forty feet in height, the tender top-shoots hanging over, meeting their neighbours, and forming long vistas of Gothic arches.

A couple of hours' run across this undulating plateau brought us to the edge of a deep valley, at the bottom of which lay our destination—Mànambònitrà—a good - sized, prosperous - looking village, surrounded by coffee-plantations, patches of sugarcanes, rice, and tobacco, and encircled by hedges of the edible passion-flower.

Having got out of the district of regular travellers' huts, we were put up in a room occupied by a Malagasy family, who themselves turned out on our arrival, without, however, taking with them the varied collection of birds, animals, and insects with whom they seemed to be in the habit of living. We began by turning out the pigs and dogs, but soon found that the noise they made scratching against and squeezing through the cracks of the slim bamboo door was worse than their presence in their accustomed corners. The pigs were very harmless, and usually lived behind a little trellis of bamboos, making a charming lullaby with their grunts. Dogs I did not like so much; they came sniffing round our beds, trying to find something to eat, and growling and tumbling over each other all night. The fowls and ducks we made no attempt to disturb, and they repaid our kindness by interfering as little as possible with our rest; the former roosting quietly on the rafters over our heads, and the latter huddled in a corner behind another trellis like that which accommodated the pigs. Of course the village cock was as offensively boastful of his early rising as in other countries, but we had the luck never to share the same hut with him. The insect population we made every attempt to get rid of, but with painful want of success. I spent most of the night having great hunts among it—lighting up every quarter of an hour, much to the disgust of Harry, who was quite insect-proof, and did not at all see the fun of being disturbed; but not being able to sleep myself, I could not resist the temptation. I found the blanket-bag in which I slept was an excellent trap; for after one or two bites they burrow in the warm wool, and can then be caught by dozens.

The next morning—the beginning of our fourth day's journey—we started at five in a good downpour, and after crossing the Mahòla river again, passed over the same sort of undulating country as on the previous afternoon. We halted for breakfast at Ambatoharànana, a dirty little village some

600 feet above the sea, at the bottom of a valley
ankle-deep in mud, and hot and steamy after the
morning's rain. Half the hut we were in was
taken up with a pile of packing-cases and hydraulic-
pressed bales on their way to the Queen; but I was
told that months might elapse before they reached
their destination. As all her transport is conducted
on the *corvée* system, the porterage has to be provided by each village in succession; and until some
one turns up to put a little pressure on the head
man, the task is indefinitely postponed. After
breakfast, threading our heads again through the
square holes of our *Poncho* waterproofs, we started
off in a regular deluge, the men sliding in every
direction, noisy as ever, and going at such a
pace that I found it impossible to hold up an
umbrella. As we went on, the features of the
country became more pronounced, and more thickly
covered with bush, which rather stopped our progress, as there was often barely room for the men
to run two abreast. The birds also became more
plentiful: we saw quantities of little green parroquets, as well as birds with metallic-looking feathers,
the size of blackbirds.

That night we slept at Ampàsimbé, "The place
of much sand," situated in a depression in the next
great step towards the central plateau, at the height
of about 1000 feet above the level of the sea—a larg-
ish, clean village, in which we were put up in a very

good hut, where, after the usual rush of the natives
to fetch water for the travellers, we enjoyed a
refreshing tub. While waiting for dinner outside
Monsieur de Vilers's big hut, we were entertained by
the women of the place, who went through a curious
performance, something between a dance and a
processional march, walking along with a curious
swaying movement, their hands outstretched from
their sides, the backs curved upwards and slightly
quivering, said to be in imitation of the flight of the
falcon, the royal emblem of Madagascar.

While we were at dinner we heard a shot fired,
and soon afterwards in rushed the little Malagasy
officer in a fearful state of excitement, asking, "Had
we heard it? Where did it come from? Who was
trying to murder us?" and a few more incoherent
questions all in one breath, at which we only burst
out laughing,—Monsieur de Vilers telling him he
really did not know, and that he had better go and
find out for himself. Off he went, shortly after
returning in great glee, having caught the would-be
murderer, and tied him hand and foot so that he
should not escape; for he felt sure the man had
intended to shoot "*Monsieur le ministre*," and that
it was his duty as a Malagasy officer to have him
punished. Our host was amused at his zeal, but
begged he would do nothing further until he had himself seen the man. So after we had had our coffee
and cigarettes we all went to interview the prisoner.

I never saw such a frightened-looking creature as this terrible criminal! Trembling all over, he explained that the revolver was an old friend, whom for years he had been trying to let off, but until then without success, and with many beseeching gestures begged that he might be pardoned for its unexpected behaviour. On examining the rusty old weapon, our party agreed that he was quite justified in supposing it would not go off, but were also surprised that, having gone off, anything should have remained of it or its owner. Nevertheless it was decided, in deference to the wish of the local authorities, that the poor wretch should be kept a prisoner until after our departure next day.

We were awakened next morning by the usual cry of "*Café!*" and starting at 4.45, soon got on to the main track, off which our halting-place lay at some little distance; and after a very steep climb for about an hour, we entered the outer belt of the great forest, following a very rough path, winding in and out, and over trunks of fallen trees, till another descent brought us down into a flat open valley. I thoroughly enjoyed the beauties of that first bit of forest, with its tangled masses of the "monkey-ropes" and creeping bamboos smothering the larger timber, as ivy does in the woods at home; and I was quite sorry when we left it for the open valley. After a few days of it, however, I found it became deadly monotonous, and longed for a breath of fresh

air and a glimpse of the sun. The curious absence
of animal life and sounds had a very depressing
effect, especially at night, when the silence was
alone broken by the weird barking of the lemurs,
the only wild animals we ever heard—and I believe
the only ones in the island—and even of these we
never caught a glimpse.

After leaving the forest, the path—mostly following the beds of watercourses—led down a steep slope
until we reached the village of Bèforana, when it
turns. a little to the northwards, and passing over a
succession of red clay hills, each a little higher than
its predecessor, plunges for good into the forest,
virgin and overcrowded, a mass of upright giants
and their fallen and decaying brethren, mingled with
every variety of creeper and orchid, but still lacking
the tropical rankness of the low-lying bush of the
coast. I should often have liked to have stopped
and had a closer look at the many strange plants
round me, but as in these narrow paths the stoppage
of one *filanzana* often brings the whole column in
rear to a halt, I had to press on. I, however, got
my men to pick me some orchid-plants to send
home, which I did with no success—on account, as
I was afterwards told, of their having been packed
in air-tight cases.

At 10.15 we stopped at the small woodcutters'
village of Ambasaniasy for breakfast, for which as
usual I was more than ready. I suffered so much

from hunger in these long morning marches that Monsieur de Vilers gave me a supply of chocolate on which to keep myself going. Once I gave a bit to one of my men, and was amused to see the friendly terms that they were all on : the one to whom I had given it, after taking a nibble, passed it on to his companion, who did the same, and so it went the whole round of my twelve bearers. I always noticed that anything they picked up was equally divided among them.

We started again at 12.10, the road getting worse at every step, running in a nearly straight line over hill and dale, without the smallest attempt to humour the gradients. We occasionally passed up and down slopes which I was told had been measured by an officer and found to be over 45°, and which, from the slippery nature of the soil in " The forest that weeps," would be very difficult, even if far less steep. Here and there a vague attempt at engineering had been made by broadening a torrent-bed sufficiently to allow of the packages for the capital to pass. These watercourses are often from fifteen to twenty-five feet deep, with almost precipitous sides ; about four feet wide at the height of a man's shoulders, and only three feet in width at the bottom. One can easily imagine the difficulties porters have to encounter, when one remembers that heavy packages, such as grand-pianos,—I actually saw one in the capital,—have to be carried along this road.

I have never seen a road so badly chosen, or one on which so little engineering skill had been expended. Not only had no attempt been made to turn the various ascents and descents encountered, but, by rigidly following the bottoms of the valleys and watercourses, the road passed alternately over tracts of level swamp and almost unclimbable slopes, when by the simple expedient of gradually ascending along the sides of the valleys both evils would have been avoided. It is a noticeable fact, that while in the central plateau of Imèrina the routes are always intelligently chosen, the path through the forest runs due east and west, regardless of obstacles, until it reaches the coast at a point nobody wants to arrive at, and thence turns abruptly along the sea-shore to Tamatave.

Harry started a theory from this that Imèrina had been originally colonised from the west, and that its semi-civilised inhabitants having lost the sense of locality common to all savages, and having, owing to the absence of the larger fauna, no tracks to guide them, were afraid to trust themselves to the forest except when following a straight line on the rising sun or along the beds of watercourses. If, he said, the road had been made from the coast by Malay pirates—one theory of the origin of the Hovas — it would, however stupidly chosen, undoubtedly have run straight inland from Tamatave ; while had it been made by pure savages, even without the first guidance of wild beasts, it would have been more intelligently laid out.

At four o'clock we reached Anàlamazaòtra, the frontier Hova station, having risen 1400 feet in the last twelve miles, the village itself being 3130 feet above the sea-level. It is a large and prosperous place, built in a big clearing. The native type here was totally different from that we had hitherto come across. The inhabitants of all the villages up to this had been black, with short curly hair and negro type of feature, and showed every sign of being of African origin. The Hovas, on the contrary, whom we had now got amongst, had complexions little darker than those of the peasantry of Southern Europe, straight black hair, rather sharp features, slim figures, and were unmistakably of the Asiatic type.

As we stood in the doorway of our hut, a huge wall of trees, distant from a quarter to half a mile, hemmed us in on every side. To the west, standing out in strong contrast to the delicate greens and yellows of the cultivated fields, the lemon-groves, thickets of wild pine-apples and passion-flowers in full bloom, it was hard and black, and, except in outline, shapeless. To the east, lit up by the setting sun, it shone in every variety of hue, through purple, bronze, brown, and olive-green to brightest emerald—a softly dimpled mass.

Although the distance covered during the day's

march had been small, the men having barely averaged three miles an hour, owing to the extra-ordinary badness of the road, they had had a hard day's work, having had constantly to stoop right down to enable us to pass under the big half-fallen trunks of trees, or else go out of their way to avoid creepers hanging like great cobwebs across the road. Monsieur de Vilers made them a present of an ox—a wretchedly lean old beast, which I had seen being led down the street, but whose fate I did not realise until, hearing a fiendish noise outside our hut while I was unpacking, I looked out and saw all the men pushing, shoving, and scrambling for the best pieces of meat, they having already killed, skinned, and cut up the poor animal.

The following day we started at 5.15 A.M., again plunging into the forest, in which we kept for about three hours, then gradually descended into a swampy valley about four miles broad, and covered with rice-fields. The young shoots were then a few inches out of the water in which they are sown. I watched with much interest the process of transplanting, which was being carried on as we passed by a number of bare-limbed and bare-headed boys and women, mostly slaves. Before the young plants are moved, about half-a-dozen oxen are driven into the small square spaces, enclosed by low mud-ridges, and are goaded and harassed by a gang of shouting boys until the poor beasts have rushed about sufficiently to tread the muddy ground into a pulp, and thus make it ready for the reception of the rice-plants. Even the hillsides had with great labour been utilised by building a series of terraces, each irrigated by a stream which flowed into the valley.

Leaving this cultivated bit, we again got into the forest, or rather a belt of it; for after a couple of hours in it, and a sharp ascent of another half-hour, we found ourselves on a high grass-covered pass, from which, backwards, we got a grand view of the forest through which we had been travelling for the last three days; while in front of us was the open valley of the Mangoro, bounded on the east by a bold range of hills. After two or three more ups and downs, some of them remarkably steep and slippery, we got on to a track which made some attempt to accommodate itself to the ground by winding round spurs and the heads of ravines, and gradually descended into the Ankày plain, on the edge of which we halted for breakfast at Mòramànga —a market town and seat of Government, with well-built brick houses.

We were welcomed by the Governor of the province—a high-born Hova, and an officer of " twelve honours," who turned out his troops to receive the Resident-General; but he — a little copper-coloured man with sleek black hair—was himself in European plain clothes, black frock-coat, and tall hat. He was invited to breakfast with us; and

K

although he could not speak French, with the help of Doctor Baissade, who acted as interpreter, made himself very agreeable. While the men of the party were smoking their cigarettes after breakfast in the open air, I, feeling very tired, lay down on the matted floor, but was soon roused by loud shouts and roars of laughter outside ; and running out, I saw all our porters trying to catch a wild-looking ox—a present from the Governor to Monsieur de Vilers—which was charging them, and sending them flying in all directions. The more they shouted, the wilder it got ; and it ended by breaking through them, and, escaping to the plain, never to be seen again by its new proprietor—although I have no doubt that it returned in due course to its original master, and perhaps lived to be presented again to other distinguished visitors.

On leaving the town we were escorted some way by the Governor—a pure matter of form ; for marching as we did in single file at top speed, any attempt at conversation was impossible ; and the porters race each other and scatter, so that he had not even the chance of bidding us farewell in a body. We were now on a stretch of grassy plain, which for the next two hours afforded good going for the men, who did not seem the least fatigued by their wild chase after the bullock. No wonder they become so excited when there is a prospect of getting meat, their usual food being composed of manioc or sweet-potatoes, and sometimes rice; but even of these they seem to eat very little during the day. In the most deserted parts of the road one comes upon two or three women sitting together by the side of the path— almost always hideous old hags—boiling the manioc- roots over a small fire, round which they have gen- erally built a mud wall, in horse-shoe shape, about four feet high. These are the restaurants on the Antânanarîvo road; and at one of them during the course of a day's march our men would stop for a couple of minutes and buy a handful of this root, all that I saw them eat between sunrise and sunset.

Towards three o'clock we reached the river Man- goro, a swift stream about 120 yards wide, running between high banks fringed with palms and bam- boos, casting lovely reflections in the water. As there was a plentiful supply of big canoes, the passage was soon accomplished, and we were each able to cross over with our *filanzana* and our twelve bearers in the canoe with us. Having reached the other side, we at once mounted a high and very steep hill, on the summit of which we stopped for a few moments, and got off our *filanzanas* to let our men take breath, and to enjoy the glorious panorama stretched on all sides beneath us. The farther slope of the hill was even steeper than that we had just climbed, and, if anything, much more slippery; and after the hard pull up they had just had, I expected that the men would go down it

quietly, but nothing of the sort! Off they started as
fast as their legs could carry them, throwing me like
a ball from one to the other's shoulders. I am not
ashamed to say I held on like grim death, for most
of the party had had falls at one time or another, so
that I was not at all sure when my turn would come.
They only stopped when we reached Ambòdinifòdy,
a small and dirty village of about twenty huts, built
in the bottom of a valley running into that of the
Mangoro, at a short distance from the point where
we had crossed it; consequently a very slight detour
would have turned the high and steep cone-shaped
hill over which we had just climbed. Having
arrived rather early, we went for a walk in the
village, where I was offered a—to me—new species
of bird, that a little boy was carrying about dead
in his hand. It was of a curious grey-blue colour,
and I now believe was of the cuckoo tribe; and I
am sorry I did not buy, skin, and send it home. But
by the end of the day's run in the open air, I always
found that my energy had nearly evaporated, and
that my chief thoughts were of dinner and bed.

We started next morning at five, leading up the
valley for a couple of hours through swamps and
rice-fields, and passing several little villages of well-
built brick houses. Then climbing a steep hill, the
last of the great steps to the plateau, we entered
what proved to be the innermost belt of the forest.

III.

Although we were now in the Hova province, and within a forced march of the capital, the forest-track, so far from having improved, was the worst we had yet met with. The succession of ups and downs seemed to be endless, huge fallen trees blocked the path at every few hundred yards, and the slipperiness of the track was too much even for my porters, who once or twice came down on their knees, without actually, however, giving me a fall. The belt fortunately was of no great width, and by eleven o'clock we reached Ankèrama-dinika, a village on its edge, and the frontier military post of Imèrina proper.

The character of the country now completely changed. Instead of dark forest, or at best open valleys bounded by ranges of hills, a rolling prairie lay before us, on the waves of which we could see our road stretching for miles ahead; while every half-hour or so brought in view some pretty hamlet of red-roofed cottages in a cluster of rice-fields.

On first leaving the forest, withered tree-stems were to be seen standing in all directions, probably the remains left by some ancient fire; but after a few miles the country became perfectly treeless, and except for one or two about the capital, I do not think that we saw a tree until we reached the forest on the western coast. Early in the afternoon we passed through Ambàtomànga, a fortified country town surrounded by a deep and wide ditch. It happened to be market-day at this place, thus affording us our first glimpse of a Hova crowd; and very picturesque the people looked, with their broad-brimmed straw hats, and snow-white *lambas* thrown over their shoulders *à l'Espagnole*—a striking contrast to the half-naked savages among whom we had been since we left the coast.

After leaving this town we got into a more rugged and barren country, here and there rocky and precipitous, but mostly covered with poor short grass. It so happened that all the rest of the party had gone ahead, and Harry was some distance in front of me when I noticed a wild-looking, half-starved bullock grazing on the side of the hill a little below our path. The beast, attracted by the noise the porters were making, looked up, snorted, and began tossing his head. I knew at once he was preparing to charge Harry's party, who did not appear to notice him, and who, going at a good pace, soon turned a corner. The brute then transferred his attentions to me. My men, I saw, realised the situation, and those running in front slackened their pace so as to keep all together. The owner, who was watching the beast, did all he could to drive him down the hill, but without any success; and having been told that whenever the porters get into any difficulty their first thought is to save themselves, I quite expected to be left in the lurch, a prospect I did not at all relish ; for, being the last of the party, there would have been no chance of my being picked up. However, I must say on this occasion they behaved very well, and stood by me until the animal was a few yards off, when I tried the experiment of opening and shutting my umbrella to try and frighten him away ; seeing which, one of my men, who evidently thought the idea a brilliant one, snatched it out of my hand and rushed at the animal, opening it straight in his eyes, with the desired effect of sending him flying, while the rest took to their heels and ran for dear life with me on their shoulders. We soon caught up Harry, and found him quite unconscious of what had been going on behind him.

Although the well-built stone houses and generally prosperous appearance of the country through which we had passed during the day had to a certain extent accustomed our eyes again to the aspect of civilisation, the first view of the capital, which suddenly burst on us as we topped a ridge, was fairly startling. The appearance of Antànanarìvo would be remarkable in any part of the world, closely built as it is on a long steep-sided ridge, rising abruptly from a treeless undulating table-land. Its church-spires, palaces, and red-pointed gables are conspicuous for miles round, and from their prosperous appearance, and in some cases pretentious style of architecture, would convey the impression of an important and well-built city even in Europe. But after a 225-mile journey through dense tropical forest, roadless, almost trackless, and inhabited only by a handful of half-naked savages, the sudden appearance of this towering evidence of civilisation almost takes away one's breath.

When we first saw the capital it was some ten miles distant, and we could easily have reached it that night; but having only taken six days on our journey instead of seven, as had been reckoned, our arrival would have been unexpected, and the various persons whose duty or pleasure it is to meet the Resident-General on such occasions would have been unable to do so; so Monsieur de Vilers decided to stop for the night at Betàfo, a flourishing suburb of two-storeyed brick villas in pretty gardens, enclosed within mud walls, surmounted by a fence of the prickly waxen-flowered euphorbia. In one of these villas we were entertained for the night by a hospitable Hova, whose civilised surroundings made me occasionally wonder whether I was not dreaming. It was so difficult to realise that, after saying goodbye to the not very advanced civilisation of Tamatave, and plunging into the forest, we could, without having retraced our steps, be really walking on polished *parquet* floors, sitting at a large mahogany dinner-table, or sleeping in a brass bedstead between

clean sheets. It was almost with a sense of loneliness that, being awakened by the banging of a
venetian shutter, I realised that the door was firmly
shut, and that there was not even a litter of pigs
under my bed, or a hen on the curtain-rods above
it. However, I woke up in the morning all the
better for a good night's rest, and gladly put up
with the slight inconvenience of not being able to
turn the contents of my tub out of the door, in
return for the unaccustomed luxury of a looking-
glass, in which I could see to do my hair without
having to emulate a professional contortionist.

Daylight showed that, in spite of its luxurious
accessories, our host's dwelling was not absolutely
perfect. Nothing in it appeared to be finished.
One window in the room was framed and glazed, the
other nailed up with rough boards; part of the
stair-banisters had no top-rail; outside, only a
portion of the roof had been tiled; and so on
throughout. I noticed this peculiarity in every
other Hova house which I afterwards saw, and was
told that it was due to a superstition that the
owner of a house always dies within a year of its
completion. As they have a rooted objection to
repairing anything, combined with a mania for
building, the result is a great mass of houses in
a state of dilapidation.

Early in the morning a mixed escort of French
and Hova officials arrived to welcome the Resident-

General and accompany him into the capital. As it
was raining hard, and he had to make a detour
through the town, we were advised to let him start
ahead ; so for once we had our early cup of coffee in
peace, and at about half-past nine started, accompanied by Doctor Baissade, for our destination.

A closer inspection of the capital did not at all
dissipate the feeling of surprise which the first view
of it had caused. Around us were the flat rice-fields
divided into squares by narrow mud-banks, some
submerged, others a mass of waving green. Out
of this chessboard-like tract, immediately in front
of us, rose a long ridge some five hundred feet high,
thickly covered with pretty little red-brick houses,
each apparently standing in its own garden ; spires
of half-a-dozen churches cut the sky-line ; while to
the left, on the highest part of the ridge, were two
huge square white palaces.

From its situation and its incongruity with its
surroundings, Antànanarìvo is undoubtedly a remarkable sight, viewed from the plain ; but there
is nothing imposing about it. The architecture is
of too toy-house and cockney an order, and its
whole aspect violates the first principle of art,
that of putting the right thing in the right place.
At Sydenham, Charlottenburg, or Saint Cloud, it
would have been a picturesque object ; in the midst
of the great African island its effect was almost
ridiculous.

While I was thinking of all this, its incongruity
with its surroundings was sharply brought to my
notice by a splash and a sudden bump, both due to
the remarkable thoroughfare by which alone the
metropolis can be reached. This consists of a track
slightly raised in the centre, some fifteen inches
wide, and occupying the whole ridge of one of the
little mud - banks already mentioned. With the
ground as wet as it was, I am not at all sure if
I could have walked along it alone ; but the extraordinary feats that my bearers had performed in
this way, made me take it as a matter of course that
they would run along it, leaning outwards like a
V. Perhaps the excitement of nearing the capital
was too much for them, but whatever the cause, the
two " wheelers " suddenly slipped, and, gliding into
the neighbouring rice-fields, left me sitting—feet in
air—on the ground. It was a good job it was not
the "leaders" who had slipped, or I should probably
have had an opportunity of seeing whether I admired
the capital more in an inverted position.

The part of the ridge for which we made is ascended by a narrow path cut out of the solid rock,
and polished by centuries of barefooted traffic. No
attempt has been made, by zigzags or other devices,
to lessen the incline, and it would have been a
steepish climb even had the road afforded good foot-
hold : as it was, I should think it absolutely impassable to any one wearing boots. Our porters, how-

ever, seemed to think nothing of it, but running at
top speed, shouting all the time to clear the way, they
soon reached Ambòhimitslmbina, the highest quarter
of the town ; then turning to the right, entered the
main street, which runs along the summit of the
ridge, occasionally turning towards the western and
steeper side, where it overhangs the precipice, supported on a rough stone embankment. After passing
through the town we left this, and entering a narrow
street, suddenly stopped before the big iron gateway
which marks the entrance to the French Residency.
Passing through this, we found ourselves on a well-
kept lawn, bounded on the right by a substantial
two-storeyed red-brick house, and commanding on
the left a fine view of the western slope of the
town. Viewed from the east, the ridge seems
nearly straight, but it is in fact kidney-shaped,
and it is on the lower or north-western projection
that the Residency is built, thus affording a view
of the whole of its one face, and the upper or
southern projection of Tàmponbòhitra, on which
are the two royal palaces. From the rugged nature
of the ground, this face of the ridge is much more
imposing in appearance than that first seen on approaching the capital from the east. Part of it is
a sheer precipice, in places overhanging the plain,
and in all parts broken by great granite masses,
giving fine effects of light and shade. Like the
eastern slope, however, its rugged beauty has been

QUEEN'S SUMMER PALACE. (*From Drawing by a Native Artist.*)

as far as possible marred by the efforts of man.
The same pretty little suburban villas, with the
surrounding walled enclosures, are crammed into
every possible site, and in some places — with
great ingenuity and at an immense expenditure
of labour in excavation, and building terraces for
their support—are balanced on the most impracticable and rocky escarpments.

Immediately below the Residency garden to the
west is a large sheet of water—I believe artificial—
with an island in the centre; in the distance a long
range of purple, cloud - capped hills; and in the
middle distance, partly hemmed in by a low range
of hills, the Kabàry plain, used as a parade-ground
and place of assemblage on *fête* days, and the
meeting-place of the Queen and her people on all
occasions when she wishes to communicate with
them *en masse*. Here the Sovereigns are crowned,
and standing in the centre of the natural amphi-
theatre, on a flat-topped rock known as the Sacred
Stone, receive the first greetings of their assembled
subjects. Here also, after her annual visit to the
summer palace of Ambòhimànga, the Queen halts
with her escort of two thousand troops, and is
received by the Court officials and inhabitants of
the city.

One afternoon I was asked by Doctor Baissade
to go down there and see a native *fête* which was
then taking place; but feeling rather lazy, I de-

clined. On his return he said that it was as well
that I had done so, as the exhibition of *mœurs
Malgaches* which he had witnessed had been wholly
unfit for my close inspection.

On the southern edge of the Kabàry ground, and
forming a link between its western bank and the
ridge of Antànanarìvo, is a curious mound, tumulus-
shaped, but some three hundred feet high, down
the sides of which run straight steep-sided trenches
about ten feet deep by ten feet wide, radiating from
the summit like the spokes of a wheel. No one
could tell me why or when they had been dug, nor
could my imagination make up for the lack of
information.

At the northern end of the lawn, and a little below it, were the barracks of the Resident-General's
escort, composed of two officers and fifty men of the
Infanterie de Marine, for whose presence, as a pre-
cautionary measure, he had obtained the sanction
of the Malagasy Government. On another day we
visited these barracks, which were particularly well
arranged and kept; and both officers and men
seemed thoroughly satisfied with their quarters,
and content to be counting foreign service in such
a pleasant and healthy locality. I do not know how
often they are changed, but I should imagine not
very frequently; for as each man has to be carried
up from the coast in a *filanzana* with twelve bearers,
the conveyance must be rather a costly matter.

Crossing the lawn, we were received by Monsieur de Vilers, who came out to meet us, and at once took us in to breakfast.

Luckily I had been partly broken in to civilisation by the experiences of the previous night, or the interior of the Residency would quite have persuaded me that I was dreaming. As a rule, even in the most luxurious colonial private houses and Government buildings there is a certain roughness and want of finish, which, however comfortable the rooms may be, afford unmistakable evidence that one is out of Europe. Here, the outer door once closed, I felt that I had stepped into France. Furniture, decoration, books, draperies, pictures, all spelt out " Paris " as plainly as if the maker's label had been attached to each; yet, oddly enough, Monsieur de Vilers told me that all the wood-carving and decoration had been carried out by Hova workmen. The rooms themselves were large and well proportioned, and though evidently designed and decorated with a view to impress the native mind with the resources of French civilisation, were both cool and comfortable. Nevertheless we were not sorry to hear that we were to be lodged in a humbler abode, the little cottage just over the way, occupied by Monsieur d'Anthouard, where Monsieur de Vilers thought we should be more independent and undisturbed. Accordingly after breakfast we strolled across, and were received by a tidy cheer-

ful-looking woman with rather a dark skin, jet-
black hair tightly plaited round her head, wearing
a cotton skirt, and a *lamba* over her shoulders.

Our Malagasy landlady.

Both she and her husband, the proprietor of the
house, were high-born Hovas; but we found him
in their little back-kitchen working at his trade,

that of a tailor, which he plied when not engaged
in his duties as an officer of several "honours" in
the Regiment of the Royal Guard. It is only by
the number of these honours that the different
grades of officers and non-commissioned officers are
distinguished. I forget the exact equivalent to our
ranks; but assuming that a corporal is an officer of
one honour, a sergeant of two, a lieutenant would
be four, a lieutenant-colonel seven, and so on.

We were shown into two very clean and cheerful-
looking rooms on the first floor, opening on to a balcony to the east; and here, after all the jolting of
the past week, we were very glad to rest till late
in the afternoon. When returning to the Residency,
we found the whole lawn occupied by a motley
crowd of natives of all sorts, conditions, sexes, and
ages — all dressed in white *lambas* and broad-
brimmed straw hats, and all squatting on the
ground. Wondering what on earth they could
have come for, we picked our way through them
to the entrance-door, at which Monsieur de Vilers
was standing. He told us with a grim smile that
they had come to welcome him and offer him gifts,
—in other words, to play again the good old game
of trying to get a penny bun for a halfpenny.
The gifts consisted of fowls, eggs, bits of cloth,
straw hats, and baskets, &c., for none of which
Monsieur de Vilers had the slightest need, and
which, from the overwhelming quantities in which

L

they were poured in, were a positive nuisance, but
for which he had, nevertheless, to give in exchange
portions of that very useful commodity, the five-
franc piece. One or two, in addition to the so-
called presents, had goods which they offered for
sale. One was unsuccessful in persuading us to
buy a cage full of lemurs—uninteresting little animals, whose sole claim to notice lies in their being
the only indigenous quadruped of Madagascar. With
another, who had a really beautiful collection of
silk *lambas*, we did some business, and, at prices
ranging from £1, 10s. to £2, bought some very
handsome strips of pure, thick, white-flowered silk,
about three yards wide by four or five yards long;
also others of equally good design in which the silk
was mixed with palm-fibre. The Hovas appear to
be excellent workmen, but have unfortunately no
inventive faculty, and I was told that these designs
were imported from Europe; and indeed I never
saw anything in the country which had any beauty
beyond that of the excellence of its workmanship.
We had a great rummage one day through the
market and all the shops we could find, but the
only things that at all took our fancy were the
straw hats, and some snuff-boxes made of polished
bamboo plugged at the ends by bits of pumpkin-
rind.

Probably the Malagasy mind does not naturally
tend towards decorative art; but I cannot believe

that such good workmen would not turn out more
objects of art than they do, did they receive any
encouragement. The *corvée* system, however, enforced on all grades of society, has exactly the
opposite effect, and makes all classes afraid of
letting their proficiency become known, for fear
of being impressed for compulsory unpaid labour.
Theoretically, everybody in the island is the private
property of the Sovereign, and consequently their
labour and produce are hers also. This in itself
would probably work no great harm, were it not
for the power to transfer her rights—the exercise
of which power leads each grade to demand, in
the Queen's name, free labour from that below it,
with the result that the chief desire of each section
of the community is to induce its superiors to believe
that it is absolutely useless and incapable.

In a way, the absence of tempting things to buy
was rather a comfort, for we got hauled over the
coals for our little shopping expedition on foot,
which we were told was a most undignified proceeding for a European or well-born native—our
guardsman-tailor-landlord would never have dreamt
of such a thing; and shopping from a *filanzana* is
such a complicated operation, that it takes away all
the charm. The process must be rather like shopping on elephant-back, if such a thing is done
anywhere, as in each case the same business has
to be gone through of lowering the carriage to

the ground, before its occupant can get out of it.
The Hova objection to walking was certainly ac-
counted for by the condition of the streets, which
were more like the beds of mountain torrents than
anything else, and in many places almost impassable,
except to the barefooted natives. Nor was passing
through them in a *filanzana* an unmixed pleasure at
this season, owing to the occupation of the town by
herds of loose bulls, which had been driven in from
all parts of the country as offerings to the Queen,
at the approaching festival of the *Fondroana*, but
which for two or three days prior to the feast were
apparently allowed to devote their whole energies to
the work of reducing the population.

I had an opportunity of studying this phase of
Malagasy life the first time we went out in our
filanzanas. We were passing down a steep and
very narrow street leading out of the market-place,
when we heard shouts behind us, of which my
porters evidently understood the meaning, for with
one bound they landed me over a low wall into a
small courtyard. As soon as I had recovered my
surprise I looked round, and saw that Monsieur
d'Anthouard had jumped off, and with his bearers
had squeezed into a doorway; while Harry's men,
whom he had somehow got into the habit of only
doing what they were told, were standing, with him
on their shoulders, in the street, down which rushed
a shouting crowd chased by two enormous hump-

backed bulls, charging in all directions, and driven perfectly wild by another crowd behind them, shouting even louder than the first, and pelting the beasts with any missiles that came to hand.

The next day, the town being still given over to the bulls, Monsieur d'Anthouard took us to see the country-place of the Jesuit mission; so getting out of the town by the nearest way, we crossed the rice-fields and the ridge beyond them to the east, and after about three-quarters of an hour's journey found ourselves outside a fine country-house, approached by an avenue of mango-trees, and situated in a good large garden bordered by the Ikopo river. We were received by two of the Jesuit Fathers, who showed us over the grounds and buildings. Everything was thoroughly simple and well kept; but the points which most interested me were the workshops and mausoleum—the former as showing the practical nature of the training given to the converts, and the latter the Fathers' complete disregard of death. In each of the workshops was one of them, bare-armed and coatless, surrounded by a group of natives, who were helping or watching him make a chair, a sauce-pan, or a pickaxe, according to his trade. Others were working in the garden or fields; and at the time of our visit, at all events, doctrinal teaching seemed to be the last thing in the minds of all. The mausoleum was a handsome building entered by an open-work iron gateway,

made on the premises, round the interior of which
were arranged rows of pigeon-holes, some closed and
inscribed with a name and two dates—some of
which showed that ripe old age was attained here
—others still open, and uninscribed. On none of
these were any written expression of regret, or hints
as to the character or history of the person whose
body lay behind the plain iron door. Pointing to
an uninscribed niche in the right-hand corner, our
guide laughingly told us that it was the recess
reserved for himself. Custom, of course, made us
assume a more subdued manner while in this house
of the dead; but our guide, on the contrary, continued to talk in his liveliest tone, evidently fully
imbued with the conviction—singularly rare among
Christians—that death is only important as being a
change for the better.

On our way home we were twice reminded of the
approaching *Fondroana:* first, by passing a number
of men carrying great fagots of dried wood—these,
I was told, were slaves who, having no property of
their own, were allowed to collect wood and present
it to the Queen in token of subjection; secondly, by
the much more objectionable offerings of the free
men. We had arrived within fifty yards of the
Residency gate without meeting any of these, my
bêtes noires, as I may literally call them, and I was
duly congratulating myself on the fact, when, turning a corner, I found that the road was blocked by

a crowd, and, looking over their heads, saw a great
bull standing in the gateway, foaming at the mouth,
and bellowing with all his might. We had to halt
for some little time while he made up his mind as
to his next move; which done, he suddenly charged
into the crowd, scattering them in all directions.
Luckily he went off the opposite way to that in
which we were coming, so we were able to slip
into the Residency without further adventures.

I was told this was the last occasion on which I
should be likely to encounter these beasts singly in
the streets; but that on the next day I should see,
from a safe place, a remarkable sight, the whole
collection of them streaming through the town in
a body. On the following mid-day we accordingly
went to the house of a Frenchman who had started
a silk manufactory, and whose balcony overlooked
the Andòhalo square, a large open space in the
centre of the town, the middle of which was now
densely crowded with men and boys, while round
its edges were erected a number of booths, beyond which again every safe nook and corner was
crammed with women and children. All this excitement was due to the fact that the bulls were
about to be let loose from the palace-yard. After
being fattened for some weeks in small backyards,
where they have hardly room to move, they are
driven—as I had already experienced—with great
difficulty into the courtyard of the Palace, where

they are penned, until on the day of the *Fondroana*
the Queen receives them as an offering from her
subjects. This ceremony over, the beasts are let
loose, and become the property of whoever can
catch them.

Soon after twelve the excitement began. First
one bull came dashing down the narrow street into
the square, followed by his rightful owner, and a
crowd of men and boys all equally anxious to secure
the prize ; then at short intervals came another and
another, then half-a-dozen abreast, driving everything before them. Soon the square was full of
beasts charging in all directions, foaming, roaring,
and panting, amid shouts and showers of sticks and
stones from men and boys, until some of the poor
beasts dropped down dead from sheer exhaustion.
It was a cruel and disgusting sight, a sort of very
feeble imitation of a Spanish bull-fight without any
of its pomp.

Harry went down into the square and photographed a bull just as it was charging at him :
unfortunately this negative, together with nearly
all those we took in Madagascar, got ruined by the
damp. However, if he did not get his negative,
he had a little excitement, which always does him
good ; while I only had a very unpleasant five
minutes, expecting every moment to see him gored.
As it happened, after he had jumped out of the
bull's way, the beast rushed at a boy just behind

ANDÒHALO SQUARE, ANTÀNANARÌVO.

him, and sending his horn right into his eye,
dragged it out. The boy, like a madman, got up
and went straight at the next beast. Luckily he
was only knocked over, and was dragged from the
scene by his friends.

I soon got very tired of this feeble and disgusting sight; but as it was not thought safe to go
through the town until all the animals had been
driven out of the place, I had to wait. One slight
variation to the scene was afforded during the afternoon. Suddenly the bulls were left to themselves,
and the whole crowd rushed to one of the booths,
from which a man was dragged by every limb in
such a way that I was expecting at any moment
to see him torn in pieces: by the time he reached
the middle of the square every stitch of clothing
had been torn off his back, and in this state he was
conducted to the Palace. It turned out that he
had stolen some goods from one of the booths, and
was being taken to the Palace for judgment.

On our way home we were treated to a little
surprise, which to my uninstructed mind seemed
as if it should have been our last. Under some
fig-trees, in a part of the road which overhangs
the western cliff, are a row of rusty old cannon
lying on the ground with their muzzles over the
precipice, exposed to all weathers, and apparently
wholly uncared for. I had often passed them on
my way through the town, but had never suspected

that any sane human being would try to let them
off. What was my horror, then, to find myself
jammed in a crowd in the midst of them, while a
man ran from one to the other with a lighted piece
of tow. First one a dozen yards to my left went
off successfully; then the next gave a fizz, and
nothing else happened; then came the turn of the
one behind which I was standing, and I fervently
prayed that it also might miss fire, but no such
luck! Off it went with a bang, jumping back
almost on to the toes of my bearers, but to
my great surprise doing no damage; and so
on down the whole row—none of them bursting,
thanks to the special providence which watches
over idiots.

The live bulls had been bad enough, but I am not
sure that I should not have preferred meeting them
again, with all their superfluous energy, to seeing
and smelling them in the *post-mortem* condition in
which they came so painfully to the front during
the next few days. For the previous forty-eight
hours abstinence from meat had been enforced
throughout the town; but the ceremony of the
royal gift over, the inhabitants made up for their
fast by a wholesale slaughter, with the result that
the whole town reeked of blood, while at every
step one ran into men carrying great hunks of
raw meat, presents, "with the compliments of the
season," from her Majesty to her faithful subjects.

We were favoured with one of these joints, which was loyally devoured by our porters.

The next day was that of the much-talked-of Feast of the Bath, during which the Queen is supposed to bathe in the presence of her people. Having received an invitation to this, we mounted our *filanzanas* after an early dinner, and at about seven in the evening alighted at the big gate of the Tranovola, or Silver Palace, where a crowd was collected to see the arrival of the guests. Passing through the guard of honour, we crossed a wide court-yard, lit with many Chinese lanterns, and entered the antechamber, a room about thirty feet square, whose ceiling was supported by a single column in the centre. On a circular table round this column were laid out the presents which the Queen had received on this and former similar occasions. Not a very valuable collection, mostly of European or rather Palais Royal origin—a clock with a china figure swinging as a pendulum, ormolu inkstands, highly coloured *bonbonnières*, and paper-weights. Birds, beasts, and fishes were there in every material except flesh and blood, and applied to every use except those for which nature constructed their prototypes. The walls of the room were covered for about two-thirds of their height with a coloured paper representing scenes in the Crimean war; above this was a strip of hideous red-patterned paper, then a frieze of a very large conventional pattern in good colouring. Four curious pictures—the product evidently of native art—were hung, one in the centre of each wall, representing a very conventional town, with a king and queen on either side sitting under a more than conventional palm-tree, upon which was perched the royal falcon of Madagascar. In one of these pictures the palm grows out of the back of an eight-winged armadillo, or crocodile without a tail.

In this room all the guests were assembled, waiting to be admitted into the Royal presence. The English contingent was represented by the Vice-Consul—Mr Pickersgill—Bishop Cornish, a good number of missionaries, and the Englishmen in the Queen's employ, as well as their wives. Another group was formed by the French in a different part of the room. The native guests completed the assemblage, most of them dressed in uniform. I heard one of them asking the Resident-General who we were. They could not make out why, being English, we should be the guests of the French—it being pretty well known that there was but little love lost between the French and English communities in the capital.

After waiting some time, an officer in uniform came and announced that the Queen was ready to receive us; so again crossing the courtyard, we soon entered the big archway of Manjàkamiadàna, or the Gold Palace, through which we passed to the door of the throne-room, where Ravoninahitraniorivo, Prime Minister, Prince Consort, and Commander-in-Chief, was standing. He is a short, well-built man, rather dark for a Hova, with a large moustache, dark piercing eyes, and low forehead. He was dressed in a patrol jacket and trousers made of fawn-coloured silk, with a silver embroidered sword-belt, all of native manufacture. Round his neck was the "Legion of Honour," and on his breast were several foreign decorations. He is said to be sixty-two, but looks about thirty-five—and no wonder; for when afterwards we were presented to him, I saw that his hair and moustache were dyed, and that altogether his face was very cleverly made up. After bowing to him, we all passed on to the centre of the room, which was divided off by red stanchions and ropes à la Buckingham Palace on Drawing-room days, and were led to the part reserved for foreign visitors, facing the throne. Harry and I were between Monsieur de Vilers and the English Vice-Consul, who seemed to be the honoured guests. The room was eighty feet square, and, like the first, had a big pillar in the centre, with more rubbishy presents arranged round it. In the corner of the room behind us was the Queen's red velvet *chaise-à-porteurs*, a great heavy unwieldy-looking thing that must be very inconvenient for the men to carry across country. Just on our right was a group of native Methodists squatting on mats. Between them and the throne

were the Queen's female relations and ladies of the
Court—most of them young, and some almost pretty

Malagasy Princesses.

—also sitting on the floor. The part of the room

between the throne and the door was railed off for
the native officials, leaving a passage between them
and us, which was lined with the gentlemen-at-arms.
The latter wore an extraordinary jumble of different
uniforms, red English infantry tunics with yellow
facings, French sailors' peaked caps with gold bands
—some with anchors, some with crowns, and one with
an eagle. Shoes were as varied, but the favourite
kind seemed to be the canvas tennis-shoe with black
india-rubber soles and toecaps. Swords and sword-
belts were also of every variety of pattern.

The throne, with its three steps covered with crimson velvet, on which the Queen was seated in an
elaborately gilt arm-chair, had over it, flat against
the wall, an arch of trumpery leaves and white paper
roses resting upon pillars of *repoussé* silver. The
Queen was attired in a crimson velvet dress, the
train being the only part we saw, as she was entirely
wrapped up in a red *lamba*. On her head was a
gold-embroidered coronet. She has regular features
and very good teeth, and would probably look pretty
were she not so sallow. Her shiny black hair was
plaited and done up in a knob. She sat there looking round her in a bored and listless way; the face
showing no strength of character, and seeming more
than twenty-five, which I am told is her age. Having seen the guests in, the Prime Minister took up a
position on the steps of the throne, but did not stay
there long, as half the time he was fidgeting about,

seeing that everything had been properly prepared in that part of the room railed off for the native guests.

As soon as we had all settled into our places the ceremony began, and a more extraordinary jumble I have never witnessed. First came a string of men-slaves carrying the different things needed for making a fire and for cooking purposes. Each in turn walked up to within a certain distance of the throne, bowed low, at the same time raising above his head whatever he was carrying. He then backed into the roped-off enclosure and deposited his burden. In the middle of this enclosure two square slabs had been laid, with bricks in the centre of each; on these fires were lit, reminding one of a gipsy camp. A big, fat, good-natured-looking native, dressed something like a French cook, who superintended the culinary proceedings, turned out to be one of the Queen's Ministers, who had for some years lived in Paris. Two enormous pots that had been used during several reigns on these solemn occasions were then placed on the tripods over the fires. Water was brought, which the ex-Minister poured into the pots, then filled one up with rice, spooning it with a big wooden ladle out of a bag held by a slave. In the other he put some meat which had been kept from the year before as an emblem of plenty, and which, as may be imagined, was fairly high. While all this was being cooked, slaves brought banana-leaves, which were given to some of the women, who cut them up, making fans to blow the fires, and square bits, with two of the corners pinned together, to use as spoons.

The time for the bath had come. A large sheet was stretched and held by three women at the corner of the room nearest the throne. The Prime Minister got up, and bowing low to his Queen, gave her his hand, helped her down the steps, and led her behind the sheet, where she remained some time, evidently longer than her husband approved of, for he was continually peeping behind the sheet during the bath. Meanwhile a strange mixture of noises was going on. Inside the room the native Methodists were offering up prayers and singing doleful hymns, while the band outside struck up wild-sounding Malagasy tunes. At intervals somebody, who took great pains to copy the intonation of an English drill-sergeant, put somebody else through the manual and firing exercise. This was without doubt one of the relics of the Willoughby reign.

At last Her Majesty emerged from behind the sheet. I at once recognised the same crimson train, so I fancy the only change she had made was taking off her *lamba*, showing an entirely European dress with its bodice cut square in front. The beautiful diamond necklace presented to her by the French Republic, and the massive gold crown she now wore,

M

made her look very magnificent. I remarked afterwards to Monsieur de Vilers that it seemed a pity she used European materials, especially as on this particular occasion she expects the Court to dress in stuffs made on the island. He told me she got all her smart clothes from Paris, and from the curious cut of the dress I imagine they are made according to what the Parisians think will suit native taste. In her right hand she held a gourd mounted in silver, full of the water she was supposed to have bathed in. Giving her other hand to the Prime Minister, she walked to the door and back again, sprinkling the contents of her cup over everybody as a sort of blessing. She then ascended the throne, and we all sat down on our heels—a position we did not in the least appreciate, as our legs soon began to ache—while more prayers were said, which she followed in her red prayer-book.

Now began the ceremony called the "Hàsina," of presenting silver coins in token of allegiance. The governors and chiefs of the kingdom walked up the gangway three at a time, bowing low, with hands outstretched as if to catch blessings and distribute them to the rest, and at the same time to defend themselves from the too great glory of the Sovereign. They halted some distance from the throne, where the Queen's sister was squatting on the ground for the purpose of receiving the coins, which they put in her hand after making short addresses to the Queen,

to which she answered in a few words. Last of all
came the Sakalavas, who, being black, cannot approach the Queen; so they made their addresses from
just within the doorway, the sister having to go
down to them to receive their offerings. After this
she walked up to the throne, and shovelled the whole
sum on to the Queen's lap in a most undignified
manner. The Prime Minister had all this time
been sitting on the lower step of the throne. He
now got up, and in his turn made a speech to the
Queen, enlivened by many gesticulations, and ended
by thanking her for all her favours, and swearing
loyalty in his own name and that of the army.
The band struck up, the officers drew and waved
their swords, while the shouts outside reminded me
of the familiar exclamation a crowd always utters
directly a beautiful rocket has exploded.

After a long grace, said by one of the native parsons, began the distribution of the meat and rice,
which was handed round to every one on plates with
the banana-leaf scoops which the women had been
making. The smell of the meat was so awful that
most of us would only taste the rice. I was much
struck with the truly British pluck of the English
Vice-Consul, who ate the whole with seeming relish.
When this frugal meal was at an end, the Queen
rose and made a short speech, at the conclusion of
which more shouts were heard, drowned by a salvo of
cannon. So ended this strange jumble of pantomime,

church, picnic, Drawing-room at Buckingham Palace, pomp, and utter want of dignity, with a considerable mixture of good honest savagedom.

We then all backed out of the room, leaving the Queen sitting on the throne. The Prime Minister came and shook hands with Monsieur de Vilers, who formally introduced us to him. The present Sovereign, Razàfinvrahìty, who was proclaimed Queen in 1883 under the title of Ranavalona III., is, I am told, his third Queen, it being the law of the country that the Prime Minister must be the husband of the Queen. They have many other curious customs, and their morals, as far as I have heard and read, closely resemble those of the South Sea Islanders.

We were informed on good authority that the reason the Methodists formerly became a great power in the country was that the Prime Minister, wishing to get rid of his too powerful brother, turned Christian, and married his Queen under Christian rites, so as to have the excuse of exiling his brother as a heathen. Later on, finding that the Methodists were getting too strong for him, he established the Church of England as a counterpoise.

Our departure from the Palace reminded me most forcibly of similar scenes in London. Having walked to the gate, we had to wait until some of the party had, after a great deal of shouting, collected the porters, who drew up with their *filanzanas* in a string, which the crowd outside was continually breaking through. Finally, we got back to the Residency about eleven o'clock, and were delighted to find supper waiting for us.

IV.

Friday morning we spent at the Residency with our host, making out all the plans for our journey to Mojànga, on the west coast of Madagascar. Having settled to start the following Monday, Monsieur d'Anthouard undertook to collect the porters. Monsieur de Vilers, with his usual kindness, had asked Monsieur Martini—a young officer on his staff, who spoke Malagasy fluently—if he would like to escort us, and to see more of the island, an offer he gladly accepted. We were also to have two other travelling companions, Monsieur Cazeneuve, a director of the Messageries line, and Monsieur Alibert, a merchant living at Tamatave.

The doctor did not approve of our leaving the capital so soon ; for we were not allowing time for the fever, which is usually contracted by travellers in the lagoons on the east coast, to declare itself. We had but little choice in the matter, however, as Monsieur Cazeneuve was anxious to get to Mojànga in time to meet the boat which was to take him to Diego Suarez.

In the evening Monsieur de Vilers invited Bishop

Cornish, his son and daughter-in-law, Miss Buckle, and Mr and Mrs Pickersgill, to meet us at dinner. The Bishop was very anxious we should see his church, so we promised to attend service on Sunday.

On Saturday morning Doctor Baissade photographed us in his garden. Harry was on his *filanzana* with his four bearers. I had chaffingly expressed a wish to be photographed with a Malagasy baby in my arms, and, to my amusement, I found waiting for me a young Malagasy mother, delighted to lend her baby for the occasion. After lunch we went to see Monsieur Rigot, who is in the Queen's employ as superintendent of the gold-mines. His house was not far from the lake, in a lovely old garden, full of fruit-trees, flowering shrubs, and many kinds of flowers. He took us to see his horse, a rarity here, as I believe there are only two in the capital, the roads being utterly impracticable for them. He also showed us a good collection of ores found in the island, which seems to be rich in all minerals except coal, which so far has not been found. We sat some time in his garden, while he described the tour of inspection he had just completed to the gold-mines, and which covered part of the route we should have to pursue from the capital to the coast. He warned us we might possibly fall in with marauding parties of Sakalavas, as on his journey he had seen two villages being attacked and pillaged by them. As he was alone, except for his porters, he was unable to render any assistance to the unfortunate inhabitants, whose shrieks he heard in the distance.

The Bétsiriry, commonly called Sakalavas by the Malagasy, are one of the western tribes of the island, a fierce and savage race, and the terror of their more peaceful neighbours. The Rev. E. O. MacMahon, who travelled through their country, thus describes the appearance of the first he met: " He had no clothing beyond a waistband round his loins, but he made up for this defect by paint and weird ornamentations, such as crocodiles' teeth, chains, and beads disposed around his head and neck; his hair was done up in large knobs."

After leaving Monsieur Rigot we went to visit Mahàzoarìvo, a country-house belonging to the Queen on the Ikopo river. The grounds were curiously laid out — a mixture of grandeur and dilapidation; but the place had to my mind one redeeming feature, the beautiful violet lotus-flowers with which part of the river was covered. That night we all adjourned to dine with the doctor in his little house in the middle of the town. We got home early, and sat on our balcony watching the bonfires lit in many parts of the capital, this being the last night of the Fondroana. The flames shot up spasmodically, giving a ghostly appearance to the groups of natives in their white *lambas*, and throwing strong weird shadows on the red brick houses.

On Sunday morning I went with Monsieur de
Vilers to the Roman Catholic church, which was
very crowded, and where we heard good music.
In the afternoon we kept our promise to Bishop

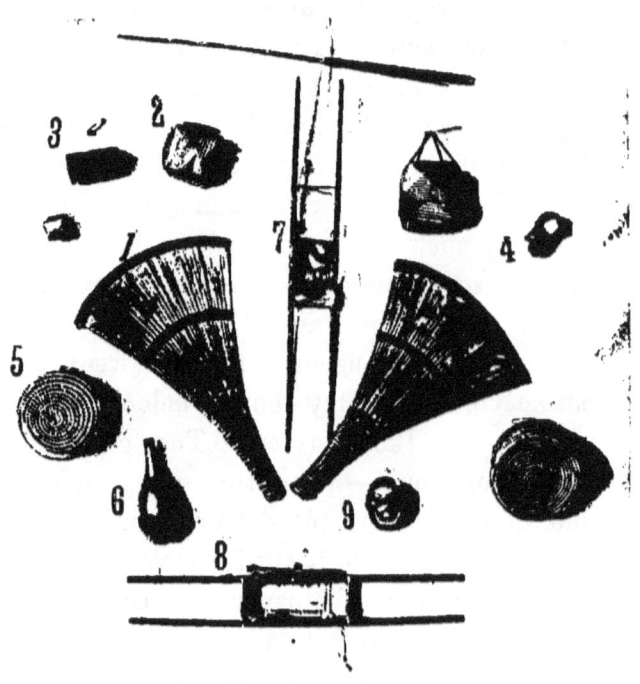

Articles of Malagasy Manufacture.

1. Fans.	4. Straw-boxes.	7. Model of man's *filanzana.*
2. Coloured straw-boxes.	5. Open work-box.	8. Model of woman's *filanzana.*
3. Bamboo snuff-box.	6. Gourd snuff-box.	9. Seed snuff-box.

Cornish, and went to tea with him after the service.
That evening Monsieur de Vilers gave a dinner-
party to the Roman Catholic Bishop, who came

accompanied by three other priests. Towards the
end of dinner, conversation somehow turned on my
having lived so much in the south of France, which
seemed to rouse their interest, and in the drawing-
room I found myself sitting on a sofa with the
Bishop beside me and two of his priests opposite.
Both of them having been born and bred in the
Pyrenees, great was their delight when I began
talking Béarnais to them, which they showed by
alternately rubbing their hands over and over, then
suddenly bringing down the outspread palms violently on their knees, and at short intervals taking
pinches of snuff, causing them to blow their noses
violently with their large red cotton handkerchiefs.

It was decided that Monsieur de Vilers and the
whole French community should escort us next
morning as far as Ambòhidratrìmo, where our kind
host proposed to give us a parting picnic breakfast.

Monday, November the 26th, we were up betimes, and after packing, went to the Residency,
where we all assembled, and started — a regular
caravan. I was quite sorry to leave Antànanarìvo,
with its curious and half-civilised people. Our road
went down into a lovely plain, with low rocky hills
springing up here and there; then led us along a
causeway fifteen feet broad, made for the purpose
of irrigation, and separating the plain from the
river Ikopo. This embankment a year ago got
into such disrepair, that the Queen used to superin-

tend the work herself, and obliged every citizen to
build one cubic metre with his own hands. We
came to two wide gaps which were bridged over
by several small trees laid side by side, making a
most dangerous place to cross; but our men went
over without flinching.

We all breakfasted at Ambòhidratrimo, under the
famous Amòntana tree, which is a landmark seen
from most parts of Imèrina. This place was originally one of the twelve sacred cities of this province.
There are a number of royal tombs still to be seen on
the top of a hillock, up which I tried to scramble,
but slipped in so doing, and fell on an aloe-leaf,
running one of its poisonous thorns into my knee,
which at once caused a good deal of pain and
swelling. After a cheery breakfast, during which
our healths had been freely drunk in champagne,
one of the party photographed us all; and then,
with many affectionate farewells, we parted; Mes-
sieurs Cazeneuve, Martini, and Alibert, and our two
selves, with our retainers, starting on our westward
journey, while the others retraced their steps to the
capital.

We soon got into an uninteresting country, and
after about four hours and a half, we arrived
at Babay. The accommodation here looked most
forbidding, the place being generally filthy, and
full of pigs—sleeping companions whose existence
we had almost forgotten during our sojourn in

Imèrina. After inspecting several huts, we chose
a two-storeyed house, the least evil-smelling of the
collection ; but the ground-floor even of this was so
appallingly dirty that we decided at all events to
avoid our four-footed companions by sleeping on the
first floor. So after the *simandous* had turned the
inhabitants out, Harry and I scrambled up a rickety

Our Party under the Amòntana-tree.

broken-down staircase, and found ourselves in rooms
a degree less dirty, though very untidy—the poor
owners in their hurry having left all their things
strewn about in such disorder that it was difficult
to find floor-room on which to pitch our beds.
In the meanwhile Monsieur Alibert, who prided
himself on his knowledge of cooking, was, with

much swearing and under great difficulties, helping
our native cook to get dinner ready. He was a
cheery little man, always making the best of everything. He was quite the type of Tartarin, and, like
that hero, was a native of Provence, and had the
broad pronunciation of that part of France. When
not looking after the cook, he devoted his energies
to keeping the servants and porters in order, and
they certainly kept his hands pretty full; but in spite
of all his efforts, I cannot say that the meal was a
great success. Our *chef* had been engaged at Antànanarìvo in consequence of his own statement
that he had been employed in that capacity on a
man-of-war; but we had forgotten to ask him for
how long, and judging from his performances while
in our service, I am inclined to doubt his engagement having lasted many hours.

The next morning we left at 5.30, keeping in
the same monotonous country — a rolling grass-
land, here and there intersected with water-courses—
which continued for about an hour. Then leaving
these rich grazing-grounds, and passing to the west
of a high rocky hill, we reached the watershed of
the Ikopo and the Andranobe, and descended into
a more populous valley, and bearing to the left,
forded the Andranobe river.

There was an extraordinary difference in the
amount of traffic on this road and that between
Tamatave and the capital. On the latter we hardly

met a single *filanzana* during the whole journey from the coast, and very rarely a human being
of any sort outside the hamlets at which we halted.
Over this road, on the contrary, there appeared to
be a continual stream of traffic, due to the attraction
of the gold-mines, to which the natives flock from
all parts of the island, and from which, dead or
alive, they make a point of returning to their own
homes. During this morning's march we met one
in the former condition, wrapped up in linen, and
strapped on to two poles of bamboo, from which
were also hung a miscellaneous collection of the
deceased's worldly goods ; among these were in-
cluded a number of guns, spears, and old cooking-
pots. Soon afterwards we were afforded a pleasant
contrast in the shape of a live and very lively Malagasy officer, in command of a company of soldiers,
making a triumphal return to civilisation, borne on
a *filanzana*, and accompanied by a bevy of his hand-
maidens, who, running by the side of his conveyance,
enlivened the dulness of the journey with cheerful
songs. Nor were we without a little music to
cheer us on our way. As they marched along, our
porters would sing their national songs in parts ;
while in the evenings we often had a regular con-
cert, the men sitting in a circle and singing to the
accompaniment of the *valia*, the only musical instrument I saw in Madagascar. It is made out of a
length of a large bamboo, part of the outer skin of

which is separated and cut into strings, tightened by a bridge of pumpkin-rind.

At 10.30 we arrived at Antoby, a deserted village of about fifteen houses, surrounded by a thick cactus-hedge, the only entrance through which was too narrow even for the passage of the *filanzana.* The houses had been left in such a filthy state that, fairly well accustomed to dirt though we were, they were rather more than we could stand; so we had our breakfast in an old Protestant church, which looked like a tumble-down barn.

After breakfast and a good rest we again started, and immediately afterwards recrossed the Andranobe river, and, ascending its left bank, gained a grassy plateau some seven or eight hundred feet above the river, and thickly dotted with herds of cattle. While on this upland a heavy shower came on, which caused our porters to put on their best pace, and sliding down the steep farther slope, we crossed the Andranobe for the third time, and found ourselves at the foot of a steep hill, on which is perched the intrenched village of Ankazobe, where we were to pass the night. Climbing the hill, we reached its outskirts, and found it to be surrounded by a fifteen-foot trench, into which, after travelling round three-fourths of it, we descended by a narrow rocky path, and climbing the other side, entered the village by a narrow opening in a mud wall, through which a miniature torrent was

rushing. After being greeted by the usual family
of pigs, we hurried on into the houses, which we
found ready prepared by the *simandou* who had
preceded us. In ours we found an unusually clean
family. Among them was a young mother nursing her baby : she could not have been more than
twelve or thirteen, by no means an unusual age
here for a married woman. We all assembled in
this house for dinner, to save my having to walk
out in the deep mud.

Next morning we were off at the usual time,
Harry and I ahead, the luggage-porters in the
middle, and the rest in the rear. This arrangement
was made as there was supposed to be some danger
of our being attacked by Sakalavas, and the baggage-
porters were utterly helpless and undefended. As we
never were attacked, I cannot say how formidable the
Sakalavas really were ; but they had certainly managed to inspire all the natives of our party with the
greatest respect ; and judging by the many villages
we passed utterly devastated by them, they seemed
to be at all events better fighting men than the
more civilised inhabitants of the country.

These precautions were, as it turned out, quite
unnecessary, for during the day's march we met
nothing more alarming than three corpses on their
way home, although at one moment our porters
had a good scare on seeing some men hiding
among the rocks ; but these proved to be soldiers

guarding the road, who had had an encounter with the Sakalavas the day before, killing three, whose grinning heads, stuck on poles, we passed a few miles farther on, while their already very unpleasant bodies lay across the road about a quarter of a mile beyond.

We halted for breakfast at Mahàridàza, a strongly fortified village surrounded by a high brick wall, outside which, at a distance of about ten feet, was a thick cactus-hedge. The entrance into it was unlike any I had ever seen before; the sides of the narrow tunnel-like opening in the hedge had been lined with rows of untrimmed trunks of trees, planted vertically about nine inches apart. Between these were dropped horizontally a number of logs, thus forming a series of barriers across the archway. These being removed, we found ourselves in a sort of square well, two sides of which were formed of trimmed cactus, the third by a most uncompromising brick wall, while on the fourth—in the same wall and at right angles to the tunnel—was a low doorway, closed by a solid mass of rock. While we were wondering whether we were to be hauled up by a rope or left where we were, the stone door gently slid aside, and passing through the archway we discovered that it was a huge disc, somewhat like a gigantic millstone, set on edge on a level platform, and which without a very great effort could be rolled backwards and forwards.

During the next day's journey the country seemed to be much more thinly populated, and we hardly saw a village, although herds of the hump-backed cattle were still to be seen grazing on the grassy slopes, with here and there armed herdsmen keeping watch. During the afternoon we got caught in a tremendous storm, and in spite of waterproofs were thoroughly soaked. I had been out of sorts all day, and this about finished me off, and by the time we arrived at Kinàjy I could hardly sit upright in my *filanzana*, and was counting every step the porters took that brought me nearer some place where I could lie down. Great was my despair therefore, to hear, on arriving outside the walls, that we must wait until we had received the Governor's permission to enter.

Kinàjy is the chief town of the province, and an important place, with a Governor and a garrison of six hundred men. After waiting outside for three-quarters of an hour, which with my throbbing head, and the deadly sickness which had come over me, seemed an age, three men suddenly rushed out, and imagining that they were the forerunners of the Governor, we all pulled ourselves together to receive him. However, taking no notice of us, they passed at full speed, and proceeded to a stream in the valley below, whence they returned shortly afterwards, still in hot haste, bearing a flowing white object, which, having nothing better to do, we watched with great interest, until, as it was borne past us, we recognised it as a frilled linen shirt, evidently the property of his Excellency, who was forced to postpone our welcome until he could appear in a suitable costume. So with as much show of patience as we could muster, we settled down to wait again, I for one heartily wishing that the great man would have come as he was, no matter what costume he might have been in.

After a time the welcome sound reached us of a thoroughly discordant band, and then, wading through the deep black mud of the narrow entrance, came the big drum, followed in single file by the trumpets and clarionets, the rear of the procession being brought up by the commander of the forces— a tall man in a green coat with a certain look of a uniform, a Tyrolese hat with a red ribbon round it, and a drawn sword in his hand—and about a dozen men, well armed, but with the most nondescript of uniforms, who, having been drawn up in a line, presented arms at the English word of command to that effect, and then turning round, preceded us into the town.

The entrance was somewhat similar to that in the outer fence of Mahàridàza, the only difference being that it was closed by a curtain of vertical logs slung on ropes, somewhat on the principle of the Indian reed - and - bead curtains. A very short journey through the little town brought us to the Governor's

house, a one-roomed hut in the middle of a palisaded
yard, in one corner of which was a small brass
cannon.   After passing through the gateway, the
band halted and struck up the "Marseillaise," followed in our honour by a strange mixture of "God
save the Queen" and the Malagasy National
Anthem ; which ceremony over, the Governor
stepped out of his doorway to welcome us.   He
was an intelligent-looking Hova, dressed in a blue
naval frock-coat, a white peaked forage-cap, and
pepper-and-salt trousers, and I have no doubt made
himself very agreeable ; but I was feeling so miserable that the only item of his conversation in which
I took any interest was that in which he told us
that on our approach he had ordered our huts to
be prepared, and that they were then ready.   On
hearing this welcome news we hurried off to ours,
and Harry at once took my temperature, and finding
it was 104°, packed me straight off to bed, and
would not hear of my going to the dinner to which
we had all been invited by the Governor.   Before
joining the party himself, he gave me a whole
bottle of Warburg's tincture, which had the desired
effect of bringing down my temperature, but did
not keep off the terrible delirium.   As far as I can
remember, the night was a succession of half-waking
nightmares and half-dozing consciousness of snarling
dogs and grunting pigs.

Next morning I was still very weak and ill, but

as Harry thought that at all hazards I ought to
be got down to the coast and on board a ship as
quickly as possible, we started early, my *filanzana*
having been converted into a kind of litter by means
of sacking stretched between the poles.   My only
recollection of the day's journey was our arrival at a
village, where they breakfasted, which had lately been
attacked by the Sakalavas, who had taken prisoners
all the inhabitants except four leper-girls, whom we
found remaining there.   After being taken out of
my *filanzana*, I was so exhausted that I lay on the
dirty floor of a hut unable to move, with the poor
lepers—disgusting sights—staring at me the whole
time.   It was not a very cheerful halting-place for
any of us; but our men were in a great state of
delight, having found a number of pits full of rice,
which the Sakalavas had left untouched.   With
this they filled the bags they always carried
round their waists, thus providing themselves with
free dinners for some days to come.   I see by
Harry's journal that we slept that evening at Am-
pòtaka, and that the country we passed through
during that afternoon was wholly uninhabited and
very monotonous.

Next morning I woke up feeling much better,
Harry having given me thirty grains of quinine the
night before, and when we started at 5.30, I was
able to sit up in my *filanzana* as usual. The ground
now began to fall rapidly to the westward, and soon

after eight we descended into the valley of the Màhamòkamìta, a river nearly a hundred yards broad, and after the recent heavy rains, rather unpleasantly rapid to ford, coming well up to the men's waists, and causing them to take off what little clothing they wore. After crossing it we turned sharp to the left down its right bank, and halted for breakfast at Màrohàrona, a small fortified village which had also been pillaged by the Sakalavas, the men being nearly all away at the gold-mines. One or two of them had since returned to find their homes deserted and their families scattered, all the women having been carried off as slaves. Thanks to all these empty villages, we were beginning to make a great hole in our store of tinned provisions, as the chickens and eggs, on which we had depended, had lately failed us, and there was no game to fall back on.

After a good rest we started again across a broad plain far more thickly populated than the districts we had been traversing, and after about an hour's march found ourselves under the northern face of the remarkable table mountain of Andrimbe, rising sheer out of the plain to a height of nearly a thousand feet, and on the edge of whose plateau was visible a large and evidently prosperous village. I was told that there was a good water-supply, and abundant pasturage at the top, and that it was inhabited by a community of robbers, who made frequent raids into the plains. It certainly seemed an ideal position for persons of their profession. This was the only instance of this sort of mountain, so common in Africa, which we came across in Madagascar.

It had been raining all the morning, and after a short lull at mid-day came down again with double force.

I noticed that our porters were going at an unusual pace, and thinking that they were probably anxious to get as quickly as possible out of the Andrimbe neighbourhood, I asked if this was the case, but was told that these mountaineers were only cattle-robbers, who would not care to attack us, and that a far more serious matter was the rapidly rising Kàmolàndy river, which lay between us and our destination, from which there was a fair prospect of our being cut off. Nor did we arrive at it a minute too soon. I happened to be leading, and for one moment my men hesitated as they saw the broad seething mass of muddy water in front of them, then boldly dashing into it, were soon well above their waists. It was with the greatest difficulty that they kept their feet, leaning hard against the stream, and moving only one at a time, and then with the most cautious steps. As I watched the torrent piling itself against the up-stream side of their naked bodies, and, glancing over the side of my *filanzana*, saw the streaks of foam rushing seawards

beneath me, I could not help wondering whether I
should not soon be accompanying them, and how
far I should get on the journey. However, we
all got safely across, and wading over a succession
of submerged fields, with here and there a hidden
ditch or water-course, into which the men slid up
to their shoulders, we climbed a small hill, and
found ourselves outside the high cactus-hedge of
Malàtsy, a large well-built village, where we passed
the night. On unpacking our baggage we found
that its passage of the Kàmolàndy had not been
quite so successful as our own ; everything we possessed was absolutely soaking. So after collecting
some wood, we lit a fire in a corner of our hut to
dry our beds, but soon wished we had made up
our minds to sleep on the floor, for there being
no proper outlet for the smoke we were nearly
suffocated, and had to run outside into the rain,
where we were promptly surrounded by a deputa-
tion of women with presents of eggs, rice, &c. We
foolishly gave them some cut money to get rid of
them, and retired into our smoke, where, in consequence of our generosity, we were shortly afterwards
invaded by the whole population, headed by the
chief of the village, bearing mangos, chickens, capsicums, manioc, and every other product of the place,
which they thought or hoped we could be induced
to buy.

Monsieur Cazeneuve having chosen a nice little

whitewashed hut for himself, we settled to dine in
it.   While in the middle of dinner, I pointed out to
him an army of big cockroaches issuing from several
holes, and soon overruning the walls. The poor man
was horrified; the one thing he could not stand was
a cockroach. He had already spent several sleepless
nights on their account, and had pitched on this
clean room in hopes of peace.   Next morning he
told us he had passed the whole of his time sitting
on a chair with a lighted candle beside him, for fear
the monsters should crawl over him.   I certainly
had never seen such a swarm all at once.   Perhaps
it was that the dirt and unevenness of the huts had
previously prevented me from doing so.   We, on
our part, spent an unusually good night, having at
last been struck with the brilliant idea of hiring a
couple of men to sit outside our hut and prevent the
pigs and dogs coming in.

The next morning we started a little later than
usual, and after travelling for some time on very
narrow and rough paths, we gradually made a sharp
descent on to a swampy plain, where the temperature became suddenly quite tropical, and which was
peculiarly and unpleasantly rife with insect life.
Soon after reaching it we entered a dense cloud of
singularly malignant little black flies, who without a
moment's hesitation went for the exposed parts of
our bodies. As in the case of our porters this was
a considerable portion, they were soon streaming

with blood, and set to work to run for dear life. We whites only fared better so far as quantity of bites was concerned. I never came across such determined or bloodthirsty tormentors; even beating our faces hard with a bunch of leaves failed to keep them off. Luckily the plague was altogether local, and we were soon clear of the infested belt; only, however, to run in the course of half an hour into a flight of locusts, which did us no harm beyond flying in our faces.

Leaving this plain, we crossed a slight ridge of broken ground. Then a further descent brought us into a region in which the familiar vegetation of the east coast reappeared, the bottoms of the valleys being thickly covered with *rafia* palms, bamboos, wild citrons, and acacias, beneath which grew species of coarse grasses and cotton-plants. We reached the pass of Màrokolòsy at 9.20, and halted for three hours in the little village of the same name, surrounded by a stockade and a double cactus-hedge. Crossing another ridge, we found ourselves after two hours' march at Ampàsorià, a gold-washing station on the Ampàsorià river. It consists of two distinct settlements, a large stockaded native village being about a hundred and fifty yards distant from the European compound, which is also enclosed in a high palisade, and in which we were put up. Our small hut was divided into two rooms, raised a couple of feet off the ground, and boasting the luxury of boarded doors and glass windows; but in point of cleanliness it was little, if anything, in advance of the native hut to which we had been accustomed, while the cockroaches were, if possible, even larger and more numerous than usual.

This village was the headquarters of a Frenchman employed by the Malagasy Government as mining superintendent of the district, who, after we had settled down, showed us over the place; and judging from what we saw, I should say the monopoly was a very profitable one. At sunset the villagers streamed into the superintendent's office bearing the proceeds of their day's work; on an average about a table-spoonful of dust apiece, which each individual emptied out of a little bag into one pan of a pair of scales, while into the other the superintendent dropped sufficient pieces of silver to balance it. With these the digger went on his way rejoicing, having received about one-twentieth of the value of his earnings. All minerals in Madagascar belong to the Crown, so that no prospecting can be done by outsiders.

The next day, Sunday, we made rather an earlier start than usual, and after traversing a varied and well-wooded country for about three hours, arrived at Antànimbàrindratsontsàraka, on the right bank of the Ikopo, here a much more imposing river than when we had last seen it near Antànanarìvo. It had there, however, the advantage of being navigable,

while it is here broken by a succession of rocky
rapids. On its banks we again found the " Traveller's
Tree," and for the first time I saw a chameleon.
After following the banks of the Ikopo for a few
miles, the road turns rather sharply to the right,
and passes through a quartz district, which, though
undoubtedly very valuable financially, was exceed-
ingly ugly, and a source of much annoyance to our
barefooted porters. As soon as we got into rather
softer ground, my men and those of Monsieur
Martini began to race for a small torrent ahead of
us, which they said was free of crocodiles, and had
good drinking-water. Being still very shaky after
my fever, I did not at all enjoy this rapid pace,
for, in addition to the actual pain caused by the
jolting, it prevented me putting up my parasol.
However, its unpleasantness made me enjoy the
more a delicious rest on a soft bed of white sand
under the shelter of an overhanging rock, near the
edge of the torrent, in which our men plunged
and splashed like babies during the whole period
of our halt, whilst troops of parroquets chattered
overhead.

The spot where we halted was on the margin
of a broad rock-lined pool between two miniature
cataracts, and was a particularly tempting one to
our dust - grimed carriers ; consequently all the
natives of the party, as they came up in turn,
followed the example of my and Monsieur Martini's

men, and plunging into the pool, made our halt rather a long one.

After leaving this place, we had a long dusty march over a tract of low barren hills, until, just as the sun was setting, we sighted the peculiar table-shaped plateau of red clay on which the town of Mavetanana is situated. After arriving at the foot of the eastward slope, our porters had a steep climb up the side of the clay escarpment, cracked by the sun into deep crevices cutting the path at every fifty yards or so, and giving us a series of exciting little jumps. On reaching the top we crossed by a drawbridge the deep V-shaped ditch which encircles the town, a fair-sized one, and containing a Government House and a good assortment of shops. After passing through it, we again crossed the ditch, and following the crest of a narrow neck of land, found ourselves on an adjoining hill, on which the gold-mining settlement is situated. Our party was put up in the house of the Inspector, who was then in France, so Harry and I were given his large dining-room, where we set up our beds and encamped for the night. There were several of the Inspector's French assistants who very hospitably entertained us at dinner, and also invited the Hova Governor, a bright intelligent young man, together with his Malagasy doctor and two Malagasy interpreters, to meet us. We sat down thirteen; but no one seemed to notice the unlucky number until next

morning at breakfast, when there was a good deal
of chaff as to who would be the victim, little thinking that poor Monsieur Cazeneuve would so soon die
of the effects of the journey, which sad event happened the day after he reached Diego Suarez. The
dinner was excellent, and was served in a little
kiosk, pleasantly cool, but whose light seemed to
attract every insect in the neighbourhood through
the open sides. The mosquitoes were a veritable
plague; while food, table-cloth, ornaments, and
everything were black with the most extraordinary
collection of flies, moths, daddy-longlegs, praying-
mantis, and all kinds of insects.

As I was very tired, I went off to bed directly
after dessert, but most of the men sat up into the
small hours, and had such bad heads next morning
that they preferred to keep quiet. Harry and I,
however, went with the Governor and two of the
Frenchmen to a small river where a crowd of women
were panning out gold. Standing in the water, they
scoop out the mud from the river-bed with shallow
flat-bottomed dishes, which they shake with a peculiar motion under water, until the lighter particles
are washed away and only the gold and the heavy
black sand remains. This is then dried in the sun,
and the sand got rid of by the simple process of
blowing with the mouth until nothing but the gold-
dust remains. Now and then they have the luck
to find big nuggets, but the gold is mostly in the

form of very fine dust. If, as I believe to be the case, enough gold is found here by this primitive process to make the mines pay well, there must be a wonderfully rich region near the river-head from which the gold is washed down, and which only requires modern machinery to develop it.

Walking slowly back, the Governor asked us if we had been attacked by any of the Sakalavas on our way from the capital. Hearing we had not seen any, he said we were very lucky, and put it down to the rains having so swelled the Ikopo that it was impassable.

On our return we came upon the final scene of our land journey,—Monsieur Martini, money-bags in hand, in the midst of a clamouring crowd of porters whom he was paying off; while behind him, with an air of calm superiority, were the cook and the two *simandous*, who were to accompany us to the coast.

Between Mavetanana and the coast is a dense belt of forest similar to that on the east, but traversed, we were told, by an even worse road than that from Tamatave to the capital, all the latter part of it being across deep swamps. Mavetanana had, however, this advantage over Antànanarivo, that it is connected with the sea by a navigable river, and down this it was settled that we should make the rest of our journey.

We had hoped to start before mid-day, but all

sorts of difficulties arose in the collection of boats and boatmen, and it was past four before we got a message from the Governor to say that all was ready for a start. Thinking that I must be tired of *filanzana*-travelling, he kindly offered to mount me on an old hornless ox; but I preferred my usual steeds, and the ox was mounted by a funny little shrivelled-up old man, one of the Governor's staff, who, vainly endeavouring to make his lumbering beast keep pace with my porters, tried to perform the duties of an equerry.

On arriving at the river-side we found that the only canoes that the Governor had been able to procure for us were two huge dug-outs, some thirty-five to forty feet in length, each requiring a large crew, and that to man the pair of them he had only managed to get seven boatmen. Monsieur Martini, Harry and I, with three men, the cook, and one *simandou*, embarked in the smaller one, and the rest of the party and the remaining four boatmen in the larger. Our journey for that day began and ended in a small shallow back-water, on the many sandbanks of which our canoe was continually running aground, much to the disgust of our crew, who were obliged every time to jump overboard and push her off, keeping the while as sharp a look-out as they could for crocodiles, with which the river abounded. At last, just before sunset, we found ourselves hopelessly aground opposite a little village, still within sight of Mavetanana. It was by the inhabitants of this village that, a short time afterwards, a French doctor was murdered in his canoe; but at this time they had no evil reputation that we knew of. The other canoe being out of sight behind us, and thinking it useless to blunder on in the dark, we settled to land for the night, and try to pick up some more boatmen. But as far as comfort or success in recruiting was concerned, we might as well have stayed on board; for after a perilous journey to the shore, perched on one of my boatmen's shoulders—the only way in which he could be induced to carry me—I found myself in an extraordinarily dirty little village, from which almost all the population had departed to the gold-mines, and now inhabited only by one man and two old women, who utterly refused to give us the smallest assistance. After wandering about for some time in the dark, peering into huts, one more evil-smelling than another, we finally settled down in one, and after a very scratch meal tried to go to sleep. As far as I was concerned the attempt was an utter failure: what with the hot muggy air, crowds of hungry mosquitoes, and a pestiferous smell from the river, which seemed to get worse every hour, I never got a wink, and gladly welcomed the first glimmer of daylight, which gave me an excuse for waking up Harry, Monsieur Martini, and the boatmen.

In spite of our early rising, it was a long time

before we got off. The other canoe had not yet
turned up, and it was as much as our three men
could do to unload ours, shove her off, and then
reload her. At last, however, we started, and soon
got into the main river, here eight hundred to a
thousand yards wide, and running through magnificent forest scenery. The country on our right
was like a thickly wooded English park, with gigantic trees of many different kinds, under the shade of
which we landed at about ten o'clock for breakfast.

But beautiful as the vegetation was, this river-
journey soon became very monotonous, continuing
as it did between unending walls of trees. In the
afternoon the sun got so powerful that we landed
for a few minutes and cut some sticks, with the help
of which we rigged up a make-shift awning with our
waterproof sheets. The only excitement of the
journey was afforded by the crocodiles, extraordinary numbers of which were apparently asleep on the
banks; but, judging from the pace at which they
flopped into the water as we approached, they were
singularly wide-awake. Even the low monotonous
chant of our boatmen was enough to disturb them;
and as we were all anxious to get a shot, we did our
best to stop this, but wholly without success. One
monster, who must have over-eaten himself, did let
us get within a fair distance of him, and received
a volley fired by all three of us, who were all confident that we had mortally wounded him. How-

o

ever that may have been, he slid into the water, much in the same manner as his uninjured brethren, and we never saw him again.

With the exception of these crocodiles, we saw hardly any signs of animal life, and scarcely any human habitations; in fact, the only village we passed was that of Ambinàny, on getting opposite which our natives took off their hats, and begged us to do the same, the place being a sacred one. Shortly afterwards we overtook the other canoe, which it turned out had stuck on a sand-bank soon after starting, and there kept Monsieur Cazeneuve and Monsieur Alibert dinnerless and bedless for the night.

Early in the afternoon we reached the confluence of the Ikopo with the larger Betsiboka river, after which the stream became very rapid, and although our boat made but little way through the water, we glided past the banks at a fair pace, and a little before sunset reached Karàmbìly, a village some twenty miles below the junction of the two rivers. Walking a quarter of a mile inland, we found ourselves in a large clean village, where we were well received by the dark-coloured inhabitants, of a totally different type from those among whom we had lately been. We were put up in large airy huts, beautifully clean, which had been carefully prepared for us. Ours looked on to an open space, a sort of village green, in the centre of which was a large tree literally covered with the beautifully made nests of the weaver-bird.

Next morning we were up betimes, hoping to reach Màravoày that afternoon, where we were to exchange our dug-outs for the dhow which would take us on to Mojànga. Loading the canoes, however, took an unconscionable time, and we waited for two full hours on the river-bank before all was ready for a start.

After leaving Karàmbily the river became far wider and the country more open, the dense forest giving place to park-like tracts, which with every succeeding mile became more tropical in character, fan-palms, tamarinds, mangos, and bananas being most conspicuous. Our journey, like that of yesterday, was again enlivened by the crocodiles, against whom we still waged a most unsuccessful war, until suddenly some way off, on shore, we saw a curious-looking, pale-coloured object sticking up out of some long grass, which our steerer's accustomed eye at once recognised as the head of a crocodile, sleeping in what seemed to be a curious position, his nose pointing straight up to the sky, showing his entire throat. It was a mean advantage to take, but Harry could not resist it, and bowled him over. This caused great excitement, and we all scrambled on shore, and helped the natives to clean him out, preparatory to skinning him at night. I had no wish to be beaten, so I went on firing perseveringly. Of course I killed a great many! but they unkindly took the burial service into their own hands, and never failed to go to the bottom. It was sad from my point of view, for now future generations will not be able to point to the stuffed trophy, and say with pride, "That is the crocodile our grandmother shot in Madagascar!"

It was nearly dark before we got into the estuary of the Betsiboka, and as the tide was flowing, the river-current got slower and slower, until it was finally absorbed altogether. Our men seemed to make no progress, and we were getting desperate, for it was long past the hour at which we should have got to Màravoày; so, seeing a canoe ahead in which several men were fishing, we made for her, and our *simandou* boarded her. A violent discussion ensued between him and the men, which resulted in his pushing two of them into our canoe. Here, again, the *corvée* was doing its work; but we determined they should be paid for their trouble. As a rule, no provision is made for their return : they take the traveller to his destination, and are there left stranded to make their way back as best they can.

We saw a good many herons and storks standing on one leg in the water, watching for their prey; and in the woods heard the wild guinea-fowls calling out, "Come back! come back!" It was now nearly seven o'clock, and still no signs of Màravoày; and

when we asked our *simandou*—who was supposed
to know the country—how far it was, he calmly
answered, "About as far before us as we were now
from the spot where the crocodile had been shot."

If we had not been so anxious to get to our destination, we might have landed and shot some of
the wild turkeys that were roosting on the trees not
far from the river-bank; but only one thought possessed us—to get on; for we had not landed to
cook any dinner, thinking we should arrive at our
destination in time to partake of that meal comfortably. The bottom of a dug-out does not get
softer the longer one sits on it, and having no room
to move about, we had got terribly cramped. As
darkness set in, we were enveloped in clouds of
mosquitoes, which seemed as hungry as their victims.
The natives hugged the right bank for fear of losing
the turning into the narrow river Màravoày, a tribu-
tary of the Betsiboka. So near the edge, the water
was in many parts shallow, and the paddles stirred
up bubbles of miasmic gases, which were most up-
setting. As we crept at funeral pace past that
unending mangrove-covered bank, the hours seemed
to be getting longer and longer; sleep was impossible, the maddening song of the mosquito for ever
in one's ear. It was like a bad dream, from which
one could not get away. I longed to get up and
walk about, or even shout at the top of my voice
—anything to break that awful monotony!

At last we turned a sharp corner, and found ourselves in the long-sought-for little river, up which,
had we arrived only an hour sooner, we should have
drifted rapidly on the flood; but now the tide had
begun to ebb just as we did not want it, and our
tired boatmen had a further struggle up stream,
which lasted till two on the following morning,

Landing at Màravòdy.

when the moon, suddenly creeping from behind a
cloud, disclosed the welcome hill of Màravòay. It
being now nearly low water, we were separated
from the shore by a stretch of deep mud, across
which the *simandou* carried me on his back. Tired
as I was of the canoe, at one moment I almost
wished myself back in it, as he sank deeper and

deeper, stumbling about till my feet ploughed up
the black slime, into which I fully expected to
subside altogether. However, with the help of two
of the men, we at last found ourselves on *terra
firma*. While they went back for Harry and
Monsieur Martini, the *simandou* and I walked on
to try and procure lodgings in the town, which was
about a mile distant. We accosted the first human
being we met; and after a great deal of talk, he
took us to a narrow door in a high palisade, round
an open space, planted with mango-trees, in the
centre of which was a large two-storeyed house.
Our guide showed us up a steep flight of wooden
steps, and we found ourselves in a sort of barn,
divided into little rooms by thin partitions, in
which were a number of sleeping men, over whom
we nearly stumbled in the dark. Our beds having
arrived, I took possession of one of the rooms, and
by the time Harry and Monsieur Martini—who had
been seeing to the safe landing of the goods—appeared, I had got the things fairly ready.

Up to the time they left the river-bank there had
been no signs of the other canoe; so, not knowing
what might be in store for us on the following day,
we turned in, determined to get what sleep we could.
This turned out the wisest thing we could have
done; for on the following morning it was still
missing, and had we sat up for it, we should
have had our vigil for nothing. We did not rise

very early, and I had hardly finished dressing when a message came from the Governor inviting us to lunch with him; but as I was feeling very ill from a second bout of fever, and Harry did not wish to leave me alone, Monsieur Martini went off by himself to see the Governor, to try and get us off accepting the invitation. While he was away, Harry and our cook persuaded a few natives to come and skin the crocodile, telling them they would be paid for their work; but either they did not believe it, or the smell of the reptile was too much for them, for they soon left their task half done, and it was only later on that two men were induced to finish it for five francs apiece.

At about half-past eleven Monsieur Martini returned, escorted by a company of soldiers and a band, and bearing a second message from the Governor begging us to accept his hospitality, and promising to provide us that afternoon with a dhow to take us to Mojànga; so there was nothing for it but to bestir ourselves, and get into the *filanzanas* that had been sent to fetch us. As we did so, the soldiers presented arms, the band struck up "God save the Queen" and the "Marseillaise," and then quite a grand procession was formed. In front were about thirty women singing and dancing; after them the band; then ourselves on our *filanzanas*; and on each side of us the soldiers in single file. Neither of us, with our travel-stained clothes and

mosquito-bitten faces, could have added much to the
gorgeousness of the show, and Harry said he felt
exactly like a Guy Fawkes being carried about on
the 5th of November. Monsieur Martini's appearance, however, was quite equal to the occasion, and
perched in the air, his gorgeous *Chasseurs d'Afrique*
uniform glittering in the sun, he was quite the gem
of the pageant.

In order to give the inhabitants every chance of
inspecting us, we were carried through the town at
a funeral pace; and it was a good half-hour before
we reached the foot of the clay-hill, with almost
precipitous sides, on which the Governor's quarters
were built. On reaching the top, we were first
ushered into what looked like a very small *châlet*,
the sitting-room of which was full of European
furniture and ornaments—no end of cheap flower-
glasses, vases, little sets of liqueur-glasses, a china
box to hold a sardine-tin, &c.—while the walls were
hung with chromo-lithographed portraits of the
crowned heads of Europe. After waiting some
time, the Governor — a "twelve-honour" Hova—
appeared, dressed in a black uniform, evidently of
his own invention, with a quantity of gold braid
sewn on anyhow. He had charming manners, and
showed the greatest interest in our journey, and
plied Monsieur Martini with many questions, particularly wishing to know how old we were, and
if I had any children. He could not understand

my coming such a long way, and leaving a baby
at home, he never having moved from this place
for the last twenty years. His wife was ill with
fever, which seemed to be very prevalent there, so
we did not see her. After a few minutes, he
escorted us across a little garden, passing under
a brick arch of a curious shape, on which were
painted life - sized figures of soldiers, dressed in
gorgeous uniforms, in the act of saluting. Over
their heads was written, *Màndrosòa*, translated to
us " Welcome." We found ourselves in a big square,
in the centre of which was a large building used as
barracks, whence there was a lovely view of the
plain two hundred feet below us. Through the centre
of this wound the Màravoày river until it joined
the Betsiboka, which in its turn could be seen
emptying itself into the bay of the same name. At
a doorway in the centre of the big building we were
received by three Hova officers, who led us to a
large room, where on a long table lunch was spread
out European fashion, only including several curiously prepared dishes.

While we were lunching, two groups of men and
women, with very good voices, sang alternately on
either side of the room, accompanying their songs
by graceful movements and gestures, so as to convey
the meaning of the words. When the leader of the
band thought one group had sung enough he rang
a little bell, upon which one set of performers rested

and the other began. The singing, besides being very pretty, saved the necessity of conversation, which was a blessing for Monsieur Martini, who had to play the part of interpreter. I was placed in the seat of honour opposite the Governor, between Harry and our French lieutenant, and delighted the natives by undertaking to carve the chickens which were in front of me. We only got away at three o'clock, when the same procession conducted us back; and on reaching our house, we found our two missing companions had turned up, and were anxiously awaiting us.

It seemed that their boatmen had completely broken down soon after sunset, and there being no place to land, they had passed a second night in their dug-out. Remembering the miseries that I had gone through during half the night in that mosquito - haunted, pestilential swamp, I was able to give them my fullest sympathy.

Monsieur Cazeneuve, feeling very ill, was all for hurrying our departure; so we again scrambled up the rickety stairs of our barn, and were busily engaged in packing when about twenty Indian merchants arrived on the scene, saying they had come to pay their respects to the Englishman, being themselves British subjects. Having no chairs, they all sat down on the floor, one acting as spokesman. He began something about the French, but Harry stopped him at once, saying he was simply a travel-

ler, and would not enter into political questions, and
that if they had any complaints on such subjects to
make, they must not come to him. They then had
a long consultation in their own language, at the
end of which the spokesman said that they had
nothing to complain of, and had only come to make
us welcome ; and bowing low, they retired, much to
our delight, as it was getting late.

We found great difficulty in getting men to carry
the luggage to the water's edge, and the Governor
turned out to be a broken reed. He had not even
taken the trouble to give any orders with reference to
our start, so Monsieur Martini had to go into the town
and find a *reis* who would undertake to convey us
to Mojànga in his dhow. As we were told that the
tide would be high at five o'clock, we started at
about half-past four, carrying most of the luggage
ourselves, and on arriving at the river-bank, found
a wretched little dhow high and dry on the mud.
The *reis* assured us the tide was rising rapidly, and
that she would soon be afloat; but, as Harry pre-
dicted, two hours elapsed before that happened.
However, thinking the *reis* ought to know best, we
went on board, and stayed there till, after about
half an hour, the mosquitoes rendered life so unbear-
able that we determined at any risk to try and
escape them. So wading across the mud again, we
settled ourselves down at some distance from the
bank, and lighting a big bonfire, huddled together

on the smoky side of it. In spite of the heat and
smoke, we were all so relieved at being temporarily
freed from the enemy, that we made a very cheery
little party : Monsieur Alibert and Monsieur Martini
even broke into song. Before we had been there
long, the voice of nature reminded us it was about
dinner - time ; and as our brief experience of the
dhow had shown us there was not the smallest
chance of getting a comfortable meal on board her,
we settled to make the most of our time on land.
So we all began bustling about to collect the necessaries ; among which, however, the most important
—the food—was chiefly conspicuous by its scarcity.
The inhabitants had refused to sell us either eggs or
chickens, and the only edible forthcoming was a
curiously shaped lump of beef, which the cook produced from goodness knows where.

Our "Tartarin," however, improvised a magnificent
dining-table out of two old tar-barrels and a bit of
corrugated iron roofing which he discovered somewhere in the neighbourhood. We had just finished
our meal when a fresh breeze sprang up, clearing
away the mosquitoes ; and as immediately afterwards
flashes of lightning in the horizon heralded the
approach of the usual evening thunderstorm, we
packed up our traps as quickly as we could and
made our way to the river, to find the dhow afloat
in mid-stream, where it turned out she had been for
some time, our stupid *reis* never having told us.

We had to get on board as best we could, one by
one, in a miniature dug-out half full of water.
Poor "Tartarin," who had stayed behind to see to the
safe packing of the pots and pans, was the last to
embark, and his lantern having gone out, he managed to step out of the canoe into the water and
was with great difficulty fished out by the crew.

However, he was but little worse off than the rest
of us ; for we had hardly settled ourselves down on
the sort of thatched awning of bamboos and palm-
leaves, the only available space on the dhow, when
the storm burst upon us, blowing apart our hastily
donned waterproofs, and wetting us through in a
minute. The wind blew the wretched, top-heavy
little cockle-shell over on to her side, until the
awning almost touched the water, and we had to
hold on like grim death to the nearly perpendicular
wall on which we were lying, expecting every
minute either that she would capsize altogether, or
that, the rotten thatch giving way, we should be
dropped off one by one among the crocodiles. The
next moment the wind whizzed her round, and
catching her other side, sent our feet into the air
and our heads resting on the ridge-pole towards the
water : all this in inky darkness, except when a
flash of lightning lit up the scene for a moment,
and showed us our craft being blown like a cork
along the water, and revealed the strange assortment of blacks and whites packed close together,

lying face downwards, with hands and feet dug
deeply into the thatch. Even in the midst of the
extreme discomfort of the situation I could not help
smiling, as each succeeding flash showed me the row
of more and more arched backs silhouetted against
the sky.

At last a lull came; the storm ceased even more
quickly than it had begun, and all seemed curiously
calm and silent. Nevertheless we were in for an
uncomfortable night; we were drenched to our
skins; the hold of the dhow was full of a confused
mass of baggage, among which no room could be
found either to sit or lie; while the thatch having
been torn by the storm from our only resting-place,
the awning, we were forced to pass the night as
best we could on a sort of gridiron. The lazy
natives let the dhow drift with the tide, taking no
trouble to steer her, so that we soon found ourselves
stuck fast in a mangrove-swamp, from which she
was only poled off with a good deal of difficulty.
After this we managed to drop into an uncomfortable sleep, from which I was awakened with a start
by an agonised voice proceeding from the depths
of the ship, repeating, " *Où sont mes pantalons ?* "
This turned out to come from poor "Tartarin," who
after his dip in the river had retired below among
the baggage, and in the hopes of getting them dried
had taken off his nether garments; but they had
unfortunately been blown overboard by the storm,

and he was forced to remain in hiding until daylight
enabled him to find his portmanteau and get hold of
another pair.

As soon as I was thoroughly awake, I discovered
that we were again at a stand-still, and the dhow at
such an angle that my feet were higher than my
head, while by the light of the moon I saw that
Harry, who was on the other side of the ridge, had
his feet in the water. Being afraid he would wake
with a sudden movement and slip in altogether, I
hardened my heart and woke him, explaining the
situation; but rubbing his eyes for a moment, he
said, "What does it matter? we are moored," and
went to sleep again. And so I found we were, the
natives having taken advantage of our slumbers to
stop and rest. This was the more annoying as we
had thus missed the whole advantage of the ebb-
tide, which had now run out; and there being no
wind, we had to wait the full six hours' flood
before we could make any progress, although by
Monsieur Martini's persuasions one or two feeble
attempts were made at rowing.

One by one we all woke up, feeling very chilly,
and with our teeth chattering; so we settled to
have some rum all round, which put a little warmth
into us, and kept us going until the dawn began to
break. Some of us had certainly got bad chills, and
suffered a good deal from acute pain.

I had been noticing for some time that one of the

crew, a shrivelled-up old man, had been busily engaged rigging up a little enclosure with a sail, and
was still wondering what it could be for, when he
came up to me and explained by signs that it was
arranged for me to take my wet clothes off. "*À
la guerre comme à la guerre*," I gratefully took
advantage of his kind thought.

At last the sun really rose, and never was it more
welcome than it was to our little party. We had
been told that we should reach Mojànga that morning; but, as a matter of fact, it was past noon before
we reached the mouth of the river and sighted the
town on the far side of Betsiboka Bay, a fine natural
harbour, and quite the best on the west coast of
Madagascar. When we got into the bay we had
the wind nearly dead against us. However, by
dint of shifting the ungainly sail, we seemed to
make some little way. Still our destination looked
like a speck on the horizon; but we persevered,
until, after a few hours, to add to our difficulties,
we again got into a flood-tide, which ran so strongly
against us that tacking was no longer of any use.
So the *reis* and his men calmly sat down, saying
they could do no more, and that we must wait
for the ebb; which meant that we should not
get in till the middle of the night. I shall never
forget my sensations of silent despair on hearing
this. I had not yet really recovered from my
fever, and the smell of the preserved, or rather *un-*

P

preserved meat, which the natives chewed on every possible occasion, had made me feel terribly sick even on the river; while the combination of a light top-heavy boat with the chopping sea of the shallow bay completely finished me. Then followed six hours of suffering never to be forgotten! I felt I must go off my head, and uttering involuntary moans, I clutched at anybody that happened to be near. Harry tells me one of our *simandous* seemed very much astonished when I flung my arms round him! I implored them to wave signals of distress to a ship we saw steaming in towards the port; but of course that was of no use, for we were a mere speck on the waters. At last Monsieur Martini, getting quite alarmed at the state I was in, got the men to paddle, which did little good till the tide turned, and finally landed us at Mojànga at 10 P.M.

Our landing was done under great difficulties. It was pitch-dark; we had no lights; and being unable to attract the notice of any one on shore, our men had to jump into the water and carry us. Monsieur Cazeneuve accosted some French sailors who were passing, and having ascertained that the ship then at anchor in the harbour was the one sent to take him to Diego Suarez, proposed that we should go with him to see the French Consul—with whom the sailors had told him their Captain was dining—and see what could be done for us. We gladly followed

THE AUTHOR ON ARRIVAL AT MOJANGA.

him, and after roaming about the streets for some
time trying to find the Consulate, Monsieur Martini
stopped at an Indian merchant's shop to ask the
way. They were extremely rude, and in an off-
hand manner said, "There is no French Consul
here," at which Monsieur Martini began abusing
them, only making them laugh. I then stepped
forward and asked them the same question in English, and got the idiotic answer, or rather question,
"Do you speak English?" to which I paid no attention, again asking them if they would kindly show
us the way to the French Consulate, feeling in my
heart that I could murder them! One of them then
got up and sent a black boy to be our guide.

Arrived at the house, we were ushered up-stairs,
where four Frenchmen were sitting smoking and
enjoying *un grogue*. Their expressions when they
saw us were amusing. And no wonder! for we were
in a most dilapidated condition. I felt positively
ashamed of myself, with my hair hanging down,
partly hidden by a dirty battered old helmet, my
clothes looking as if I had slept in them for a
fortnight, a Malagasy spear in my right hand, and
appearing, as well as feeling, more dead than alive.
The French Consul was most kind, making us sit
down and have some supper. We were also introduced to the *Commandant* of the ship, with whom
Monsieur Cazeneuve discussed our plans, telling
him of our anxiety to get back to Africa as soon as

possible, so as to catch the next English coasting-
boat, which we knew was to touch at Mozambique
in a few days. The French Consul having told him
we might be here for weeks without finding any
opportunity of getting away, he decided it would
not cause him any great delay to take us across.
Our difficulties were at once swept away, and our
gratitude knew no bounds.

The Consul's *filanzanas* had been brought round,
and we were just starting for the ship when I
suddenly discovered that the crocodile was being
forgotten; so going into the room where the luggage had been collected, we were nearly bowled
over by the smell proceeding from the precious
trophy. The poor *Commandant* smiled a sickly
smile when he was asked to take it on board; but
he very good-naturedly agreed to do so, taking the
precaution, however, as soon as he got it, of having
it carefully nailed down in a packing-case full of
salt. After bidding an affectionate farewell to
Monsieur Martini, who was returning to the capital
by another route, we made our way to the ship's
boats, and were soon comfortably settled on board.

BOOK V.

THE LAND OF SLEEP.

WE sailed from Mojànga at five the next morning
—Saturday, December 8th—and arrived at Mozambique the evening of the following day. To our joy,
as we steamed into the harbour we found the English coasting-steamer "Courland" (of the "Castle"
line) at anchor, and were at once taken on board
her by the *Commandant* to see if we could procure
a cabin. The Captain being ill, the purser did the
honours; and having told us they had plenty of
room, and were only to sail the following afternoon,
our kind *Commandant* invited us to remain on his
ship that night.

Next morning, having taken leave of our French
friends, we went on shore to get our tickets from
the agent. Mozambique looks a clean but sleepy
little town, with its white houses built close together,
forming narrow shady streets. We landed at the
well-built pier, which took us on to a wide boulevard, planted at regular intervals with the beauti-

ful flat-topped, scarlet-flowered *flamboyant* acacia. Near this was the agent's house, where it took us a good quarter of an hour to rouse anybody. Having done so, and obtained what we wanted, we walked through the streets, full of little shops, which I inspected with care, in the hopes of buying some curiosities. I found nothing but the bare and uninteresting necessaries of life, all in the hands of the Indian merchants, who looked only a degree less sleepy than their landlords the Portuguese. Having no object in visiting the numerous churches, and the heat having become intense, we went straight to our new ship.

I was prepared to find the crocodile again a source of difficulty, for his covering of salt having partially melted, his odour had become decidedly obnoxious. I warned Harry I was ready to have a good fight, if necessary, to get the box on board; and seeing the Captain at the top of the companion-ladder, I walked straight up to him — a native carrying the crocodile behind me — and chaffingly said that the contents of this box were so precious that if he wished to have us on board he must take it also, assuring him that if only he would provide me with more salt he would never be aware of its existence. He laughed and was really most kind, ordering one of his men to open the box and refill it with salt. I honestly confess I was glad the job did not fall to my lot!

Having settled all our things in the cabin, we had a good look round at our fellow-passengers, most of them Portuguese except two Arabs, one of whom turned out to be the Vizir of the Sultan of Johanna —one of the Comoro Islands—who seemed to have some grievance against the French, but what it was I never could exactly make out. He told Harry that they had taken his country, in which his wife and children still were, and that if he went back to get them out, he was sure the French would cut off his head. To me, however, he told quite a different story, that his wife and children were at Cape Town looking after a shop, which was doing very well, and that he intended soon to go to France to interview the French President and get redress. Whatever the merits of his case may have been, he was a fine old man, and seemed to have seen a good deal of the world.

After two days in smooth water, we arrived off the bar at the mouth of the Kwa Kwa river—twelve miles up which lies the town of Quilimane—a formidable-looking mass of surf as I viewed it from the bridge, but which did not give us any trouble; and after running the gauntlet of the breakers for a few minutes, we found ourselves in smooth water, and were boarded by the pilot, who had taken good care not to offer his services until all chances of his having to risk his life had passed. A couple of hours' run up a broad river, lined with swampy

mangrove-covered banks, brought us abreast of the
town of Quilimane, off which we anchored.   During
our passage up we passed several hippopotami; but
in spite of, or perhaps in consequence of, their
assuming the familiar Zoological Garden pose with

The Quilimane Pilot.

only two nostrils and the bump of veneration in
view, I should certainly have failed to recognise
them had not the Captain pointed them out to me.

Soon after casting anchor, the Vice - Consul came

on board, and saying we should be devoured by mosquitoes if we stayed on the ship, very kindly invited us to stay with him during the forty - eight hours she remained there. So putting a few things into a small bag, we accompanied him ashore, where we were promptly pounced upon by the Portuguese custom - house officials, who insisted on searching into every corner of our diminutive piece of baggage. Passing through the broad boulevards—planted with palms and *flamboyants*—of the scrupulously clean but deserted-looking little town, we arrived at the pretty palm-fringed garden in the middle of which is built the British Consulate. Here our host and his young wife made us thoroughly comfortable, and there being but little to see in the immediate neighbourhood of Quilimane, we enjoyed a thorough rest, and at the same time learnt much that was then new and interesting of the geography and politics of that part of Africa, though recent changes, both in the maps and the political situation, have now made all that we then heard completely out of date. There was one bit of information, however, which I obtained from a prospectus of the African Lakes Company, shown me by our host, which completely astonished me, and may still have the same effect on many of my readers—viz., that it was possible to take, at the offices of the Company in England, a through ticket for one's self and baggage from London to Lake Tanganyika.

We left Quilimane early on Friday, our Captain being anxious to get to Chiloane the following morning, as the bar at the latter place would be impassable late in the day; but, as it turned out, we might have passed several more hours comfortably in bed at the British Consulate without causing any delay; for after a sultry afternoon, during which the glass fell steadily, a storm burst on us at about sunset with so many ominous signs that our Captain, fearing a cyclone, stood out to sea, where we passed the whole of the next very miserable day. Early on Sunday morning, the weather having begun to improve, we stood in, and soon after noon crossed the bar without any further difficulties than the usual ones caused by shifting sands, and the absence of the buoys, perpetually promised but never provided by the Portuguese authorities.

The town of Chiloane is situated on the inland end of the island of the same name; but on account of the shallowness of the channel, big ships have to anchor just inside the bar. Opposite our anchorage on the island was a small Government building, in which goods from the interior are collected for shipment, and as we had been expected the day before, our cargo was ready to be put on board at once; and after only a few hours' delay we steamed out to sea again—rather a disappointment to me, as I had been hoping for a chance of running up the river and seeing the town, and also had been looking forward to a quiet night.

The following evening we anchored off Inhambane, whose houses, dazzlingly white in the moonlight, looked very picturesque between a dark background of feathery palms and the belt of silvery ripples which separated them from us. The next morning we amused ourselves watching some splendid turtle swimming about all round the ship; for the heat was so stifling that we had to wait till late in the afternoon before we went ashore, when, accompanied by the Captain, we took a stroll in the town.

The houses, painted in various colours, give the town a bright appearance, but it has nevertheless a very deserted look : grass grows up between every chink in the paving-stones in the streets of the European part of the town; while the roads in the native quarter — never properly made — are now wholly neglected, and over ankle - deep in fine white dust. The outskirts, however, are decidedly pretty, consisting of groups of beehive - shaped Kaffir kraals, shaded by palms and acacias, and each enclosed in high palisades of bamboo inter-laced with palm-branches. We walked into one of these enclosures, where a group of women were collected, who laughed and talked most amiably with our Captain. I wanted very much to see the interior of a little hut, and was just peeping in when one of the women rushed up, putting herself between me and the entrance. On being asked why she would not let me have a look round, she explained that if she let strangers go in the whole of her family would be sure to fall ill, apparently looking on us as possessors of the evil eye. Beyond the suburbs the road ran between high hedges of creeping asparagus—well known in English greenhouses —and farther on were palm-groves and a number of small trees, in size and growth somewhat like the English crab-apple, bearing a fruit resembling a small shrivelled-up apple, of a brilliant red-and-yellow hue, with at the end a hard excrescence, which I can only compare, from its shape, to a big haricot bean, and which, I was told, was a species of nut very good to eat when it was fried.

After two days at sea, during which I had a return of my Madagascar fever, we steamed on the morning of the 20th of December into Delagoa Bay—a magnificent harbour, and indeed the only good natural one on this coast, and which only requires the addition of a few buoys and beacons to make the entrance a perfectly simple matter. At nine we anchored off Lorenzo Marquez, at the mouth of the English river, and on its left bank. The town is by far the most prosperous-looking of the Portuguese East African possessions, and certainly its appearance does not justify its evil sanitary reputation. The houses are mostly large and well built, and arranged round airy squares or broad

INHAMBANE.

boulevards, well planted with eucalyptus. On the east and north-east it is open to the full force of the sea-breeze; while above it, to the west, rises a high escarpment, apparently a perfect site for residential dwellings. The terminus of the then unfinished Transvaal Railway, situated on the river-bank, and surrounded with lighters full of stores, gave to the place an air of life and work which is wholly wanting in the other seaports of this colony.

Soon after anchoring we landed, and after walking through the big square, named after the inevitable Vasco da Gama—whose name meets one at every turn on this coast—and marching up and down two or three dusty glaring streets, we reached the British Consul's house. Once there, we found ourselves so comfortable, and Captain Drummond—the Consul—so hospitable, that we managed to while away the greater part of the day in the broad verandah.

Towards the cool of the evening, Captain Drummond having mounted us, we rode off to call on Mr Knee, manager of the Delagoa Bay – Transvaal Railway. We soon reached the swamp which separates the town from the high land, and which is the chief cause of the former's unhealthiness. Nearly all the Portuguese towns are built either on islands, or on land protected by swamps from landward attack. All danger of this has now passed; and the swamp is now Lorenzo Marquez's worst enemy.

The authorities are filling it up as fast as they can; but the work will take considerable time before it is completed. Crossing the swamp by a broad causeway, a good road—the first I had seen since leaving Aden—led up the head of the bluff, and took us on to an extensive plateau commanding a magnificent view of the town, harbour, and country to the east and south-east. On the edge of this, surrounded by a pretty park, was Mr Knee's house, where we were most kindly received, and where we also met Colonel M'Murdo, who held the Government contract. Hearing that we intended to visit the Transvaal, Mr Knee kindly offered to send us up by rail to Komati Poort, and thence in his own mule-cart to Barberton, where we could catch the Johannesburg coach. The trip would have been a most interesting one, and we were greatly tempted to accept his offer; but as all our baggage and some important letters were awaiting us at Durban, we were reluctantly forced to decline it.

Mr Knee had the most interesting collection of Kaffir curiosities, which delighted me; and also some lovely seeds quite new to me. They are about the size of an ordinary acorn, but three-sided, one of these sides being much flatter than the other two; and at the end where the acorn's cup would come is a beautiful scarlet top, which does not shed the seed as the cup does the acorn, and always retains its colour.

On the following morning we started at daylight, and after a thirty hours' steam sighted the Natal coast, whose slopes, divided into fields and covered with cultivation, formed a remarkable contrast to the untended growths of nature to which we had so long been accustomed.

BOOK VI.

THE LAND OF GOLD.

Soon after noon on December the 22d we cast
anchor in Durban Roads, and the tide being too
low to allow of the "Courland" crossing the bar,
we decided to go ashore in the tug which was
soon seen approaching us, alternately balanced at
the top of an enormous breaker, and then apparently
disappearing under the water. The prospect was certainly not an inviting one, but anything was better
than the roll of the ship as she lay at anchor; so,
stepping into a sort of bird-cage hung from a derrick,
I soon found myself swinging in the air over the
tug, which at one moment was yards below me, at
the next almost touching my cage. A favourable
opportunity being chosen when she remained for a
moment stationary on the top of a wave, the cage
was suddenly lowered, seized by the crew of the
tug, and unhooked. Then followed an incessant
rearing, kicking, and bucking of the tug, until we
found ourselves gliding through the smooth water

of Durban harbour, and a few minutes later were made fast to the wharf at the Point.

We had hoped to get to Durban early, draw some money from the bank, and go on to Maritzburg by the afternoon train; but it took so long to collect our luggage, which had been sent on from Tamatave, that it was late in the afternoon before we got into the town, and being Saturday, the banks were closed: so we had to stay on till Monday.

As the crocodile was a positive nuisance, and we thought that we should have no further use for our two camp-beds, we handed all three to the innkeeper, asking him to have the former properly dressed, and to send the latter to England. It happened that we met him again in Cape Town, where he had come on a trip, when he told us that he had mistaken the two parcels, and sent the beds to the bird-stuffer, from whom he had had a message saying that he could stuff most things, but that camp-beds were quite out of his line. I do not know whether he attempted to do so and failed; but whatever the cause, the camp-beds have not yet turned up, although the crocodile arrived safely in due course, and is now reposing in an outhouse at home, still smelling as energetically as ever!

We were met at Maritzburg by Harry's friend Mr Matterson, to whom we had telegraphed news of

Q

our arrival, and who invited us to stay with him and his wife. Gladly accepting his invitation, we spent a happy fortnight in their pretty little house outside the town.

During our stay we "did" the neighbourhood thoroughly in our host's "spider"; and one day having been lent the Commissariat waggonette by Colonel Curtis — commanding the troops — Harry and I drove over to Falkland to visit some old friends of his whom he had not seen since he had been on the Staff in Natal. The road ran for many miles across the veldt, with here and there only a track to guide us over the succession of steep grass-covered hills, whose monotony was only broken by an occasional Kaffir kraal. It was the wildest spot imaginable — the little house covered with vines, surrounded by a garden where flowers and shrubs grew luxuriantly at their own sweet will. The hostess being a great invalid, our host did the honours, and walked us off to see his ostrich-farm, which was extremely interesting; but I cannot say I found these tall ungainly birds attractive. He said it did not then pay, as there was no market for the feathers. He then proposed to lend us two ponies if we cared to ride some distance off to see the banks of the Umgeni river, an offer I gladly accepted. While the black servant was putting the saddles on, our host and his daughter brought out two large bags of feathers, and chose a handful of

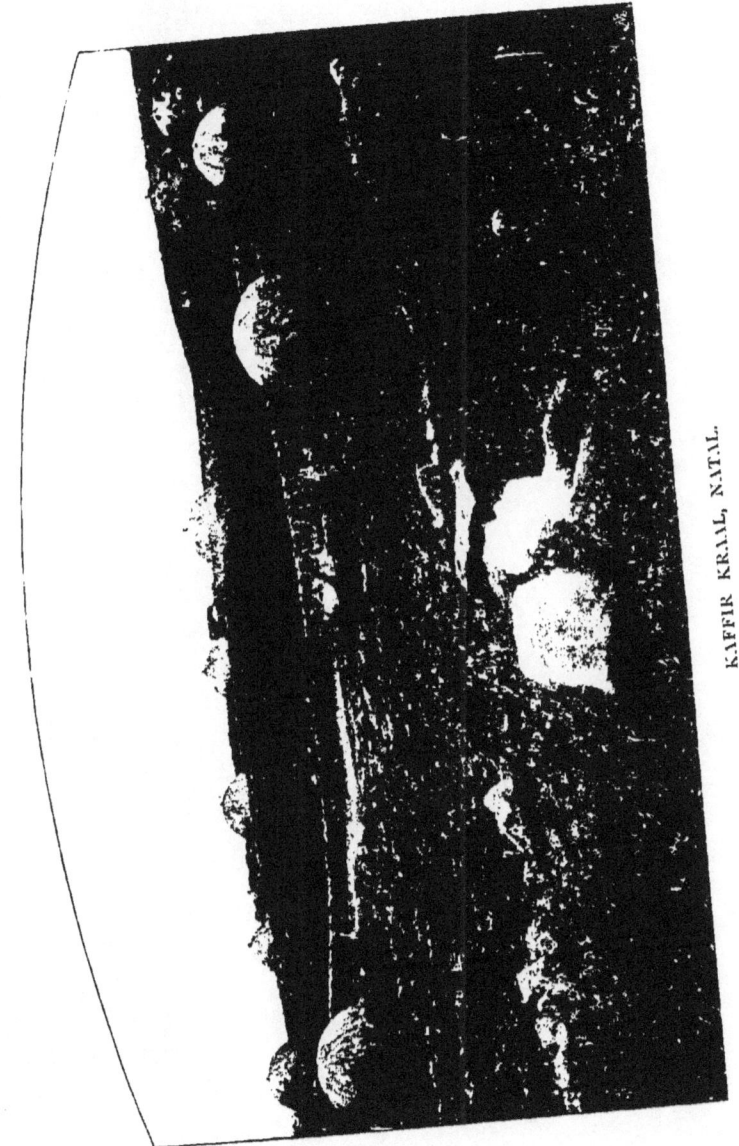

KAFFIR KRAAL, NATAL.

lovely black ones with white tips for me to have made up when I got home.

The ponies ready, off we started. As it was getting late, and a storm was brewing, we galloped all the way, and finally reached the edge of a precipice overlooking the lovely gorge through which the Umgeni here cuts its way. Opposite us, at the distance of about three-quarters of a mile, an overhanging red cliff, about on a level with that on which we were standing, separated the rolling expanse of veldt from a steep bush-covered slope, radiant with every possible shade of green, and at that distance looking like a soft bed of variegated moss. Below this again was a strip of gigantic boulders, among which the Umgeni—five hundred feet beneath us—foamed and tumbled, or collected into glassy pools, reflecting every shade of the neighbouring foliage, and finally disappeared a couple of miles to the east round the corner of a huge red bluff. On our side of the river the same gradations of boulder, bush, and precipice were repeated, but, seen from a bird's-eye point of view and at a shorter distance, assumed a totally different aspect, the green tree-tops, as we peered down upon them from the overhanging cliff, looking like a huge creeper-covered trellis spread to save wayfarers from falling into the inky darkness below.

As we rode back again, we suddenly heard terrific bellowing. Away to our right stretched long slopes of hilly pasture, on which great herds of cattle were feeding. Two of these herds, each headed by a bull of immense size, were advancing towards each other, the leaders preparing for battle, pawing the ground and tossing their heads. The loneliness all round, the gloomy sky overhead, and the evening creeping in, combined to produce an uncanny feeling, mixed with a sort of superstitious awe. I was glad when I found myself back in the waggonette driving homewards, though by that time night had fallen and the storm had burst. It was all I could do to hold the horses, terrified as they were by the flashes of lightning which from time to time lit up the scene. Somehow we eventually got back safe, though we had several times missed the track in the dark.

One night Harry and I dined at Government House with Sir Arthur and Lady Havelock; and another night Mr Matterson got up a Zulu dance for our amusement, which was performed by his Kaffirs. It took place in the garden, a lamp having been arranged so as to throw a light on the dusky group, who, with torches in their hands, and clad in Highland costume minus the kilt, stood in a semicircle; and while one came forward and executed a strange war-dance, the others clapped their hands, uttering curious sounds, and clicking their tongues as an accompaniment.

After passing Christmas and New Year with our

friends, we started on the 7th of January, after dinner, and arrived at the terminus of the line, Elandslaagte, at seven the following morning. Two coaches were waiting ready to start; so, having secured the box-seat for me, we hurried back to the train to see after our luggage. Great was our dismay at finding that no portmanteau was forthcoming. They assured us it must have been taken out by mistake at Ladysmith; so after telegraphing to the stationmaster asking him to forward it by the Harrismith coach on to Johannesburg, we started with just what we stood in, besides Harry's dressing-bag. By great ill luck, just as we were leaving Maritzburg on the previous evening, Harry's master-key had stuck in the lock, which we had to break open; and being in a great hurry to catch the train, I had forgotten to take out my diamonds, which I had foolishly brought with me. On learning that they would have to travel all through the Transvaal after us in an unlocked portmanteau, I quite made up my mind that I had seen the last of them.

Our small coach, or rather post-cart, with two wheels and no springs, was driven by a fat, cheery old man called Hans, full of chaff, and for ever talking to his six horses. After travelling for some hours over a comparatively smooth road, we breakfasted at the "Fox and Grapes" Inn; after which our team was increased by two, and the road became rougher, with frequent steep hills. In the afternoon a farm on the hillside, not far from

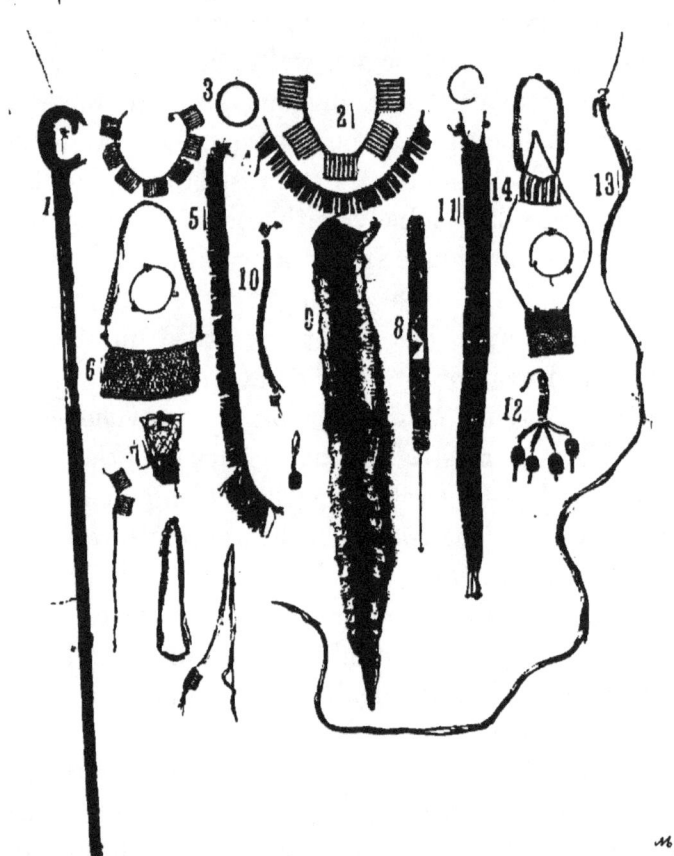

Zulu Dresses, Ornaments, etc.

1. Zulu walking-stick.	6. Girl's girdle.	11. Bead waist-band.
2. Necklace.	7. Seed snuff-box.	12. Snuff-boxes.
3. Copper-wire bangles.	8. Waist-band.	13. *Keimpji.*
4. Wooden necklace.	9. Puff-adder skin.	14. Girl's girdle.
5. Woman's girdle.	10. Bead necklace.	

the road, was pointed out to me as having belonged to Mr Rider Haggard. Directly after this
we drove down a slope at a great pace into New-
castle, a small town of slightly built houses mostly
roofed with corrugated iron, and which owes its name
to the coal found there. After securing rooms in
the "Plough" Hotel, we went out to try and buy a
few necessaries; but articles of clothing for me were
impossible fo find.

Five o'clock the next morning saw us galloping
off again, and at about nine we forded the river
Ingogo, which, thanks to the recent dry weather,
was fairly low. A little farther on we came to the
foot of Majuba Hill, barren, steep, and rocky, and
bringing back bitter recollections on which it is useless to dwell; and shortly afterwards we drove over
Lang's Nek, an insignificant little roll in the ground,
which made one wonder how it could ever have been
such an impassable obstacle. We halted for breakfast at Mount Prospect Farm, a nice little house, well
sheltered by big trees, where the peace was signed
between the English and the Boers. Some way off
was pointed out to us a little improvised cemetery
where Sir George Colley is buried.

At about twelve o'clock we reached Michelson's
Store, situated on the open veldt, and the frontier
station of the Transvaal. He was described to me
as a Polish Jew, who had begun life hawking cheap
jewellery up the country, and had made an enormous

fortune in gold-mining speculations, with which he
intended to take London by storm. In front of his
store is the Boer monument, erected, as the inscription on one side of it tells, by the " Burghers of
Wakkerstroom, in grateful memory of countrymen
who died fighting for freedom." On each of its
other three faces is a list of those killed at Lang's
Nek, Ingogo, and Majuba—*i.e.*, eight at Lang's Nek,
fourteen at Ingogo, and two at Majuba. Oddly
enough, a little inscription at the base told that
it had been made by the enemy—J. Smith, of
Pietermaritzburg. At Ingogo there is also a monument of exactly the same shape, bearing a terribly
long list of English names on its four sides.

Our post-cart was now emptied, and everything
transferred to what they call the "bus," a sort of
roughly-made waggonette with a round-topped hood
open at either end, in which a kind man gave me up
the box-seat. I quite mourned the loss of the fat old
Hans, his successor being gloomy and uninteresting.
About four o'clock we stopped at one of the halt-
ing-places, in a dirty little shanty, on unsheltered
open ground, where a Dutch family gave us some
squashy bread, and pale-brown hot water which
they insisted on calling "coffee"; for which
luxuries they made us pay an exorbitant price.
During the afternoon a heavy storm came on, and
when we reached the Vaal-*drift* the river was in
such strong flood that the driver at first thought

there was too much water to risk the crossing. He
hardened his heart, however, and by the skin of our
teeth we got through all right, the horses swimming
their hardest against the current, which was drifting
the coach away from them, knocking its wheels
against the rocks, and threatening to turn it over
at any moment. The last miles of the drive were
across vast grassy plains, so that the pitch-darkness
that surrounded us did not make us miss much of
interest. That afternoon we saw a good many
widow-birds, curiously tail-heavy, but still very
attractive in their deep mourning. We reached
Standerton in the Transvaal at nine, and put up at
the "Blue Peter" Hotel.

We had been told we must start the next morning
at three, and a little before that hour we were all
suddenly awakened by a horn, which we took as a
signal that the coach was only waiting for the passengers to start. While we were sitting in the bar
waiting for some hot coffee, a man with a woman,
evidently just arrived, walked through. The innkeeper then explained that the horn we had heard
was that of the up-country coach, which had just
come in, having lost its way in the storm, and that
ours would not start before five o'clock; so, with
many grumbles at being stirred up before our time,
we returned to our room, which, much to our
disgust, we found in the possession of the new-
comers, to whom our cute landlord had promptly

let it, thus pocketing four charges for " apartments "
for about six hours' use of his wretched little cabin.
We therefore had to content ourselves with two hard
chairs in the sitting-room, the sofa and the floor
being already occupied with sound sleepers, and
cold and tired as we were, there spent two long
weary hours.

The up-country landlord of South Africa is about
the most remarkable specimen of his class that I
have ever come across; and I can quite believe the
story told of an inexperienced traveller, who, finding
neither milk nor sugar with which to flavour his
coffee in some Transvaal hostelry, was presumptuous
enough to ring the bell, and, getting no response,
repeated the operation, with the result that the
landlord rushed into the room, angrily asking—

" Did you ring that bell ? "

" I did," replied the traveller.

" Then if you do it again, I'll wring your ear off."

The rain was still pouring when we started. At
10 A.M. we reached Widepoort, a pretty but forlorn-
looking little place in the midst of a treeless veldt
rolling away for miles and miles. There we found
a tidy-looking English couple, who cooked us an
excellent breakfast : they kept a store, where numbers of old English uniforms were piled up, which
are all bought by the natives. The track was
getting less hilly, but as bad as ever for the horses,
being through heavy and marshy ground. We

arrived at about 4 P.M. at Heidelberg, a pretty little town, with a nice clean inn, and after dark we reached Boksberg, a coal-mining place just started, its little houses having sprung up as rapidly as mushrooms.

I had noticed that one of our passengers had been getting very excited and had frequently looked at his revolver as we approached this place; it turned out that he had been warned that a man who had got a deadly grudge against him was waiting for him there. I believe he was terrified, for as soon as we arrived he slunk into a house and disappeared until it was time to go on again.

The evening was glorious as we entered Johannesburg at about eleven o'clock, and after getting rid of our mail-bags, we drove through the streets with a great clatter to the best hotel. There was not a corner to be had. One of our fellow-passengers, who lived there, tried to find rooms for us in several places. While he was doing so, we stood waiting with our bag on the pavement in front of a well-lit-up and most noisy bar, from which peals of laughter were issuing, especially from the neighbourhood of the two fat rosy-cheeked girls who stood behind the counter. At last our kind fellow-passenger returned, having found a room at the "Grand" Hotel, of which he gave us the address. One of those delightful two-wheeled "spiders" with a hood, used there as cabs, happened to be passing, so

we got in, not knowing how far we had to go. As it
turned out, it was just round the corner, not fifty
yards distant, a journey for which the driver — a
perfect gentleman in appearance—calmly charged
us 10s.! and as there are no rules and regulations
about fares, we had to pay.

I shall never forget the room we were taken to!
The hotel proper consisted of one low building,
looking on to the street, in which were the public
rooms. After passing through two of these, we
found ourselves in a large courtyard, on either side
of which was a narrow three-storeyed wooden house.
In front of each floor ran an open wooden balcony
connected to that above it by a narrow flight of
wooden steps. We reached the second floor by one
of these, and with the help of a dim lantern groped
our way over many pairs of boots into a room, or
rather a pigeon-hole, with a little window about
one foot square, under which was what they were
pleased to call a bed. This, as I discovered the next
morning, was simply a pile of dirty mattresses
heaped one on the top of the other on the bare
floor. Dead beat, I tumbled into the ready-made
bed without inspecting anything; while poor Harry,
about a foot longer than the room, lay down on the
floor with his knees tucked up, as, not knowing what
our neighbours might be, I did not like leaving the
door open for him to put his legs through. When
daylight appeared, I shivered with horror as I looked

at the sheets that I had been sleeping in. Miner after miner must have slept in them for weeks!

Next morning we walked out to see this marvellous town of two years' growth, with its curious mixture of grand public buildings, large hotels, and rows of corrugated iron houses of all sizes. The streets are wide, but very dusty; the shops good, but everything ruinous in price. There was plenty of money flying about the town; the rage for speculation was at its height, and there was a boom in gold shares, which were being run up by the English market. Enormous fortunes were being made just then, with the natural result that it was impossible to get servants or clerks. Every one speculated on his own account, and did not see the fun of working for other people. Round the Exchange there were always groups of busy-looking men; otherwise the place had a deserted appearance, and one could hardly realise it held twenty thousand inhabitants. In the large square in the centre of the town a good many waggons were drawn up, some of them outspanned, a very neat operation: every yoke, as soon as it is taken off, being laid down on the ground in its proper position, so that the full span of sixteen oxen can be put to again in a moment.

In the afternoon, after bargaining with three drivers, and at last inducing one to come down to a reasonable price, we drove to the " Robinson " mine, situated just outside the town, and one of the most important in the district. We were taken all over it, and shown the working of the machinery. They have now got down about seven hundred feet below the surface, and still find gold in as great quantities as ever. The gold-bearing quartz is placed in trucks, which are run through narrow galleries up an inclined plane to the mouth of the mine, and there passed along another line of rails to the stamp-room, where forty stamps are always at work. The quartz is first put through a crusher like a sort of coffee-mill, then pounded in machine-mortars, next mixed with water and run over amalgamated zinc plates. It then passes through a sluice covered with blankets, in which the larger pieces of gold are caught. They told me that the £1 shares of this mine were at that time worth £70.

Round Johannesburg is all bare and desolate veldt, no trees to give any shelter, and very little to suggest to one that riches lie so near at hand. Some turned-up earth, a few trenches, and little heaps of stone, are all one sees. As the Irishman said who travelled with us next day to Pretoria, "They tell me there is gold here. Where is it? I can't see any—only bits of rock and stone about." We started at 7 A.M. in a totally different class of conveyance from that in which we had travelled from Natal, more like an old royal mail-coach hung on powerful C-springs, holding twelve people inside, of whom six faced the

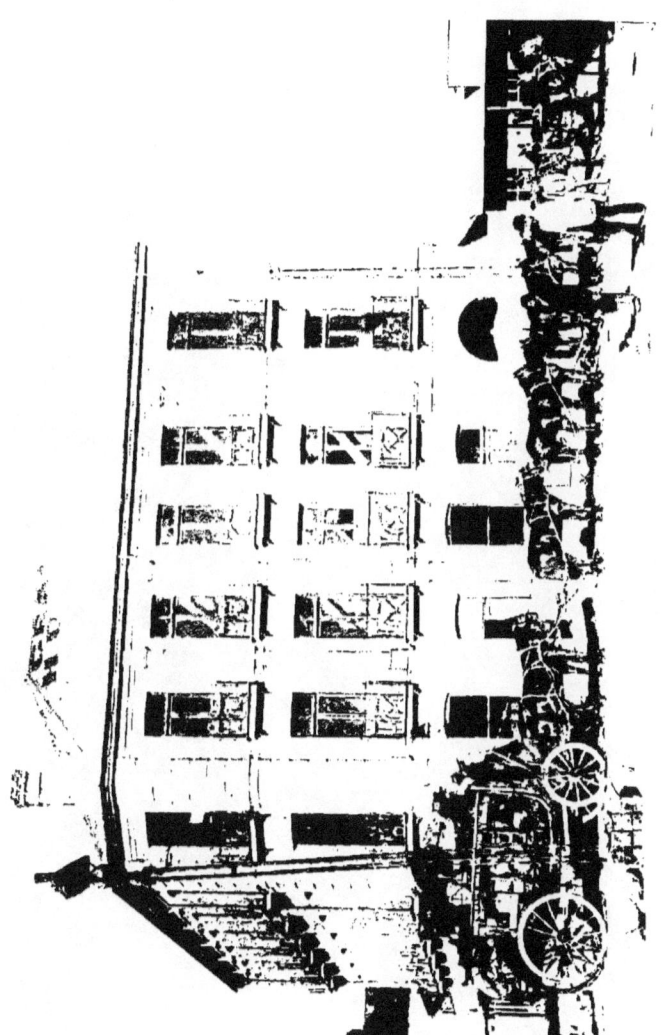

THE PRETORIA COACH.

horses. On the top were two rows of seats, the rest of the roof being entirely taken up by luggage. The road was a fair one, and we travelled along at a good pace, changing horses three times, and break-fasting at the "Half-way House," a well-built hotel in a lovely spot, surrounded by great boulders of rock, among which grew mimosas covered with their little yellow sweet-scented balls.

At twelve we reached Pretoria in the middle of a heavy shower, the last part of the road being very pretty. I never saw anything more unlike one's preconceived ideas of a capital; it was far more like a large English village, composed chiefly of pretty little one - storeyed houses, each standing in its own garden, bright with the pink blossoms of the oleander. The streets, however, are very broad, so as to allow the long teams of the ox - waggons to turn; and down their sides are *sluits*, open ditches of running water. After one hundred and fifty miles in the Transvaal, in which we had so far come across hardly any one who was not English, we had expected that here at all events we should be able to study the Boer at home, but we were sadly disappointed. Pretoria outwardly is as English as Johannesburg. Even the hotel to which we were directed was called "The Fountain," not *Die Fontein*, as I should have expected in the capital of Boerdom. Finding this was full, we went on to "Strachan's," where we were received by a thoroughly English barmaid, of whom Harry asked if there were any rooms to be had.

Her answer was, " What's your name ? "

" Colvile."

" Then I'll run and ask mamma."

She soon came back saying they had a room, and led us out of the front-door, down a verandah facing the street, and into a sort of loose-box opening out of it—a dirty little hole with a door which would not shut, so that we were practically in the street.

The first thing we did was to set out and shop. Being so long parted from our luggage, we were obliged to buy things as we went along. This done, we went to call at the British Residency, and were lucky enough to find Mrs Williams at home, who invited us to stay to lunch, so as to make sure of not missing her husband, who was out. This was a most comfortable house, charmingly done up, with a nice verandah looking on to a lovely little garden. It was certainly jumping from one extreme to another to sit here after our late experience of hotels !

After lunch, Mr Williams offered to drive us to the race-course to see some sports, the wind-up of their race - week. It rained in torrents the whole time ; still it amused me to see the different types by which England was there represented—the Dutch, with the exception of one or two emigrants from Cape Colony, holding completely aloof from this class of entertainment. They are a homely people, and the womenkind not above doing their own housework, which I do not wonder at, considering how difficult it is to train and keep the natives, who at a moment's notice ask for a holiday, go away, and never come back. Mrs Williams told me she had at last to send to the Cape for her servants.

Harry went after the races to call on General Joubert, victor at Lang's Nek, &c., to whom he took a great fancy. He described him as rather of the type of a dark-haired Scottish farmer, with a slightly grey beard, small twinkling eyes, and singularly sympathetic manner, but showing nervousness by constantly twiddling his thumbs. The General said that since the war the Boer forces had been entirely rearmed with the Martini-Henry, which he believed not only to be the best rifle in existence, but the best that would ever be invented. On Harry asking him if they were ever troubled with cartridges jamming, he said they had hardly ever had a case, which he attributed to the men's habit of using a pull-through with a bit of suet attached, with which they cleaned out their rifles during any pause in the fight.

On Sunday afternoon, while I was resting, Harry called on President Krüger, by whom he was received in a large bare room, furnished with a few uncomfortable chairs, two large Bibles on a round table, and pictures of Von Moltke, Prince Bismarck,

R

and General Joubert. The President was a coarse but rather cunning-looking old man, with a Newgate frill, large flat ears, and a red nose with spreading nostrils; to whom Harry took as great a dislike as he had taken a fancy to General Joubert.

That evening we dined with Mr and Mrs Williams, and met a young Dutchman, who had been brought up in England as a lawyer, and went to the Cape in that capacity. He had been given a high legal post in the Transvaal, and when the rebellion took place, he volunteered and joined the English. He spoke very bitterly when he told us that for a month he worked for England like a slave, and at the end never received a word of thanks, much less any recompense. He naturally lost his appointment, and now has to make a fresh start and begin life over again. He said the Cape Dutch in the Transvaal had learnt a bitter lesson, and that whatever might happen in the future, England must not count on them as allies. They would either leave the country or go against us.

During dinner we were told, as an instance of the cruelty of the natives, that a few days ago in Swaziland, instead of hanging a man, they tied a rope round his neck and another round his feet, and pulled contrary ways until he was in a horizontal position. The ropes were then drawn tight, and little taps given to them, until the victim literally died of shocks to the system. We also heard many interesting details of Mr and Mrs Williams's trip to the Zambesi. I believe she is still the only white woman who has ever been to the Victoria Falls. It took them fifteen months to go there and back in their own waggon. She gave an amusing account of how, having run out of articles for barter, she fell back on her cloth dress, in exchange for strips of which they got their daily food when there happened to be no game to shoot.

On Monday we were taken into a little backyard in the town, in which was kept the tombstone which had been erected over the British flag when it was buried here after the peace of 1881, near the spot where the bishop's church now stands. I quote the address delivered at the burial service from the 'Transvaal Argus' of August 6th, 1881 :—

"FRIENDS, SOUTH AFRICANS, AND COUNTRYMEN,—We are assembled here to-day to perform the sad and solemn rites of consigning to its long last resting-place the remains of one whom we have honoured and revered from our birth. While yet in the greatness of her power, the magnificence of her dominion, the pride of her sway, she has bowed her proud head, and fallen, not, alas! from any inherent weakness, but in the midst of her glory, by an insidious blow from the hands of her most trusted adviser. For a thousand years she has inspired her sons not only with energy to conquer the greater portions of the world, but with virtue and moderation to rule it. For a thousand years her colours have floated with equal majesty from the torrid to the arctic zone; neither has trouble shaken nor

has time weakened the affections which have beat for her
in the hearts of her people. In all quarters of the globe
where her standard has been raised, she has been looked to
as a refuge for the troubled and the oppressed. Her sons
have scattered themselves over the face of the earth,
bearing with them the tidings of justice and freedom.
People have flocked to her standard, whole nations have
lifted their eyes to witness and their voices to proclaim
her coming. At the magic influence of her presence the
fetters have fallen from the limbs of the slave; but the
rippling laughter of the happy and the free has been heard
on every side, while the moderation of her sway gave
peace and contentment throughout the lands. But, O
friends! in this our adopted country all has changed.
That flag, for which our forefathers gave the choicest of
their treasures, and for whose honour so many offered up
their lives, has been laid down in the dust. Wounded to
the heart by an unkind thrust, shorn of a portion of her
honour, her crown of glory taken away by those whose
prime duty it was to guard her with most jealous care, she
has come to an untimely end. The flag we loved is dead!!
and with that flag (the emblem of justice and freedom),
justice and freedom themselves in this land seem also dead.
We lay in that grave before us the flag which may no more
in this country unfurl herself. Our hearts, too, are in that
grave. And now, gentlemen, dwelling no longer on the
past, with the past we bury all rancour and animosity,
turning ourselves to the future with that hope which has
ever sustained us. Friends and countrymen, we are not
cast down; though we have lost our flag we have not lost
our courage. Though the emblem has gone, the sentiments
she inspired still remain with us. Though our poor dear
flag lies in that grave, the principles she taught shall live
as long as the sun shall shine. The future of this land—we
had hoped a bright and glorious future, when all this
wide domain from Table Mountain to the Zambesi should

have been welded in one harmonious whole under this flag,
—the future of this land now lies in the eternal mainten-
ance of those principles of truth and justice without which
no country can prosper. *Go, then, all of you,* and let the
influence we spread and the lessons we teach be the
influence instilled into us and the lessons gained by us
under the shadow of that flag whose loss we so deeply
mourn."

On the tombstone was the following inscription:—

In loving Memory

OF THE

BRITISH FLAG IN THE TRANSVAAL,

WHO DEPARTED THIS LIFE
ON THE 2ND AUGUST 1881,
IN HER FOURTH YEAR.

"In other climes none knew thee but to love thee!"

On the same morning Mr Williams drove us to the
fort in which the English troops had been besieged
during the war, now occupied by the new Boer
artillery. In it were two new armour-plated huts,
very like similar contrivances which we had seen at
Massowah, and which were said to be very useful
for savage warfare, though they seemed to me very
cumbersome things to take about on an expedition.
We were shown over the fort by a German officer
who had been private secretary to Dinizulu —
Cetewayo's son.

We started again for Johannesburg by the one
o'clock coach, nine inside—a Salvation Army girl,

several bookmakers, and a broker or two — and several on the top. After the first stage the driver went off the usual track to avoid a bog, instead of which he got into one. Suddenly we heard a crash and came to a standstill, and found ourselves axle-deep in mud ; and in trying to pull us through, the traces and iron chains snapped, the leaders going off at full gallop up a hill and disappearing over the sky - line, leaving the helpless wheelers still fast to the coach. As nothing could be done till the six horses had been caught and brought back, most of us got out and walked to the " Half-way House," hoping to reach it in time for lunch ; but we found it was far farther off than we expected, and after being disappointed a dozen times as we reached successive ridges from which we expected to see it, we were finally overtaken by the coach within sight of its doors.

We got back to Johannesburg at seven, and found that our coach for Kimberley was to start at four on the following morning, so we lay down in our clothes and got what rest we could.

Groping through the dark streets we arrived at the coach, and at once settled down into our places, two seats at the back facing the horses, which had the advantage of allowing their occupants to rest their heads when the coach was not jolting too violently ; but, on the other hand, the construction of the seat in front made it impossible for them to stretch their legs; while the occupants of this seat, although given a fair amount of liberty in that direction, had no support for their heads, their seat being simply a bench backed with a narrow strap supported on stanchions; and as the coach jolted across the veldt, their heads bobbed and bumped together every time they dropped into a doze. Opposite their seat was another similar one, and behind it one like ours, both having their backs to the horses, so that twelve of us were seated inside the coach, all under slightly varying conditions of discomfort. Soon the companionship of suffering brought us on friendly terms; and we temporarily exchanged seats, and practically tested the disadvantages of our neighbours' position, till a partly dislocated neck in our case, or a numbed leg in theirs, made us again exchange and return to our own places.

As the day broke we found ourselves in an uninteresting country covered with yellow mimosa. We arrived in time for lunch at Potchefstroom, a pretty little well - timbered place, which offers a pleasant contrast to its treeless surroundings, and is approached by a most picturesque wooden bridge, at each end of which grow two large weeping-willows. Thence we continued our journey on to Klerksdorp, which we reached at eight o'clock, after nearly sticking fast in several bogs.

We thought we were to sleep here at "The Smiling

Morn," as the hotel was called; but on entering the bar—called " The Smiling-Room "—we were told we should only dine and change coaches, as the Johannesburg coach went no farther. So after a good wash and an indifferent dinner we were off again by nine, and had a beautiful clear night for our drive. The whole coach was soon off to sleep. We were awakened at about 1 A.M. at a changing-station where hot coffee could be got, and then travelled on till daylight, when we stopped for breakfast at Makosospruit, and for lunch at Bloemhof. After leaving this last place, one of the back-springs broke, and we had all to get out of the coach and take the luggage off, so as to allow the spring to be roughly patched up with cow-hide. It was a great bore, as we were still some miles from Christiana, which we consequently did not reach till late that evening.

About two we crossed the Vaal river, about three hundred yards wide. The coach and horses were driven on to a ferry-boat and towed across, we sitting in our places the whole time, and in spite of our sleepiness enjoying the beautiful moonlight view of the river. On the far bank we had a five minutes' halt for a cup of coffee; after which, with the exception of a few minutes' halt in the early morning, when we got a mouthful of bread-and-butter, we had nothing to eat until we reached Kimberley at noon.

On arriving there we drove to the Central Hotel,

which had been recommended to us as the best; but finding it full, went on to the Queen's, where we had no more success! Our flyman then proposed the Grand, where, as at Pretoria, we were offered a loose - box, this time actually opening into the street without even an intervening verandah, the hotel itself being full. We had to take it and be thankful; for the whole of Kimberley was over-run with cricketers, a team having come from England to play the Colony. Having secured a resting-place, we again went to make inquiries about our luggage in hopes that it might have been sent straight on, but nothing had been heard of it; so we went back and rested till dinner-time, having certainly earned repose, for we had left Pretoria on Monday the 14th, slept from 11 P.M. to 3 A.M. at Johannesburg, went on travelling night and day all Tuesday and Wednesday, arriving on Thursday the 17th at Kimberley, having only been allowed daily half an hour for breakfast, half an hour for lunch, an hour for dinner, and about five minutes at every outspanning stage. It was not so much the rough-ness of the road, but the want of sleep, and the cramped position that one is in all the time, that makes it so exhausting.

Next morning we called on Mr J. B. Currey, manager of the South African Exploration Com-pany, whom Harry had known in Cape Town, and who kindly gave us a note to Mr Pickering, manager of the " De Beers " diamond-mine, asking him to show us over the works. On arriving there we found we were unfortunately too late to see the diamond-washing, so were taken over the " Compound" where the miners live. Mounting a steepish slope, we found ourselves in front of a heavy locked door, which being opened by the porter in answer to our ring, we entered a large square, with an asphalt floor, surrounded by a fence of corrugated iron ten feet high. On two sides of it are the canteens and the Kaffirs' quarters, and on a third those of the white overseers. In the centre is a big swimming-bath next the schoolroom, in which I noticed one of those gongs with copper tubes of different lengths which I have often seen at home; on this they learn to play tunes. After visiting the hospital, a cool, airy, high-roofed shed, where there were forty wounded men, laid up mostly with broken arms and legs — casualties that had happened in the mine — we were taken through a door that is always kept locked, into a passage; reminding me of the covered bridge by which passengers cross from one platform to another in a large English railway station, and ventilated at intervals by small iron - barred windows. At the end was a big square hole in the floor, through which we could just see the top of two narrow iron ladders side by side, by which the diggers have to go up and down to and from the

THE COMPOUND, DE BEER'S MINE.

mine. The black miners are engaged for three
months, during which time they cannot leave the
"Compound." At the end of this period, if they
like to re-engage themselves, they can ; and some
of them were pointed out to us as never having
been outside the place since it was started two
years ago. Even the overseers cannot go outside
without a ticket-of-leave. No money is used inside
the " Compound," all articles being bought and sold
in exchange for brass tokens of different fictitious
values.

In the afternoon we drove with Mr Currey to
" Du Toit's Pan " mine, a huge quarry with precipitous sides several hundred feet deep, at the
bottom of which, as we peeped over the edge,
the workers looked like ants. The sides are
covered with a network of wire-ropes, each pair
running over two wheels and working a tub by
which the men ascend and descend the mine, and
the blue clay is brought up. We were very anxious
to go down in one of these tubs, but I was already
feeling very ill with another return of fever, so we
were taken instead to see the washing of the clay
at the " De Beers " mine, which we had missed that
morning.

On our way there we passed through many hundred acres of what appeared to be ordinary ploughed
fields of a bluish clay, and which certainly gave no
indication of the immense wealth which they con-

tained. It is in these fields that the diamond-
bearing clay is exposed to the air for some months
before being washed. They were only separated
from the highroad by a light and easily climbable
fence; and it struck me as very curious that such
extraordinary precautions as we had seen in the
morning should be taken while it is dug out, and
that it should then be left apparently at the mercy
of any passer-by in the open fields. When it has
been sufficiently loosened by the action of the
weather, the clay is taken to the washing-station,
and thrown on to a sort of gravel screen, where it
is washed under a jet of water, the lighter particles
being carried away, while the gravel and diamonds
remain, a smaller-meshed screen beyond catching
any stones which had passed through the first.
After it is thoroughly washed, it is spread out on
tables, and the men sort it carefully, picking out
any diamonds they come across, which are easy
to see from their whiteness as compared to other
pebbles. Mr Currey told us he was going to gravel
his garden-paths with this refuse, which is considered of no value, the garnets, of which the
gravel is composed, being too small to be worth
cutting. He told me also that a lady, who had
been given some for the same purpose, had found
three diamonds while walking about her garden.
Even stones found accidentally like this have to
be reported at once, for the laws are so severe

that any one who does not do so is liable to find himself in a very awkward position.

On Saturday afternoon, January 19th, we left Kimberley by train at 2.25 for Cape Town. Luckily Harry had secured a reserved carriage, for my attack of fever had gone on increasing from the day before, and the terrible sickness still continued; so my recollections of the first twenty-four hours are of the vaguest. Towards the evening of the next day, however, I began to feel better, and was able to enjoy the grand scenery we were passing through, the line winding in and out among the mountains. It got more beautiful after nightfall, with the bright moonlight casting deep shadows in places, and in others showing up the clear hard line of the rugged mountains. Many were the different profiles of human faces and shapes of animals that they assumed.

We arrived at Cape Town at about seven o'clock on Monday morning, and spent nine days there vainly trying to find any sort of ship to take us to Mossamedes, where we could have found a West Coast boat in which to continue our coasting trip. With this object in view we pestered every possible person connected with the sea, from the local timber merchant to the Captain of a French man-of-war, who had incautiously put in for a little holiday. While not thus engaged, we were making the lives of steamship and railway officials a burden to them on account of our lost luggage, which, however, never turned up until months after we had reached England. Strange to say, the lockless portmanteau arrived exactly as I had packed it, with every diamond intact—a rather remarkable fact, considering that it had followed us the whole way from Ladysmith through the Transvaal and the diamond-fields.

BOOK VII.

THE FORTUNATE ISLES.

FAILING to find the ship we wanted, or our luggage, we embarked on Wednesday, January 30th, on the "Hawarden Castle," and after an uneventful voyage, landed on Wednesday, the 13th of February, at the port of Las Palmas, the capital of Grand Canary; and thence drove about two miles into the town, where, after several fruitless endeavours to obtain accommodation, we finally put up at the Grand Hotel.

Las Palmas at a distance has rather an oriental appearance, and the expectations thus raised are fully gratified on closer acquaintance, as far as the population is concerned, the natives being the most arrant beggars I have ever come across, children of all sorts and sizes crying incessantly, "Johnny, give me a penny," while their elders, with equal pertinacity, demanded cigarettes. From behind latticed windows too—reminding one of the Egyptian *mushrabieh*—rows of dark eyes peeped out at us as we passed, their owners seemingly living, during the daytime at all events, the ordinary harem life.

A closer inspection of the streets, however, reveals the very unoriental quality of extreme cleanliness. The houses are of a dazzling white exterior, many of them adorned with massive handsomely carved

Washerwomen, Las Palmas.

doors; but their most marked features are some curious cannon - shaped wooden gutter - spouts projecting three or four feet from just under the eaves, and which must form a rather trying series of shower - baths to the foot - passenger on a rainy day. The four principal sights of the town are the cathedral, the museum, the new opera - house, and the cemetery, all of which we duly "did." The exterior of the cathedral is decidedly imposing, but the interior to my mind was not worthy of it, its only marked feature being its Gothic roof and arches, which were very fine. The museum contains a good collection of plaster-casts and implements of the original inhabitants of these islands, the Guanches; also a remarkable assortment of bottled monstrosities, as to whose date and origin I did not inquire. The new opera-house is a fine cream-coloured stone building, the interior of which was not yet finished, but which, if it has not been spoilt by paint and gilding, should now be very handsome. All the mouldings are beautifully carved in pitch-pine, and it went to my heart to think that they would soon be covered up, and made to look like ordinary plaster-casts.

The cemetery is a very peculiar institution, its most remarkable feature being the short tenancy enjoyed by most of its occupants. A large part of it consists of a quadrangle whose surrounding walls are pierced with niches for the reception of coffins, which only remain in them for the period—longer or shorter, according to the means of the deceased's relatives—during which they are hired. At the end of this time the coffins are removed, broken up, and their contents thrown on to a heap of similar remains in a sort of backyard adjoining the quadrangle. In this we saw piles upon piles of skulls

s

and bones all bleaching in the sun, with here and there a skeleton from which the skin had not yet wholly disappeared. The caretaker was so accustomed to this ghastly sight that he thought nothing of walking about on the top of these, picking up different specimens to show us.

During our walks in the country, my curiosity was aroused by seeing many large fields of prickly-pears, the top shoots of which were all carefully tied up with bits of rag. On inquiring, I learned that it is on these plants that the cochineal insect feeds, and that for fear of these precious little bugs dropping off and getting lost, they are thus made prisoners on their feeding-grounds, until the time arrives when they are collected by the women in little wooden trays, and then left to die and dry up in the sun.

In the course of one of our walks near the town, we came across some curious cave-dwellings in the face of the cliff, the entrances to which, being coated with a circle of whitewash, had a clean look at a distance; but the appearance of such of the inhabitants as we saw did not tempt us to explore the interiors.

Not caring much for Las Palmas or its neighbourhood, and hearing that the next outward-bound boat for the West Coast of Africa would not start until the 9th of March, we determined to pass the remainder of our enforced stay in the Canaries at

BONE YARD IN LAS PALMAS CEMETERY.

Orotava, in the island of Teneriffe. We were told on the third day of our stay at Las Palmas that the boat was sailing for Teneriffe that evening, and we went to the agent's office to secure our tickets, hurried back to the hotel, and after getting a little dinner, started off for the port. As there was no one to take our things on board, we asked the manager if he could get it done for us, to which he at once answered that he would go and do it himself as soon as he could be missed!

At nine o'clock we embarked on board the "Leone Castillo." She was a small uncomfortable boat, and it struck me she might be very nasty if there was any sea on. Luckily it was beautifully calm, and bright moonlight. We were received by the steward —a fat, dirty little boy—who followed us like our shadow. I happened to ask him what were the green lights I saw ahead, so he comfortably installed himself in a chair opposite us, and lighting a cigarette, told us it was the wreck of an Italian ship which had raced a Spanish merchant-ship into the harbour some days before. A collision took place, and she sank so rapidly that seventy lives were lost, though they were only two hundred yards from the breakwater.

Not being able to get rid of this objectionable boy, we retired to our cabin, where we luckily discovered in time that our sheets were quite damp, and had again to make use of our blanket-bags.

The night was to prove sleepless for me, thanks to the " Spanish kangaroos," as I heard some one describe them at Las Palmas. I had been told that if I went on deck about 3 A.M. I should see the beautiful Peak of Teneriffe, and the wonderful shadow it casts on the sea on a moonlight night; so in the middle of the night I crept up, but saw nothing but banks of clouds.

We arrived at six, anchored off Santa Cruz, breakfasted there, and started off about ten o'clock to drive to Orotava, where we stayed for a fortnight. Being in great want of rest, we went no excursions, and our life there was a very idle one, and would have been thoroughly enjoyable but for the cold, which we, coming straight from the tropics, felt acutely, although the other English visitors, lately arrived from the chilly North, were complaining of the heat. My one excitement was my daily lesson on the guitar from the barber of the place, after he had shaved Harry; and with reading, sketching, and taking photographs, our days were filled up in this lovely quiet spot. The Carnival began the day before we left; and a party of us went into the streets to see the masquerade, and got well pelted with eggs which had been emptied of their contents, filled with sawdust and flour, and then secured with a piece of paper stuck over the hole.

We went back to Santa Cruz on Tuesday, March the 5th, where we came in for a second egg-pelting

as we drove through the streets. We stayed there
two nights, but I saw nothing of the town, being
laid up with one of my ever-recurring attacks of
fever; and having booked places for Sierra Leone,
we left Santa Cruz on Thursday the 7th of March,
on board the "Benguela."

BOOK VIII.

THE LAND OF DEATH.

I.

THE West Coast boats had always been painted to
me in such gloomy colours that I had expected that
I should now begin really to "rough it," and was
therefore very agreeably disappointed to find myself
more comfortable than I had been in any ship since
leaving England. The Captain, a dear old man,
seemed to think everything would be too rough and
uncomfortable for me on the West Coast, so he did
his very best to make things on board as nice as
possible. We had the large ladies'-cabin, airy and
with a big skylight, and which, with its good-sized
table and berths, turning into sofas by day, was
more like a sitting-room than anything we had yet
seen on board ship. We always found it a cool
and quiet spot, where we were able to spend many
hours reading and writing.

There was a great mixture of nationalities on

ON THE ROAD TO OROTAVA.

board. Two young Belgians, who were on their
way to the Congo accompanied by a young Syrian
interpreter, Suliman, whom they always called
Salomon, a sly, thin, cringing, despicable piece of
humanity, like most of his class. A Dane, who
spoke English easily, and looked like a Scotsman.
A Russian missionary with a kind intelligent face,
who seemed full of the work he was about to undertake : he did not know a word of the language of
the people among whom he was going, but said he
would very soon pick it up, as it had only taken
him six weeks to learn English, which he spoke as
fluently as he spoke French and German. A red-
bearded Englishman going out to Bonny as head-
clerk in the telegraph office. An Irishman, who had
come out as the ship's doctor just for the trip. A
French-Swiss. And last, but not least, a very short,
fat man, who seemed to suffer very much from the
heat, and who, we were told, was a German-Swiss
called Schmitt. From his conversation we gathered
that he dabbled in commerce on that coast, and had
done a little exploring up country from Sierra
Leone. Since my return home I have found out
that our friend Schmitt—whose name we discovered
later was really Zweifel—was no other than the great
Swiss explorer, and discoverer of the sources of
the Niger. From the look of him one would never
have guessed that he could have gone through so
much walking and roughing it as he must have

undergone in his many journeys up country quite alone, with the exception of a few natives to carry his goods.

We began by having very cold weather, as instead of getting into the trades, we had an unusual south-west wind blowing against us, making our progress slow. The ship was as full as she could hold, and a great part of her deck was covered with "sleepers" for the use of the Loanda Railway.

Very often in the evening the Belgians used to call Salomon on deck to amuse us with his extreme sharpness and powers of mimicry. The only other time of day we ever saw him was early in the morning smoking a cigarette in his shirt-sleeves, the dirtiest of the dirty. He always had a penny whistle in his pocket, and when asked for a song he played the accompaniment first, then sang the words, and so on verse after verse. His imitation of two Frenchmen conversing was very clever, full of gesticulation, with the longest words he could find in his vocabulary. His mimicry of animals was equally good, and he seemed to have a whole menagerie in his throat. He generally ended his performance by singing in Arabic, with that curious droning nasal sound that runs through their songs.

On Tuesday, March the 12th, we got well into the trades, and it became pleasantly hot with a smooth sea. The next day we anchored off the island of Goree about 10 A.M., and were disappointed to find

that Dakar on the mainland was too far off for us
to have time to visit the town before the ship sailed
again. The agent for the line of steamers came on
board to make arrangements for embarking French
blue-jackets on their way to join their ships in the
Gaboon, and on his return to Goree he took us
with him, and left us to see the town by ourselves.
The island is very small, and after having walked
through a few streets, we had seen the whole of
the French settlement, except the fort, which is
situated on one of the points. A steep hill leads
up to it, which we climbed, and found ourselves
in front of a closed doorway. All was so quiet
we began to think there was no one there. We,
however, knocked on the chance, and were answered
by a volley of threats and abuse in French, to
which I replied by again knocking and asking if
we might come in. A soldier then came, and smiled
when he saw us, saying he had thought it was
the little black boys who amused themselves by
hammering all day on the door. The Captain then
appeared, a very nice man, who took us to see the
view of the surrounding country from one of the
highest parapets. We then went and sat in his cool
little sitting-room. He seemed so pleased to get one
of his own class to talk to, as he could not often go
over to Dakar. It must be a trying exile for a man
like that to live so much alone, and with no comforts to make life easier. He accompanied us down

the hill to the town, where we took a sailing-boat and went off to the ship.

About three o'clock the French sailors arrived from Dakar in a lighter towed by a steam-launch. There was not room for all on board, so some had to remain behind and wait for the next steamer that would take them. It made me quite sad to see some of them—mere boys just come straight from France — going to live in such a deadly climate, where probably half their number would not survive. The part of the ship chosen for them was that already crowded with "sleepers" under the awning, which left them so little room that most of them had to sleep out in the open, and cook their food as best they could. Their high spirits never failed them, and it was only when in the evenings they sang in chorus some beautiful and touching songs in which were ever-recurring regrets at having left "La belle Patrie," that one felt how well they realised that it might be for the last time they had said farewell to their country.

We were at sea all Thursday and Friday, and nothing occurred worth mentioning — beyond a heavy swell which made the vessel pitch badly— until Friday evening, when a tornado came on. The first sign we had of it was a bank of black clouds ahead making a hard line against the other part of the sky, which was clear and lit up by the moon. The Captain warned us the storm would break suddenly, and told us to be ready to run down below. The wind got up, and before we knew where we were a tremendous shower came down. The poor French sailors got their bedding quite wet, and went about trying to find a dry corner to sleep in; not an easy matter, as such heavy rain went through all the awnings. In a few minutes it was over, and the air felt fresher, though still very " hothousey."

On the morning of the 16th we steamed into the mouth of the Sierra Leone river, a broad and beautiful estuary lined with luxuriant tropical vegetation, on the left bank of which rises the high green ridge from which the colony derives its name, and on the slope of which is situated the capital, Freetown, off which we cast anchor at 6.30 A.M. We were soon boarded by a clamouring crowd of negro boatmen, but were able to dispense with their persistently offered services, thanks to the harbour-master, who took us ashore in his gig. In spite of the early hour we at once called on Major Crookes, the Governor's A.D.C.—the Governor being away down the coast—who kindly volunteered to show us about the place.

Viewed from the sea, Freetown is as pretty a place as one could wish to see anywhere, but the same can hardly be said of it when seen at closer quarters. The streets, though broad, are dirty and ill kept, and there is a general appearance of mildew and decay about the houses which has the most depressing effect. Even the flowers, beautiful as they are, are so heavily scented as to heighten the depressing influence of the climate. The only lively objects about the place were some little birds with bright metallic-looking plumage, which flew hither and thither among the trees. We had but little time to form a personal opinion of the much-abused Sierra Leone natives. We, however, visited the market, full of cheery negresses cackling over their varied wares, among which I noticed some immense plaited hats, which, owing to the ends of the straws having been left sticking out about three inches, had a curious shaggy appearance. We also went to a chemist's shop to buy some photographic chemicals. Stumbling over a little monkey gnawing a banana in the doorway, we entered a long barnlike room, along whose length ran a counter, over which the proprietor, a gentleman of colour, was leaning in conversation with an overdressed negress. So interested were they in each other, that it was a full quarter of an hour before either of them deigned to notice our presence. At the end of that time the man condescended to inquire whether we wanted anything. So leisurely was he in his movements that by the time our modest ¼ lb. of hyposulphite of soda had been weighed out and paid for, the hour had arrived at which our ship was due to leave; so hurrying back, we returned on board.

All the passengers were on deck watching her

Majesty's ship "Archer" steam into the harbour, with
the exception of Schmitt; and as we were just getting under way, I inquired if he was not likely to
be left behind. I was told, however, that he was
safe on board, but concealed in his cabin. It seems
that during one of his explorations he had killed
some Sierra Leone natives in self-defence, and that
although he had been tried for this and acquitted,
their relations had vowed vengeance; so that his
assumed name and temporary retirement were due
to his fear of being lynched.

Soon afterwards we steamed off again to the
southward, generally keeping well in sight of the
long low line of palms, the strip of sand, and the
fringe of breakers which are characteristic of this
part of the African coast. In the early morning
of the second day we anchored for a short time off
Sass Town, a large village on the Liberian coast;
and again, an hour later, off Grand Sesters, the
latter a very large native village of conical-roofed
round mud-huts, most picturesquely situated in a
banana-grove between a thick forest and a large
tract of cultivation.

One object of our call at both places was the
collection of " Kru boys " for the coast factories; and
hardly had the echoes of the gun announcing our
arrival died away than the whole male population
were afloat, racing towards us in canoes big and
small, but all of the "dug out" class, and all ex-

tremely rickety and dilapidated-looking. Much to
our Captain's disappointment, however, none of them
wished to engage themselves, and I do not know
why they were in such a hurry to come out, for
they had nothing to sell — not even themselves.
They seemed thoroughly to enjoy themselves, bobbing up and down in the swell, and chaffing our
crew, while the little boys made expressive signs
that they would like some food, and one and all
addressed me as "Mammy." The "Kru boy"
seems to be a very good-natured hard-working
savage, of magnificent build, and, I believe, both
honest and amenable to discipline while fulfilling
his usual one or two years' engagement with a white
trader, but, I am told, makes up for it on his return
by utterly defying the Liberian Government—whom
he speaks of contemptuously as "them Melican
man"—and showing a general disregard for the Ten
or any other Commandments that may be brought
to his notice. It is, however, certainly on him that
the prosperity of this coast depends, he being the
only living thing that can be induced to do a stroke
of work. The "Kru boys" seem to be very quick at
picking up the curious pigeon English which they
talk, or indeed any other language except German,
of which they say, "German mouth too much
hard;" but I must say their English is rather remarkable, and difficult to understand. For instance,
if one of them is asked if he has found something

CAPE PALMAS.

which he has lost, he answers, "Yes, I no found him." The following is a *menu* concocted by a "Kru-boy" cook, which, with its translation, has been lately given to me :—

10*th Sept.* 1892.	10*th Sept.* 1892.
Book.	*Menu.*
Soup crazy.	Soup cressy.
Big fish cold.	Cold salmon.
Fowl small chop.	Fowl cutlets.
Beef no catch brain.	Braised beef.
Cow-belly.	Tripe.
Fowl for pot.	Boiled fowl.
Dem peach.	Peaches.
Bla for piccin.	Rice pudding.
Plum for soft side.	Stewed Plums.
Stink butter.	Cheese.
All dem sweet mouth.	Dessert.
DEM BIG HOUSE FOR HILL.	H.B.M.'S CONSULATE-GENERAL.

Early next morning we rounded Cape Palmas, a pretty palm-covered promontory, boasting the unusual luxury of a lighthouse, but nevertheless adorned with wrecks ; then changing our course to the east, we anchored at noon off Tabu, near enough to the land to get a good whiff of miasmic gases, which reminded me strongly of Madagascar. Tabu has one large European factory on a big black rock overhanging the sea on the left bank of a pretty little creek, beyond which is the native village and its usual background of palms. I was anxious to land and have a stroll, but the surf

was so bad that the Captain would not let me, so
I had to content myself with sketching it from the
ship; while to console me for missing a "curio"
hunt, Mr Fothergill, the purser, gave me a native
piano, a closed box about seven inches long by
three wide and one deep, ornamented with burnt-in
designs, on the top of which are fixed eight strips

Tabu.

of bamboo fastened at one end, the other being
raised by means of a little wooden bridge.

Our change of course brought us a fresher breeze,
and as we also stood out farther to sea the temperature was very pleasant; but, on the other hand, we
missed the amusement, which we had between Sierra

Leone and Cape Palmas, of watching through a glass the various aspects of the palm-fringed shore, with its succession of native villages. During the next two days we only sighted two of these, Winne-bah and Barracoe, the former a pretty spot backed by high land, and possessing several large European houses, while the latter is marked by the appear-ance, for the first time, of square huts in place of the bee-hive shape of farther north and west.

A little before mid-day on the 21st we reached Accra, the capital of the Gold Coast, an imposing-looking place, built on a high bank overhanging the beach. We landed in the surf-boat that came off for the mails. I was told that this safe roomy con-veyance has only been used on the Coast since the Ashanti war, when they were brought out for the purpose of landing troops and stores; and after my experience in her, I felt very thankful that King Koffi Kalkali had been evilly advised to defy us, and thus bring about the introduction of some more seaworthy craft than the native dug-out.

Our steamer having anchored some way out, we had a twenty minutes' row, or rather paddle, to the shore, and I had ample opportunity of studying the boatmen and their ways. The boat was manned by eleven strong well-built natives of varied types, one of whom steered in the stern with a paddle, while the others, five on each side, sat close against the edge of the boat, each steadying himself by a ring

T

of rope through which he passed his great toe. The boat standing high out of the water, they had to bend right over the sides at each stroke to reach the water with their short three-pronged paddles, all the time uttering curious sounds, which grew louder as the waves got higher. At first it seemed as if a continuous line of surf cut us off from the shore, but as we got nearer I noticed that there were openings in this here and there. Steering for one of these, the men paddle slowly on until they see that a larger wave than usual is about to overtake them ; then putting on a spurt, the boat is impelled forward at furious speed on the top of the boiling breaker, whose roar the men try their best to silence by the ever-increasing loudness of their song. Blinded by salt foam, deafened by noise, and bewildered by the rush of waters, I had hardly time to wonder what was going to happen next, when a crash brought me to my senses, and on to my nose, and I found myself seized by four strong black men, and carried safe but dripping to the beach.

Ascending a flight of steps cut in the face of the cliff, and followed by a crowd of little naked blacka-moors, we found ourselves on the edge of the town. We went first to see the Comptroller of Customs to find out if the Governor was then at Accra ; but as he was at Christiernbourg, an old Danish fort on a rather high part of the cliff about two miles to

the eastward, we found that we had not time to
drive over to see him.

While we were waiting, an ambassador from one
of the chiefs of the interior, with whom the Comptroller had been having an interview, came out—
a most curious-looking individual, whose appearance
reminded me forcibly of the picture in a child's
book of Bible stories of the high priest, dressed as
he was in long garments, and wearing suspended
on his breast a square embossed gilt ornament, the
size and shape of Aaron's breastplate. Behind him
walked three black boys, the centre one carrying,
in an upright position in front of him, a very
formidable-looking weapon, the blade of which was
a foot wide, tapering down to the point and handle,
and having a pierced design all over it. The handle
was in shape and size like a gilt pine-apple of
medium size, and starting from it was what looked
like a snake coiling up the blade, the whole thing
being about three feet in length.

After our short visit to the Comptroller, we started
off to see the town, accompanied by a little black
boy whom he lent to us as a guide. Though lacking
the distant beauty of Sierra Leone, the town is far
superior to it on closer inspection. The houses are
large, clean-looking, and well built ; the streets broad
and well kept ; even the native huts are far better
than any we saw elsewhere on the coast ; and the
place has certainly a general air of prosperity, and

even healthiness, though in this respect I fear appearances are rather deceptive. The shops, too, seemed good and plentiful, mostly full of European goods, among which were some very pretty cotton prints, and great varieties of coloured beads. It was studying the natives, however, that most interested me. A great many of the small boys had their one garment kept on by two rows of beads fastened round their waist, while most of the women had only a piece of checked duster stuff hanging from their hips down to their knees. Their hair is done up in curious tight cones four inches high, standing straight up on the top of their heads, somewhat like a clown's wig; but two women whom we met looked most civilised in European hats of a long-past fashion, though their short-sleeved cotton dresses with low-cut bodices made a strange contrast with their dark skins.

After wandering through many small streets we entered the main one, and soon found ourselves in the shade of the fine gnarled old cotton-tree which stands in the middle of the market-place. A veritable Nijni Novgorod of Western Africa it seemed, containing specimens of all varieties of its sons, from the light-skinned white-robed Moor, his darker brother in faith the Houssa, the half-nautically dressed " Kru boy," and the black-coated " coloured gentleman " of Sierra Leone, to the untutored and unclothed inhabitants of the lower Niger.

NEGRESS, ACCRA.

The goods on sale were as various as their sellers. Long flint-guns, pipes, tobacco, calabashes, cotton stuffs, straw hats—broad-brimmed, narrow-brimmed, and brimless—looking-glasses, tin mugs, skins, meat, fruit and vegetables of all kinds, the latter being mostly offered by contented-looking old negresses, who squatted by the side of their baskets without making much effort to dispose of their wares. Not so, however, the owners of the carved wooden stools of the country. Having bought one of these—I suppose at an exorbitant figure—we were pestered all the way back by would-be vendors of these articles, the word having apparently been passed down the street that we were willing to relieve all families of their superfluous furniture. It was the hottest part of the day, and in spite of a nice breeze we were beginning to feel that lunch, and a nap in a deck-chair afterwards, would not be amiss, so we refused most of the numerous offers to step inside; but in response to one man, whose mysterious manner led us to believe that he had something particularly tempting, we followed him up a narrow passage, through a dark court into a low stuffy room, from a corner of which he produced an ordinary green parrot. But as I had been told that I should probably return home in a ship full of them, I declined his offer.

On returning to the ship we found the sea had risen a good deal; and as the surf-boat could not be kept

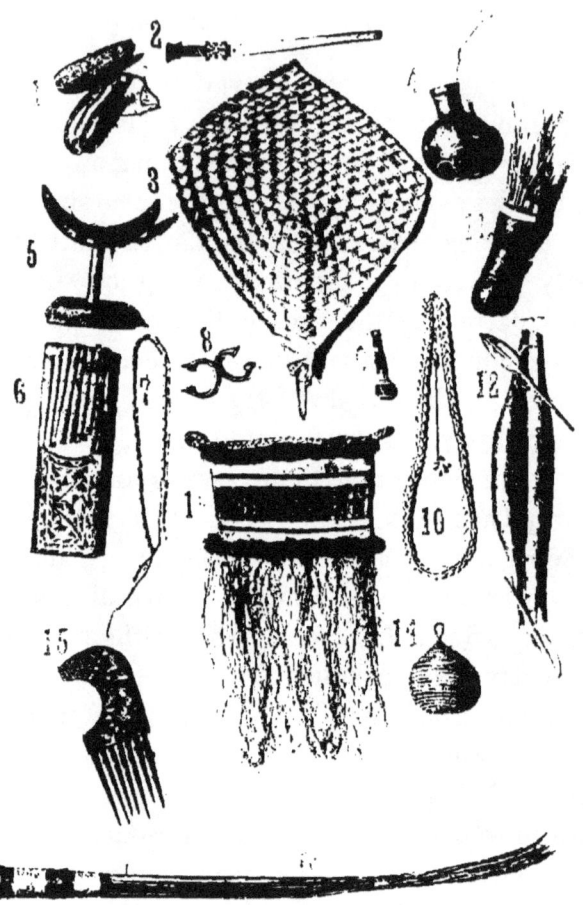

West African Wares.

1. Loofas.
2. Kru boy's tooth-brush.
3. Accra fan.
4. Earthenware musical jar.
5. Wooden pillow.

6. Kru boy's piano.
7. Girdle of cowrie shells.
8. Manilla coins.
9. Needle-case.
10. Girdle of cowrie shells.
16. Broom.

11. Carved gourd.
12. Model of canoe.
13. Grass haversack.
14. Round basket.
15. Accra comb.

alongside the companion-steps without fear of breaking them, I had to climb up a rope-ladder.

Our ship ought to have gone round the Bight of
Benin to Old Calabar, and then southward; but as
the Captain thought it desirable to land the French
sailors as soon as possible, he made straight from
Accra to the mouth of the Gaboon.

On Friday afternoon we had another tornado,
which seemed as if it was going to blow us out of
the water while it lasted, but it left the air deliciously cool, and was succeeded by the most lovely
phosphorescence I have ever seen, the wake of the
ship being a positive blaze of light.

We passed close to Prince's Island the next
evening at eight, when it was unfortunately too
dark to see it. I was very sorry for this, as, judging
from the account of it in the 'African Pilot,' which
I quote, it must be a remarkable sight. It is only
nine miles long, and " consists of a series of steep
and rugged mountains surmounted by gigantic
obelisks of most fantastic shapes, the whole culmi-
nating in a peak 2700 feet above the sea, and is
in its physical features and aspect one of the most
remarkable in the world." It is also interesting as
being one of the six volcanic cones which run in a
straight line in a south-westerly direction from the
Cameroon Mountains, 12,700 feet above the sea.
A glance at the map shows that a line drawn from
the Rumbi Mountain to Anna Bom Island passes

through every one of these peaks, all evidently the result of one vast volcanic upheaval.

We ought to have sighted the mouth of the Gaboon on Sunday morning the 24th of March, but owing to a pouring rain nothing could be seen a mile ahead. The ship was stopped several times that soundings might be taken; and having got to fifteen fathoms, the Captain felt sure that land must be near; so he anchored, hoping the heavy rain would soon clear, and let him know his whereabouts. We then all had lunch; still nothing was to be seen, when suddenly on our right, instead of ahead of us as was expected, the land appeared quite close. We were just opposite the mouth of the Gaboon, into which we steamed between Cape Joinville and Pongara Point, and two hours later were at anchor off Libreville, on the left bank of the broad estuary, which takes its name from the larger of the three rivers flowing into it. The heavy rain had perhaps a depressing effect, and at any rate obscured all view of the distance; but I certainly was not struck with the beauties of the place, which consists of a small cluster of European houses situated on the slope of the low range of hills lining the left bank of the estuary. The right bank is low and uninteresting, and between it and Libreville extends a broad expanse of lead-coloured water. I was told that the settlement was much less flourishing than it had formerly been, the chief cause of diminution of trade being the heavy duties imposed and the new markets opened. Before the European scramble for Africa began, the Gaboon was the only port within reach to which natives of this part could bring their goods. Now, with the Congo on the south and the Germans on the north, the native naturally paddles his canoe down the river which happens to lead to the best market.

The harbour, however, is a magnificent one, and in it were lying three French men-of-war : "L'Alceste," used as a guard-ship, "Le Pourvoyeur," and "Le Sané," on board which we had dined at Cape Town, and on whose Captain we at once went to call. We were nearly blown out of our boat by a salute, at extremely close quarters, of—I forget exactly how many guns—in honour of Admiral Brown Coulston, whose ship, "L'Aréthuse," was just steaming in ; and found our friend Commandant Fournier in full tog, just preparing to step into his gig to meet the Admiral. So arranging to meet later in the day, we went ashore and explored as much of the place as was to be seen in the drenching rain.

After walking for about a mile down a pretty avenue of cocoa-palms by the sea-shore, we found nothing more interesting than a *café* full of Frenchmen enjoying a Sunday chat and *vermout;* so, turning to the right, we struck inland, and describing a semicircle, re - entered the town by the Governor's house and the barracks, into both of which the occupants had very sensibly retired. Finding ourselves back at the pier and drenched through, we determined to follow their wise example, and hailing a boat, were on the point of giving the order "Home," when we were invited to go over "L'Alceste." We found her a comfortable old-fashioned ship, with big square port-holes well out of water, and chiefly given up to hospital accommodation: on board her were several of our late fellow-passengers, the French sailors, comfortably settled down, and very pleased to have a deck over as well as under them.

At 6.30 on the following morning we steamed out, and turned again to the northward, with much regret on my part, as I was very anxious to visit the Congo, about which I had heard so much from all on board.

It continued to rain all that day, being still the rainy season on the part of the coast nearest to the Equator. On the next day, however, we got into the district where the rains begin in April and end in September. They begin later and later as one ascends the coast, lasting from May to September on the Gold Coast, from June to October at Sierra Leone, from July to October at Bathurst, and so on.

On the morning of the 26th of March we got into the long swell which marks proximity to the coast-line in the Bight of Benin, and at about noon sighted a spire, which we were told was part of Bonny

Cathedral. Shortly afterwards some corrugated iron roofs became visible ; and as we continued our course, a straight dark line just showed itself above the waters, and gave us our first view of the land portion of the Niger delta. As I glanced at the Captain's chart I wondered how we should ever find our way through the labyrinth of channels into which we were entering — a doubt by no means lessened by a view of the apparently unbroken lines of surf and expanses of mud-coloured shallow water which lay between us and the shore. However, after many twistings and turnings, and the guidance of the solitary buoy by which this channel is marked, we finally glided into smooth water, and cast anchor in the Bonny river—a broad estuary, bounded by banks of mud, almost awash at high tide, and far below the level of our eyes as we paced the deck of the "Benguela." On the left bank were some half-dozen two-storeyed European buildings, with corru-gated iron roofs, behind them a broad expanse of bush, of which the straight outline was here and there broken by a gigantic cotton-tree. As it neared the river's mouth, the bank's few feet of elevation gradually dwindled to nothing, until it merged into the broad, wet, sandy foreshore, which in its turn melted into the sea-horizon. There was no sign of native habitations, the town, or rather towns, of Bonny being, as we afterwards learnt, situated on creeks a little farther up and down the river. Some fifty yards from the shore was moored an old hulk, connected with the land by a wooden pier.

The right bank of the river, about a mile and a half distant, presented an absolutely flat and unbroken horizon, and, when shortly afterwards we entered the ship's boat to row ashore, disappeared altogether beneath the sky-line. Up-stream the view, equally flat and unbroken, afforded rather more variety of colour. The broad stream stretched away—an unruffled streak of light—till it melted into the haze of the northern horizon; the green foliage and brown gnarled stems and roots of the unending mangroves stood out sharply on an island in midstream a few hundred yards above us; whilst on the left bank, above the factories, mangroves again showed a sheet of less brilliant green, gradually fading in the far distance into the grey of sky and river.

The hulk just mentioned was a remnant of the older style of trading, when merchants sent their own vessels, which, casting anchor in the rivers, were covered with mat awnings and generally made comfortable,—remaining for weeks or months until their original cargo was exhausted and replaced by barrels of palm-oil. Later on they took to leaving one ship permanently on the coast, moored to the shore, dismantled, and turned into a floating house and fortress; for in the good old days of the "Palm-oil Ruffian," the vocation of merchants on this coast

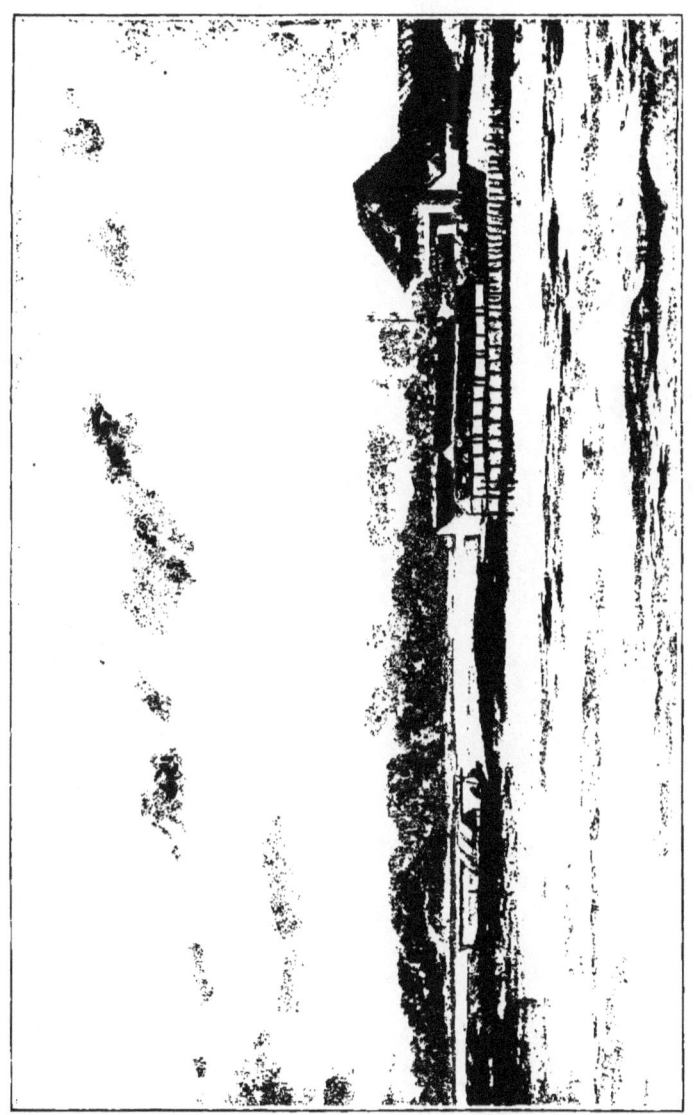

FACTORY, BONNY.

was anything but a peaceful one. Now goods are all sent out by the regular lines of steamers, and the merchants' representatives live in comfortable houses on the dry land.

Soon a smart gig put out from the shore, and brought on board Captain Boler, one of the oldest English residents on the coast, and Major—now Sir Claude—Macdonald, the British High Commissioner for the Oil-rivers, who had just arrived from England on a special mission. The former kindly invited us to stay with him while we remained at Bonny; and finding that we were likely to have to wait some days before the arrival of the "Nubia," which was to take us to England, we gladly accepted his offer. So, packing up our traps, we reluctantly bade farewell to the "Benguela," her captain and officers, and accompanied Captain Boler ashore.

His residence was a substantial two-storeyed building, of which the ground-floor was entirely devoted to merchandise and coopers' workshops, for the repair and manufacture of the casks in which the palm-oil is sent to England. The first and residential floor was reached by a broad wooden staircase outside the house, but under cover of the wide verandah which encircled the whole building. On to this verandah all the rooms gave. At the top of the staircase and facing the river was the dining-room, occupying nearly all the centre of the house; to the right and left of it large airy bedrooms opened, giving respectively as well on to the northern and southern verandahs; while on the other side were the offices, Captain Boler's own rooms, and those of his clerks.

II.

In the afternoon Major Macdonald took us to see the cathedral. Soon after starting we came to a narrow tidal channel, and were anxiously debating as to the best means of passing it, when three naked little blackamoors appeared, one of whom, pointing at me, said, "Me carry them man;" and as good as his word, he lifted me on his shoulders and carried me across. Our way to the cathedral lay through Bonny Town, a dirty and intricate collection of huts: some with wattle-and-daub walls and palm-leaf thatched roofs; others of mud-brick and corrugated iron roofs; and some again a mixture of the two styles of architecture, but all out of repair, and, as far as I could see, filthily dirty. The chief feature of the place appeared to be the extraordinary number of broken square-face "Holland's" gin bottles which were strewn about its streets, and which afforded ample evidence of the thirsty temperament of its inhabitants. Gin is one of the most important exports from England to our new Protectorate, and so highly appreciated by the natives that they even have a few bottles buried with them

when they die; and as I learnt from a wooden
image of a god which was given to me, they have
promoted it to the dignity of the ancient nectar
—the deity in question being represented with a
"square-face" bottle in each hand.

Two minutes' walk, however, sufficed for the
passage of King Ja-ja's capital, and brought us to
the margin of a deep pool surrounded by gigantic
cotton - trees, whose heavy shade and buttressed
roots would almost have made one imagine one's
self in some early English cloister, but for its
human occupants, whose behaviour and appearance
were as far as possible opposed to all ideas of peace
and dignity. Here King Ja-ja's female subjects
come to draw water for their households : fat elderly
negresses, swathed in two or three particoloured
square dusters; slim agile young matrons, looking
anything but matronly in half a yard of the same
material; girls of all ages, from six to sixteen, with
no fraction of a duster, but adorned with a single
string of cowries pendant from their hips : all carrying huge water-jars on their shoulders—in the case
of the children, almost as large as themselves—and
all laughing and talking and splashing to the utmost
of their powers. Accompanying them were the
unemployed youths of Bonny—apparently a large
proportion of the population—helping the women,
as idle young men do all the world over, by causing
endless giggles, and rendering the proper business

on hand perfectly impossible. I was too far off to hear what was said, and even had I been nearer, was unacquainted with the Yoruba dialect spoken at Bonny; yet I understood every word that was uttered as well as if I had been watching a similar scene being enacted in an English ball-room, or on the area-steps of a London house. The consequences of the Tower of Babel have no doubt been most annoying to serious-minded persons in search of information; but to the truly frivolous they have caused but little practical inconvenience, nor will, until a second and worse Babel inflicts on mankind a confusion of giggles.

Our road lay through thick bush, in which a broad "ride" had been cut, marked by narrow interlacing tracks which the bare feet of its users had worn. Half an hour's walk brought us to Archdeacon Crowther's house, a pleasant dwelling in a well-kept garden facing the river. We were most amiably received by the Archdeacon and Mrs Crowther, who showed us over their beautiful church and well-built schools, the former capable of seating a thousand persons, — a number which, I am told, the Archdeacon often draws within its walls. The mission-buildings are all situated in a clearing in a part of the bush which was formerly sacred to the local god, and from which his votaries, ever anxious to secure a human sacrifice, were in the habit of pouncing out on unsuspecting wayfarers.

COTTON-TREE, BONNY.

Although it is an open question whether the West African negro has yet arrived at a stage which fits him for the reception of our religion and civilisation, with their attendant liberties in the matter of gin, gunpowder, and forms of worship, and restrictions as to sexual relationship, there can be no doubt that the world at large can no longer tolerate the cruelties and abominations attendant on ancestral and devil worship, nor live cheek-by-jowl—as it must nowadays with all seaboard populations — with a people which practises them. Whatever may be thought of the advantages of missionary work among members of more advanced religions, the thanks of the civilised world are certainly due to the missionaries,

Ju-ju Priest.

who have at all events stamped out the outward and more objectionable forms of West African superstition. Among these Archdeacon Crowther, and, as I heard on all sides, his father, the Bishop

U

of the Niger, belong to the very highest class; and being themselves natives, have an amount of influence which no white man could hope to attain. Like their American brothers, some of the black parsons are decidedly quaint in their methods of teaching. One who acted as *locum tenens* for the Archdeacon some time ago, attracted great crowds every Sunday by his violent anti-white sermons. In one of them he was telling his congregation of God calling the lambs into His fold. "Which did you think God called?" he asked; "the white lambs, or the black? Nay, my brethren, not the white, but the black. And why?"—here a solemn pause—"Because he grows wool"!

Many were the stories told us of cannibalism and human sacrifice—the former, I fancy, mostly exaggerated; for, as far as I know, cannibalism has never been practised in this region except as part of a religious ceremony; but the latter is still so openly practised in the districts out of immediate European control, only a few miles from Bonny, that it is certain to have flourished there equally until it was suppressed by force. Only a few weeks before our arrival, for instance, thirty slaves were killed at a place not fifty miles from Bonny, in order that their late master might not be unattended in the land of spirits; while the relations of another deceased chief, also in the immediate neighbourhood, had lately buried alive two of his slaves in his grave, and had hung up two more, head downwards, by hooks passed through the sinews of their heels; in which position they remained until the flesh rotted away, and the poor wretches, still alive, fell into a pit full of spikes, on which they were impaled.

Among the rites formerly practised at Bonny, the most horrible, I think, was the monthly sacrifice of a virgin to the shark-god. At the first low water of every spring-tide a victim was led out to the water's edge, there bound to a stake, and left until her agony was ended by the slowly rising tide, or the sharper but more quickly striking fangs of the hungry sharks.

Horrible as this religion is, it has the advantage of putting enormous power into the hands of the rulers, and thus enabling them to maintain a degree of order which our milder methods fail to effect. Men who had travelled in the interior told me that, in point of honesty, the civilised compared most unfavourably with the uncivilised parts. One traveller in a hitherto unvisited region having lost his gold watch and chain, wished to offer £30 reward for its recovery; but the chief of the village would not hear of such a proceeding, saying that it would disgrace him for ever were it known that a stranger had been obliged to buy back his own property in his territory; and issuing a proclamation, the watch was soon found and returned to its owner.

Judging from the experiences of Archdeacon and

Mrs Crowther, the inhabitants of the Kru coast, who, from their frequent employment on board European ships, have become fairly civilised, do not share these fine scruples. While they were returning from a trip to Sierra Leone they were shipwrecked off Cape Palmas; and in spite of the fact that they were personally well known to many of the natives, the latter had no compunction in robbing them of everything they possessed. Mrs Crowther, being a very plucky woman, felt so indignant that she took off her wedding-ring and threw it into the sea rather than let the natives have it.

In justice to the Kru boys, however, I must say that they treat the stranger no worse than their own friends and relations. After one of them has been working up and down the coast for months or years, and has collected a nice little "pile," and a fashionable outfit, consisting of a tall hat, a red cotton umbrella, and the tunic of a Guards drummer-boy, he begins to yearn for his native village; so balancing himself—or otherwise—in a keel-less dug-out of fifteen inches beam, he bids farewell to civilisation, and charging the surf, lands with a bump on his native shore. Immediately following him is a gigantic roller, and in the excitement of the moment it is many chances to one that the welcoming crowd forget to drag the canoe out of the way with sufficient rapidity, and that she—bottom uppermost,— the tall hat, the umbrella, and the tunic, are all

BISHOP AND ARCHDEACON CROWTHER AND CLERGY.

gaily dancing in the surf. A score of strong arms
are soon beating the water to their rescue, which is
speedily effected, without much advantage to the
rightful owner, but to the great joy of the lucky
swimmers who secure the prizes. Then after toiling
all these months away from home, the welcome
wanderer cannot be allowed to burden himself with
all those heavy bags that hang from his waist, and
many willing hands are stretched out to relieve him
of his load, with the result that he re-enters his
home much in the condition in which Job entered
and expected to leave this world; nor does he again
have the pleasure of handling an umbrella or a gin-
bottle until a fresh arrival from the ships of Christ-
endom affords him also the opportunity of assisting
at the home-coming of some one else.

On our return home Major Macdonald had at once
to start for Opobo, where he was due to attend
a "palaver" on the following morning. As no
steam-launch was at hand, he had to travel in a
native canoe, winding his way through the intricate
network of channels which intersect the Niger delta
in every direction, most of them wholly unexplored,
and many even utterly unknown. It is strange to
think that within a short distance of Bonny, constantly frequented as it is by English men-of-war,
there should be miles of water-way less known and
more un-mapped than the distant upper reaches of
the Niger or the Zambesi.

Next morning I was awakened early by the loud beating of tom-toms, so lifting up my mosquito-curtain and peeping through the blinds, I spied a procession of long war-canoes advancing down the river laden with barrels of palm-oil, and each containing a king and some fifty of his subjects, who, by the peculiar manner in which they handled their long-pointed paddles, showed to the initiated to which particular monarch they had the honour of owing allegiance. These paddle-strokes are some of them curiously fantastic and intricate, and must add enormously to the labour of propulsion, and, I should imagine, are only reserved for state occasions. They are, however, as distinctive as the tartan of a Highland clan, the camel-marks of the Sudanese, or the tattooing of a South Sea Islander.

This, it appeared, was the day of the week on which the neighbouring kings — who have taken upon themselves the lucrative post of middle-men— come down to exchange the palm-oil collected from up-river markets for European goods. Later in the day I had the honour of being presented to all their sable majesties, some of whom rejoiced in such un-royal and un-African names as "Black Face," "Green Head," "Dublin Green," "Charles Holliday," and "John Brown"; the only exceptions to this rule being "Oritchie" and "Oko Jumbo." They were mostly pleasant, fairly intelligent-looking men, with good white teeth, which they continually

showed, and the regular Christy Minstrel laugh.
One or two of them had been to England, and wore
European clothes. These seemed there to have lost
a good deal of the simplicity which lends a charm
to the untravelled and uneducated West African,
without having gained very much instead. One of
the kings quite won my heart by a little bit of
flattery on my artistic powers, about which I myself was not particularly confident. Looking over
my shoulder as I was sketching a lovely palm-tree,
the resting-place of a troop of white doves, which
stood just under the verandah, he remarked, pointing at the sketch, " Them all same like tree."

On my asking Captain Boler for information as to
the class of goods for which the palm-oil was exchanged, he suggested I should come and inspect
them myself. We accordingly descended to the
store. Such a curious collection ! Knives, hatchets,
bales of cloth, looking-glasses, straw-hats, blue-and-
white-striped jerseys, beads and knick-knacks of all
kinds; among which were some very fine pieces of
coral, much used by the wealthier natives as an
ornament. Captain Boler showed me one piece,
about an inch square, which he said was worth £70.
Some time ago the experiment was tried of sending
out some imitation coral, which, however, had no
success. The first chief to whom it was offered,
after looking at one of the strings of beads, put it
to his lips, and uttering a contemptuous " Tcha ! "

—Pooh !—handed it back and went off, accompanied by all the others. They are also most particular about the composition of some coins known as *manillas*—in shape like a thick plain bangle with thickened turned-up ends, which gives them the appearance of a capital C. To please them, these coins must, when hit, give out a certain ring which they alone can accurately recognise. The choice of cotton prints for this market is also a matter that requires great care on the part of the exporter. Often whole cargoes of stuffs are found to be almost unsaleable, and have to be got rid of for what they will fetch. In many parts cotton - stuffs are not accepted unless they are printed on both sides ; the ordinary prints, plain on one side, or, as the natives express it, " Them no have two face," being looked down upon as worthless.

In the midst of Captain Boler's motley collection I noticed some rolls of fine red damask, and on in- quiring by whom that was purchased, I was told there was a great demand for it among the kings, who used it for the purpose of winding-sheets. The same ideas as to a future state which cause slaves to be sacrificed at their master's death, lead to the interment with the corpse of all such necessaries and luxuries as would ensure his comfort and dignity in the land of spirits. As it is the custom to bury a man beneath the floor of his own house—which, in the case of the head of the family, is then abandoned

—it is probable that the tumble-down and unprom-
ising-looking old shanties of Bonny Town will yield
some rich treasures, should its inhabitants ever
become sufficiently advanced to feel the need of
drains.

In the afternoon Captain Boler took us to Ju-ju
Town to pay " Black Face " a visit.   It was a three-

Ju-ju Town.

mile row, mostly through narrow channels between
islands densely covered with mangroves, whose dark-
green foliage, perched on the top of a framework of
earthless roots, presents a strange and unnatural
appearance even by day; and in the twilight, mag-
nified and rendered indistinct by the rising mist,
these tangled roots look like bunches of some writh-

ing reptiles pendent from the dark walls that hem in the narrow stream on either side.

A wonderful stillness pervades these West African creeks. Except for the gentle ripple of the water among the mangroves, hardly a sound was to be heard ; and the only sign of life was afforded by an occasional crane, which, startled by the sound of our oars, reluctantly abandoned his fishing and flew heavily away ; and by the families of little red crabs collected on the snaky-looking roots, that edged into the water as a splash from the oars warned them of our proximity.

Turning a sharp corner, and passing under an archway of overhanging branches, so low that we had to duck our heads, we found ourselves in a small shady creek, bright with the reflection of the glorious vegetation that lined its banks. Just in front of us was a high palisade of stout poles, above which peeped the palm-thatched roofs of the village. Stopping at an opening, we were received by " Black Face," " John Brown," and " Green Head," who helped us out of our boat, and led us into the hut of the first-named king. It was a curiously civilised abode to find in such a place and among such savage surroundings,—glazed windows, well-painted walls adorned with some fair prints, and mahogany chairs, sideboard, and dining-table, the latter covered with siphons, with of course a due proportion of the inevitable " square-face." Having partaken of a mix-

JU-JU PRIEST.

ture of these, and uttered the mystic word "Boo," which is *de rigueur* on such occasions, our hosts offered to show us their war-canoes; so skirting the town, we followed a narrow path and dived into the bush, a tangled mass of lovely flowering creepers and gigantic ferns, over which towered some of the largest cocoa-palms I had ever seen. A short walk brought us to the shed in which the war-canoes were kept—huge unwieldy-looking things dug out of the trunk of a single tree, about three feet broad and fifty or sixty in length. They present, however, an imposing appearance fully manned, with the fifty paddles simultaneously flashing in the sunlight. Close by was the old *barracoon* in which the Portuguese used to store the slaves prior to embarkation, —a long, low, one-storeyed stone building without windows, a very dismal dungeon in which to spend the last hours on one's native land.

On the margin of the creek close by, half buried in the mud, I saw an odd-shaped earthenware bowl, curiously ornamented with bosses. Being always on the look-out for *curios*, I at once asked if it had been thrown away, and finding that it had, I whispered to Captain Boler to try and secure it for me, which he kindly did; and I triumphantly carried off my trophy, which, it turned out, had belonged to a neighbouring and now disused Ju-ju altar, and was one of the vessels in which the blood of the human sacrifices had been carried — with songs and dances—through the town, to be tasted in turn by the inhabitants. In the town itself we found another altar still standing, and adorned with a collection of curiously carved images, bowls, bits of pottery, and brass rods. These were by way of

Idol and other Articles from Bonny.

2. Grass cap.	5. Grass plate.	8. Grass-woven basket.
3. Accra stools.	6. God from Bonny.	9. Sacrificial jars, Bonny.
4. Carved pumpkin.	7. Paddles.	

having been discarded and thrown away by the present chiefs, who are Christians; but from the fact of the altar and all its appurtenances having been left intact, I suspect that, at the best, they have but added our religion to their own. Near this altar was a group of women squatting on the ground, who were singing the wildest of tunes to the accompaniment of tom-toms made of square pieces of wood hollowed out from beneath, and of an even simpler instrument—an ordinary narrow-necked earthenware jar, from which they produced various deep notes by beating on the mouth with the palms of their hands. These jars varied in height from about three feet down to a few inches, according to the depth of note they were intended to produce. While the women were singing and playing, the men and boys danced—not the war-dance, which is nearly always performed by the males of savage tribes, but rather the class of that of the "Gawazi" women on the Nile, or, I should imagine, the Nautch girls of India.

On the following afternoon H.M.S. "Pheasant,' with Major Macdonald on board, arrived from Opobo, which she had been blockading for some weeks in consequence of the behaviour of the local kings, who, acting as they do as middle-men, were anxious to prevent all direct communication between the buyer and the producer. With this end in view they had placed booms across the river, and other-wise made themselves thoroughly obstructive; the result being that the crews of two of her Majesty's ships had been obliged to spend most of their nights for some time past in patrolling fever-stricken creeks, with hardly any greater opportunity of excitement than that afforded by the occasional capture of a dug-out and her crew of two small boys, and cargo of half-a-dozen long-legged chickens.

We dined on board that night, and heard a great deal about the miseries attending the blockade of West African rivers, and how the damp nights in the swamps and the monotony of the work had played sad havoc with the crew, a very large percentage of whom, and several of the officers, were down with fever. The Captain had wished to show us the war-dance of his " Kru boys "; but just as they were about to begin, the doctor asked him to postpone it, as the Chief Engineer, who among others was seriously ill with fever, had suddenly taken a turn for the worse, and was in a very critical condition.

Soon after our return to England we were grieved to hear that Captain Johnson himself had succumbed to the effects of this deadly coast.

We had a very pleasant dinner, at the conclusion of which Captain Johnson had again to get under way to proceed to New Calabar, where Major Macdonald was due for another " palaver." We were invited to accompany them, and offered a cabin on board ; but the " Nubia," which was to take us home, was due the next day, and being afraid of crossing her *en route*, we had reluctantly to decline. As it turned out, the " Pheasant " returned from her trip before the arrival of the "Nubia"; so that we should, after all, have had plenty of time to see this, to us, new bit of country.

Before leaving, the Captain gave me the following letter, which he had received the day before from an Opobo chief, and which I reproduce as a good example of "English as she is" writ in the Niger delta :—

"SYLVANIA VILLA,
OPOBO FARM, *March* 26, 1889.
"Captain JOHNSON, H.M.S. 'Pheasant.'

"SIR,—I herewith much pleasure to send you one young Parrot by my boys.

"I have tried all my best to send you and old Parrot, but sorry that I cannot succeed. I therefore beg you to receive this young one, and I think please God he will in future become a good bird to play with. I am very sorry indeed of not getting you old bird, who is already speak well. However, if you teach this young one he will surely be a good Bird.—I remain, sir, your most obedient servant,

"APPIAFI."

At about noon on the following day we rowed off to see King "Charles Holliday," whose plantation lies on a small creek about two hours up the river. Our route lay through the same sort of scenery as we had passed going to Ju-ju Town, but the creeks were narrower, and much more intricate ; and in the utter absence of landmarks, one wondered how any one could find his way about this watery labyrinth.

On arriving at "Holliday's" landing, we found him awaiting us with a few of his men, and were

escorted by him through the village to his compound. Passing through a broad arched gateway,
we entered a high-walled enclosure some two hundred yards square, in one corner of which stood a
well-built European-looking house giving on to a
covered courtyard. Going up a broad flight of
wooden steps, we were ushered into the dining-
room, a nicely decorated apartment, whose most
prominent feature was a large coloured photograph
of our host, which had been enlarged from an
amateur's negative sent to England for the purpose,
in which the large coral bead that he always wore
was done full justice to.

After a short time a little slave came in with two
dishes—on one a substantial piece of roast-meat, on
the other palm-oil " chop "—quite the most delicious
mixture that I had ever tasted of shrimps stewed in
palm-oil, with just a pinch of ground chillies. It
was so good that I have often regretted that by the
time palm-oil reaches England it has lost its fresh-
ness; and although doubtless excellent for the purpose for which it is imported—the manufacture of
soap, and the bright-coloured but rather unsavoury-
smelling grease which is applied to railway-carriage
wheels—it is no longer suitable for culinary purposes.

Everything eatable on this coast is described as
" chop "; and judging from our host's answers to
various questions of mine on the flora and fauna of
his estate, he seemed to divide nature into two

great classes. "Them make chop," or "them no good for chop," was the only information I could extract from him on any subject connected with natural history. Being a practical man, the "make-chop" class was greatly in excess of the other, as we noticed when after lunch we made a tour of his scrupulously clean village and well - kept estate, which was chiefly planted with cacao and coffee shrubs.

I had been wondering during our stroll at the remarkable absence of population, and imagined that the people must all be away at the markets or elsewhere, when the mystery was solved by the appearance round the corner of two women carrying water-jars, clad in the scantiest of possible costumes, whom "Holliday" imperiously waved away the moment he caught sight of them. I asked why he had done so, and he explained that his people not being dressed in a style to which I was accustomed, he had ordered them all to remain in their huts during my visit. As we were anxious to secure some photographs of native types, this was the last thing we wanted, and the king was accordingly asked to rescind his order.

I also photographed "Holliday" with his six wives and their numerous offspring. As the scene was a good typical example of a West African house-hold, I will try to describe it.

The left third of the picture is occupied by the

x

wall of a two-storeyed, gabled wooden house, built
of alternately light and dark painted boards, and
pierced by casemented windows, with diamond-
shaped leaded panes. The eaves, projecting some
twelve feet, form a broad verandah, supported by

"Charles Holliday" and Family.

tall wooden uprights, the feet of which rest on a
dwarf stone wall, supporting a wooden platform, surrounded by a balustrade, and approached by broad
stone steps. At right angles to these steps, and
running diagonally across the picture from the

entrance-door on the first floor to the platform, is
an open wooden staircase, of a step-ladder style of
architecture. In the background is a long low shed,
its walls hidden by a collection of palm-oil barrels,
and surmounted by a corrugated-iron roof. On one
of the lower steps of the platform stands " Holliday "
himself, scratching his chin; on his head is a Pan-
ama straw-hat, with the broad brim turned down.
A green cord is fastened round his neck, threaded
through a large single piece of red coral, which,
hanging in the centre of the upper opening of his
white linen jacket, takes the place of collar, necktie,
and scarf-pin. A red-and-blue-check duster, wound
round and round the waist beneath the coat, reaches
a little below the knees, showing a few inches of
bare black leg above the white cotton socks and
black leather laced ankle-boots. Leaning over the
balustrade to his right are two of his wives—one
fat and thirty, the other equally fat, but not more
than twenty years old, each dressed in a single piece
of check duster material passed round the body
under the arms, rather higher than a European low
dress, but more than making up at the skirt for its
superfluity above. Legs and feet are bare, and a
checked handkerchief wound tightly round the head
completes their attire. On " Holliday's " right and
left, sitting on the stone steps, are two other wives,
dressed like the first pair; while a fifth, swathed
in a wrapper of broad blue-and-red stripes, stands

slightly in the background. All have little black piccaninnies astride their hips. At the top of the wooden steps, forming the apex of the pyramid, is the hope of the family, the king's eldest son — a cheery boy of twelve, who, dressed in a white linen shirt many sizes too short for him, is preparing to slide down the banisters. In the foreground, seated on a stone outside the platform, the youngest wife, aged eleven, is playing with two little slave-girls, probably rather her seniors—one dressed like the elder women, in a coloured check cotton wrapper, the other in the costume of Eve before the Fall. She, on the contrary, is arrayed in the smartest of European low-necked, short-sleeved, frilled frocks, evidently made for a child of six, beneath which her patent-leather shod feet dangled in the air, apparently suspended by half a yard of white cotton pantaloon. In the lower right-hand corner of the picture, marking the extremity of the pyramid's base, is the most important personage of all—a young gentleman of about three summers, who, decked in a scarlet cloth shirt, which has prudently been constructed to allow for the growth of its wearer, is standing in the place and position proper and habitual to him—well to the front, in an attitude of command.

As the day was getting on, and we had another visit to make, we had to bid farewell to our pleasant and hospitable host far sooner than I should have

wished.   After winding our way among the creeks
for half an hour, our boat shot through the usual
almost hidden entrance to that on which "Dublin
Green's" village was situated.

The scene was very different from that which presented itself in the "Holliday" domain,—a dirty,
badly kept village, looking damp and gloomy beneath the shadow of large overhanging trees; crowds
of men and women with little clothing, and apparently less to do, sprawling in groups near their door-
steps; while naked children of various ages stag-
gered under the weight of enormous water-jars, on
their way to and from the river.   The appearance of
one of these, I must own, at first rather startled me
—a perfectly white child of some ten years old,
naked as the day she was born.   A closer inspection,
however, revealed the white hair and pink eyes of an
albino, and explained the cause of her appearance.

Like that of "Holliday," the house of "Dublin
Green" was surrounded by a walled yard, after passing through which, and ascending some steep steps,
we were ushered into a stuffy untidily kept room, in
which the head wife was sitting.   She was a fat,
dirty, middle-aged woman with a loud laugh, and
was apparently much amused at our visit.   After
drinking some tea we took our departure, and none
too soon, for a chilly dampness was rising from the
river, and before we were clear of the creeks it was
pitch-dark.

III.

On Wednesday, April the 3d, the "Nubia" steamed in, and the following day saw us homeward bound, very sorry not to be able to stay any longer under Captain Boler's hospitable roof, from which he had promised us many interesting expeditions. His parting words were, "You must come back again and do the rivers thoroughly;" an invitation which we still hope some day to accept.

The next evening we stopped at Quitta, on the Gold Coast, which consists of a few factories, a fort garrisoned by Houssa police under an English officer, and a native village in a palm-grove, all situated on a low strip of land between the sea and the chain of lagoons, behind which the country stretched in an unbroken line of mangrove-swamps as far as the eye could reach. This is the place from which Sir John Glover started on his expedition up the Volta during the Ashanti war. It is now a great place for poultry-breeding, and the recognised victualling station for homeward-bound vessels. Soon after the gun was fired, a fleet of canoes was seen racing towards the ship, which shortly became the centre of a tremendous hubbub. The natives had to stand upright in their small dug-outs to throw up their provisions, an operation that caused many upsets, to which, however, they seemed perfectly indiffer-

ent; and soon righting their canoes again, throwing
one leg over them, they jerked themselves into an
upright position, and at once began to bale out their
little crafts. Before many minutes the sea had
become covered with a mass of bobbing heads, poul-
try, and vegetables, the latter in every variety of
colour. Purple "alligator" pears, yellow plantains,
emerald-green limes, and scarlet chillies made a
charming contrast to the slaty colour of the sea.
In the midst of this the righted and the yet un-
capsized canoes darted about, their owners annex-
ing all that came within their reach to a chorus
of invectives from the submerged proprietors.

The sight was very curious, and would have been
amusing had it not been for the cruelty to the poor
fowls, which had to go through the same acrobatic
performance as the vegetables; and being tied together in bunches of about eight or ten, they had
not a chance of saving themselves. As these living
bunches were thrown up by the natives, the poor
things flew about in various directions, and being
all fastened to the same centre, it needed a very
quick man on board to catch them; and even when
this was done, hardly a bundle arrived without
several broken legs and wings.

It was great fun watching our "Kru boys" offering
the natives anything they possessed in exchange for
their beloved dried fish; a bar of blue soap would
purchase a dozen. While I was watching them

bargaining, my attention was attracted by the sight of a curious dark mass, mysteriously advancing towards us without any visible means of propulsion. When it got close to the ship, the middle of it suddenly disappeared, and on looking through my glasses, I discovered that it consisted of a number of cocoa-nuts ingeniously fastened together, leaving a hole in the centre through which a native had passed his head, and quietly swum under his load.

Next day we reached Accra, where we did not land again, as I had a slight attack of fever, and there was a very heavy surf on ; so we amused ourselves watching the crowd of natives who came off in canoes with specimens to add to our menagerie—which was already pretty well stocked—monkeys of many kinds, parrots, parroquets, and cockatoos being chiefly conspicuous. These are bought by the crew as a speculation, but most of them die on the homeward journey.

On the evening of the same day we passed close to Cape Coast Castle, whose old red fort forms a picturesque object on this rather monotonous coast. Standing as it does high above the sea—in comparison with the towns on the Niger delta—it was difficult to realise its remarkable unhealthiness. Next morning we stopped to pick up the mails at Assinie, a deserted-looking French station, consisting of four stone European houses, and a native village on a

low strip of shingle backed by cocoa-palms. I do
not know if it produces any particular source of
wealth, but I was told that at Axim, a few miles to
the east, gold could actually be panned out from the
sand in its streets. Nevertheless the difficulties of
labour and the expenses of white supervision are so
great, that no gold-mining company on this coast
had hitherto paid. The surf was so bad that the
mail-boats were upset twice while coming off to us;
and as a view of the place which I got from the ship
did not reveal anything sufficiently tempting to
make me run the risk of a swim among the sharks,
I stayed on board.

A few hours' steam brought us to Grand Bassam,
an equally uninteresting place of the same class, at
which steamers do not usually stop, but off which
we anchored in consequence of a signal from the
shore that there were passengers to embark. After
two or three narrow escapes and several duckings,
these arrived, and were found to consist of three
black men, a black woman nursing a small monkey,
and two Frenchmen, one of the latter of whom was
so ill that he had to be hoisted on board in a tub.
The other was Captain Binger of the *Infanterie
de la Marine*, the French explorer who had left
Senegal in 1887. He had been given up as lost,
and mourned by his relations, until some weeks before our arrival the Governor of Grand Bassam
heard that there was a white man at Kong, a large

town about thirty days' journey to the north. On receipt of this news, Monsieur Treich-Laplène—who was no other than the almost dying man just brought on board — volunteered to go and meet the traveller, and if necessary assist him. Arrived at Kong, he found that the white man was the missing Captain Binger, and the two proceeded to the coast: but Monsieur Treich-Laplène got an attack of fever from which he never really recovered; and although he picked up a little on the ship, I heard that he died shortly after his arrival in France.

We soon made the acquaintance of Captain Binger, who was a most agreeable and interesting companion, and who helped to while away the monotony of the voyage by a narrative of his adventures. As it has since been published in his ' Du Niger au Golfe de Guinée, le pays de Kong et le Mossi,' I will not try to condense it; but it was a source of great interest to me at the time, and it has always been a satisfaction to me to recall that I was fortunate enough to hear it from him at the very moment of the completion of his journey.

Considering the hardships he had undergone, he appeared to be wonderfully well, although he said that both he and his native companions had suffered a good deal from fever, chiefly brought on by hunger and fatigue. Although the greater part of the country through which he had passed had never

CAPITAINE BINGER.

before been explored by a white man, he found that
the inhabitants were for the most part Mohamme-
dans, and fairly civilised, among the exceptions being
the Gurunga, the tribe to which belonged the girl
whom I have already mentioned. One chief of this
tribe was nevertheless remarkably friendly, and in
proof of his goodwill insisted on presenting the
traveller with a handmaiden, an addition to his small
party which Captain Binger at first looked upon as
anything but desirable. One of his native followers,
however, volunteered to lead her to the altar, and
her status being thus satisfactorily settled, she became a most useful member of the expedition, and,
accompanied by her little monkey, followed it faith-
fully through all its dangers. Her husband had
come on board very lame, having in his leg one of
those unpleasant pests of this coast, the guinea-worm.
I do not know how it enters a human body, but having once lodged itself, it grows at a marvellous pace,
until one day it incautiously protrudes its tail from
the ulcer which it has formed. This habit being
known, the appearance of the tail is anxiously
waited for by the patient and his medical adviser,
the latter of whom at once pounces on the protrud-
ing member, and proceeds to wind it carefully round
a small piece of wood, giving it a slight turn day
by day, until the whole of the parasite has been
reeled off. I am told that this operation is one
requiring great delicacy, the breaking of the tail

being fatal to its success, this being a very vulnerable part of the guinea-worm, who after his decease makes himself even more obnoxious than during his life : or perhaps the proverb, " Once bit, twice shy," is as applicable to guinea-worms as to the higher orders of creation ; and the intelligent animal, having been once treated like a reel of cotton, takes very good care not to risk a repetition of the process.

Another of Captain Binger's men ·had been poisoned by mistake in one of the villages where they had slept. He had taken shelter in a hut where the owner was sitting down to his meal, at which, according to the usual custom, he was invited to join, not knowing that the food had been poisoned for his host's benefit. The poison is very deadly, but takes months to operate, its only symptom being a gradual internal swelling.

I had heard so much traders' " shop " talked since I had been on the coast, that I had begun to take quite an interest in the matter, and asked Captain Binger his views as to the advisability of pushing markets inland. He seemed to think that trade transacted in the interior would rarely pay, as time being no object to the natives, they are just as willing to bring their goods to the coast—in fact prefer it, as there they get better bargains. For instance, a piece of cloth which would cost them 10s. on the coast, would be charged twice as much if the European merchants had to take it some distance inland.

When not enjoying Captain Binger's conversation, or dozing in my deck-chair, or trying to catch flying glimpses of the passing coast, I spent a good deal of my time watching the habits of the many kinds of monkeys that were being taken home by the men as a speculation. Poor little things! Happily a very large percentage of them die on the voyage, and are spared the long term of imprisonment, with a ruined liver, for which they are intended. Most of them seemed thoroughly to realise their fate, and expressed on their faces as clearly as they would have done to Professor Garner with their lips, their utter weariness of life. There were two exceptions, however, to the general rule of solitary confinement and boredom—a baby gorilla and a chimpanzee. The former on account of his value in Europe, and the latter from his superior intellect, were allowed to roam about at will. Being too young to remember his forest life, the little gorilla seemed quite content to be carried about in his owner's arms, or to walk up and down holding on to his hand, looking just like a little black child of three or four years old. The poor little chap had got a nasty cough before we left the ship at Goree, and it is doubtful whether he ever lived to realise the £100 which it was hoped he would fetch at the end of the voyage. The

chimpanzee fully acted up to the converted black
boy's maxim, " Me Christian now, me get drunk all
same like master." The crew looked upon him
quite as one of themselves, to be bullied, played
with, or treated to liquor, as the humour seized
them. They, however, usually took the precaution
of chaining him up before indulging in the first
pastime—his temper being none of the best,—while
after the last he certainly walked away from his
instructors in the matter of gracefulness; for whatever other good points he may have, grace is not
the most marked characteristic of a drunken sailor.
Yet ugly though the monkey was—the very image
of a sallow-faced old woman—he never for a moment
lost his sense of the picturesque.

For the next three days we hugged the shore,
stopping at every village where a signal was hoisted
and a barrel of palm-oil was to be collected; but as
all were very much alike, and all approached through
a belt of breakers, without the advantage of the
big English surf-boats, as at Accra, in which to
face them, I showed the better part of valour and
remained on board, until at noon on the 11th we
anchored off Monrovia, the Liberian capital, a lovely
spot situated on a high well-wooded promontory on
the left bank of the St Paul river.

As we were to remain here for some hours, and
the bar was a fairly passable one, we went ashore,
and were well rewarded by a walk through the most

MONROVIA.

remarkable capital that I have yet come across,—the strangest mixture of mushroom growth with gradual decay, careful architecture with utter neglect, superabundance of vegetation with lack of human life. Broad, well-laid-out streets, in which half-a-dozen four-in-hands could drive abreast, are choked with rank grass, and occupied by a few stray half-starved curs; broad airy *stoeps*, under which the eye naturally seeks for a well-to-do Dutch farmer or merchant smoking his pipe and counting his gains, are either deserted and rotting, or occupied by a fat negro lying dozing in a hammock. Monrovia is distinctly a good town gone wrong, and at first it surprises and almost shocks one; yet one can hardly expect it to be otherwise. Built in 1823 by a society of American philanthropists, a ready - made negro population was despatched from America for its occupation, and left to carve out its own destinies. Now the male Liberian, happy in the possession of the title of Right Honourable, General, or Admiral, rests in his hammock, and dreamily ruminates over his superiority to the surrounding "niggers," only occasionally waking up to discuss some globe-stirring event, such as the Franco - German war, during which, after a prolonged Cabinet meeting, it was formally announced by the President that he "guessed Liberia would remain neutral"!

This pleasant sense of superiority to the aborigines appears to be wholly due to a process of subjective reasoning, the hard facts of the case being that the benighted heathen outnumber the Liberians by nearly forty to one, and have given them the most uncompromising thrashing whenever the latter have brought such unpleasant subjects as taxation too prominently forward. Even the white trader has, I regret to say, sometimes taken a hint from the " Kru boy " in this respect. Having noticed two brass cannon rather ostentatiously placed on one of the coast factories which we passed, I inquired the reason, and was told that they had been purchased by the owner in consequence of a demand for taxes from the Liberian Government, to whom the reply was sent that it had better come and get them.

Of the Monrovian ladies I am unable to speak, not having seen one of them ; but as they were not asleep in the *stoeps*, it is probable that they were hard at work somewhere. At any rate, I am sure that none of the male population would have shown the energy displayed by our late visitor, Mrs Martha Ricks.

After wandering about for some time with a vague sort of idea that we must have missed our way and strolled into one of the buried cities of the Zuyder Zee, we returned to the wharf, and, there being no boat to take us off, sat under the shade of a ruined shed, and contemplated the famous harbour off which a disabled British war-ship was warned, for fear she should sink and spoil the approach. At five that

evening we steamed off again, and soon got into a
tornado, whose accompaniment of blinding rain
necessitated—at least so the Captain said—the further discomfort of the fog - horn, which kept me
awake all night, but which had the advantage of
attracting the notice of the outward-bound ship of
the same line commanded by our Captain's son-in-
law, with whom, having cast anchor in mid-ocean,
he had an hour's chat.

Friday the 12th saw us again at Sierra Leone, but
too late at night for the health officer to come on
board. However, he turned up early next morning,
and took us across to the Government yacht
"Countess of Derby," which had just steamed in,
having on board the Governor, Captain—now Sir
James—Shaw Hay, who had been on an expedition
to Sulima. He was suffering from a bad attack of
fever, but nevertheless kindly invited us to breakfast at Government House, where we all repaired.
It is a large, rather rambling building, with fine
airy rooms, and a broad terrace in front overlooking
the luxuriant garden, and commanding a fine view
of the town and harbour. Yet it is hardly a cheerful abode. Like everything else about the place,
it shows the effects of damp in every corner, and
would certainly give me the " blues " had I to live
in it. We had, however, a most pleasant breakfast,
after which, as our time was up, I was carried down
to the pier in a most comfortable sort of bath-chair,

Y

a conveyance that bore about the same relation to my Madagascar *filanzana* that a dowager's barouche does to a bagman's gig.

The following day and night were spent at sea; and at sunset on Monday the 15th we sighted Goree, where we were to leave the "Nubia" and embark in a Messageries boat for Bordeaux. We cast anchor at about eight, again too late for the health officer to come on board, much to the annoyance of our Captain, who was in a great hurry to get away, and who repeatedly fired off his gun, but without producing the desired effect. I, on the contrary, was by no means displeased at the official reluctance to turn out, as I knew that there was no hotel at Goree, and did not at all enjoy the prospect of a long open-boat voyage in the dark to Dakar.

Having received *pratique* early next morning, we went ashore with Captain Binger, first to Goree, where we were entertained by the *maire* and his mulatto wife while Captain Binger did some business, and then to Dakar, where we found a most comfortable hotel, and an excellent *chef*, black as a lump of coal, but scrupulously clean and neat in the regulation white cap and apron. The waitress was of the same complexion as himself, but most stately and graceful in her movements. She wore on her head a red-and-blue handkerchief, somewhat like a turban, with one of its corners hanging down on the left side, and was dressed in a loose cotton

robe, cut exactly the same shape as a surplice, only
instead of having the sleeves hanging down to her
wrist, she had gathered them on the top of her
shoulders, leaving bare her well-shaped arms.

Dakar is divided into two distinct portions,
the French and the native quarters. The former
has a remarkably prosperous and well-to-do look.
Approaching from the sea, one lands on a broad
stone wharf, lined with coal-sheds, warehouses, and
merchants' offices, and traversed by a continuation
of the St Louis Railway, the terminus proper being
a few hundred yards down the shore to the south.
Round an open space, looking down the wharf, are
the Government buildings and one of the barracks;
while farther inland, broad well-laid-out *boulevards*,
lined with good two-storeyed houses, extend for the
best part of a mile. Through this part of the town
we took a stroll with Captain Binger, who showed
us as much as he could in the time, as he was starting by the evening train for St Louis, where he
had to make arrangements for his followers' return
to their home at Bammaku.

After seeing him off by train, we went for a
further stroll in the country; but beyond the large
native town—composed of neat, cleanly-kept conical
huts, inhabited by a good-looking and very intelligent people, who live almost entirely by fishing—
and the hospital, built on a plateau looking towards
Cape Verd, we did not find much to interest us,

and rather lamented over the information we had received earlier in the day, that the Messageries boat which was to take us home was not due for two days. Had she arrived at once, I should have been so much nearer home, which by this time I was quite ready to reach; or had her arrival been postponed for a week, we might have accepted

Native Town, Dakar.

Captain Binger's invitation to go with him to St Louis. As it was, there was nothing to be done but try to kill time in this highly civilised but rather uninteresting place.

In their due course, however, the hours slipped away, and at about five in the afternoon of the 18th we stepped out of the shore-boat into the

Messageries ship "Portugale," in which we were to
return to Europe.

We had been warned that it was very necessary
to arrange the price with the boatmen beforehand,
and had done so; but they proved too sharp for us,
for having still got our baggage in the boat after we
had boarded the ship, they proceeded to ask us for
more money, and on Harry saying that he would
not give them another sou, they smilingly replied
that they would take our things back with them.
Harry was furious, and was just preparing to spring
into the boat again when he was stopped by one of
the officers, who said that the ship was in quarantine owing to yellow fever at Rio Janeiro, whence
she had come, and that no one could leave her.
So there was nothing for it but to pay up and
make the best of it.

With this final experience of the simple black
man we bade adieu to the confines of his garden,
arrived at Bordeaux on April 26th, sent a wire
home to our servants, and the evening of Saturday
the 27th found us dining quietly in our little house
in Chapel Street, hardly able to realise that we had
ever left it.

INDEX.

PRINTED BY WILLIAM BLACKWOOD AND SONS.

www.ingramcontent.com/pod-product-compliance
Lightning Source LLC
Chambersburg PA
CBHW021339110726
47900CB00005B/1537